THE OTHER

The Other Women

A Story About Three Transsexuals

Pamela Hayes

iUniverse, Inc.
New York Lincoln Shanghai

The Other Women
A Story About Three Transsexuals

iUniverse books may be ordered through booksellers or by contacting:

iUniverse
2021 Pine Lake Road, Suite 100
Lincoln, NE 68512
www.iuniverse.com
1-800-Authors (1-800-288-4677)

This is a work of fiction. All of the characters, names, incidents, organizations, and dialogue in this novel are either the products of the author's imagination or are used fictitiously.

ISBN-13: 978-0-595-43256-1 (pbk)
ISBN-13: 978-0-595-87597-9 (ebk)
ISBN-10: 0-595-43256-5 (pbk)
ISBN-10: 0-595-87597-1 (ebk)

Printed in the United States of America

CHAPTER 1

It was a warm April morning, a Saturday, and Lenore was in her Ford Taurus driving to Charlottesville, Virginia, her new home. Her new life.

Behind her in a U-Haul, she had rented, were two strong, muscular dudes, Bubbie and Tyrone. In the car next to Lenore was Maureen, a friend of Lenore's and Bubbie's, girlfriend.

Lenore was paying the guys $100 apiece to lug the heavy stuff off the truck.

Earlier, they had lugged it onto it. After she was moved into her new digs, she was going to treat everybody to dinner and fill up Maureen's car with gas.

Their assistance was a steal. No moving service would have relocated her almost two hundred miles for a couple hundred dollars, the price of a meal and a tank of unleaded.

Since Maureen was a friend, and she and Lenore had done the shopping/lunch thing, and Lenore had watched Maureen's kids, Bubbie was used to her, but Tyrone appeared a tad uncomfortable dealing with her.

And although Tyrone was uneasy with her, she could tell by his expression that he was impressed with her appearance.

And who wouldn't be? Lenore was a good-looking girl. Facially, she was unspookable—black transsexual slang for not being able to tell that a male-to-female transsexual was a biological male.

She was 6'0, slender, with clear, silky skin the color of apple juice, intelligent eyes that danced with merriment and thick shoulder length auburn hair.

Lenore always wore tastefully applied makeup and delightful smelling perfume, fashionable attire purchased from stores and catalogs specializing in clothes for tall ladies.

Some people thought Lenore's beauty and feminine appearance was the work of a plastic surgeon.

But her looks were natural.

Electrolysis and hormones helped to effectuate her softness.

No, no, no way, I'm living without you, Jennifer Holliday sang from the radio. *I just want to be free.*

What a voice, Lenore thought. And she could so relate to the part about wanting to be free, which was why she was moving to Charlottesville.

Through the straw, she took a sip of the Big Gulp she had purchased from 7-11 before starting her journey.

The sun was radiant. Maybe that was a sign that life in Charlottesville would be filled with happiness and cheer.

That certainly was not the case back home in Hampton. Because she was a transsexual, she often found herself in more dramatic scenes than the characters on *Young and The Restless.*

Her family had a major-league problem with her decision to change her sex.

"It's wrong," shrieked her mother. "Immoral." How two-faced of her, considering what Lenore knew about her past.

"If God wanted you to be a woman, he woulda made you one," said her judgmental Aunt Carolyn.

"I don't want you coming around my kids. I want them to grow up right," said her annoying sister, Elvira.

When Lenore started living full-time as a woman, people whom she had considered friends refused to go out in public with her. When she was Travis, and wore trousers and shirts, she was quite the social butterfly, flitting around with her gay pals, going to restaurants, to concerts. Visiting wineries, sampling this Chardonnay. That Merlot. She frequently visited Barnes and Nobles, where she and her friends sipped gourmet coffee and gabbed about books.

Life was good.

But when her hair became longer and she started wearing makeup and female garb full-time, her "friends" vanished.

The phone stopped ringing. Knocks on the door became infrequent. People avoided her and gave her the cold shoulder when she contacted them. They treated her like she had a infectious disease.

She had had gay and straight "friends."

Maureen, with her sweet self was the only one that hung in there.

Lenore had expected more support from the gay boys.

WRONG. They didn't want to be bothered. Didn't even want to dance with her when they bumped into her in gay bars. "I don't dance with drag queens," lisped the effeminate Phillip. He said drag queen like it was an expletive, and she had known the jerk for three years.

Also, because of her decision to switch genders, her boyfriend, Michael took a hike.

Asshole.

But he wasn't always an asshole. In the beginning, he was as sweet as a bowl of sugar cubes.

Her thoughts regressed to Michael. For three days, she was out of town in Texas attending a Gay Pride Parade.

Lenore hated being away from home. And she missed Michael.

And when the taxi dropped her off at the apartment that she shared with him, she was elated. On the plane coming home, she mused about how marvelous it would be to see him.

When she entered their dwelling, holding her suitcase, the room was dark and felt empty, although the sofa, the TV and artwork were still there. "Michael," she called. And received no reply. For some reason, she didn't expect one.

She entered their bedroom, hoping to find him, snoozing, with a book, a newspaper or magazine on his chest. But he wasn't there. Her eyes shifted to the opened door of the walk-in closet, and Michael's shirts, sweaters, pants and shoes were gone.

A lump formed in her throat. She could feel herself began to disintegrate. *Keep it together,* she muttered to herself.

Crazily, she dashed to the living room, and checked for his favorite CDs and books and they weren't there. She had known they wouldn't be.

Needlessly, she rushed to the bathroom, and Michael's cologne, toothbrush and shaving equipment were gone.

Oh, God. He's left me, she thought as tears sprang to her eyes.

And she hadn't seen it coming. She thought they had a great relationship.

In fact, he frequently paid for her hormones and electrolysis. He had gone to the mall with her and helped her select clothes and purses.

So, yes, he had been supportive.

But oftentimes, gay guys dumped their boyfriends when they started dressing as women.

If I want a woman, I'll get one, some gay men argued. *I don't want a guy that dresses up as a woman. I don't want a transsexual.*

Evidently, that was how Michael felt. And why didn't he tell her to her face that he wanted out? She deserved an explanation, damn it.

She rushed to the wall phone in the kitchen and with trembling fingers, clicked seven numbers, rolling her eyes as she did so. She truly didn't look forward to this conversation. But it was unavoidable. Perhaps, the person she was dialing could shed some light on the mystery of Michael's whereabouts.

"Hello," the woman greeted pleasantly.

"Mrs. Tate," Lenore said.

"Yes," Mrs. Tate said in a tone as sweet as maple syrup.

"Uh, this is Lenore Cavanaugh."

"You mean, Travis," Mrs. Tate spat.

"I mean, Lenore." She had had her name legally changed.

"What do you want?" Mrs. Tate asked belligerently. Mrs. Tate was Michael's mother, and she never approved of Michael being gay. And she damn sure didn't approve of his relationship with Travis/Lenore.

She refused to step foot in their apartment. And she told Michael that Lenore was not welcome in her house. Once Michael had taken Lenore (when she was dressed as a guy) to the house and his mother said, "Y'all just gone somewhere with this gay mess." Her expression appeared as though she was viewing flies swarming around feces. "I don't want the shit in my house."

And one Friday night—morning, actually—it was after one a.m., Lenore and Michael were in bed, watching a movie and the phone rang. Lenore answered it.

"You and my son betta check your damn self before you wreck your damn self," Mrs. Tate slurred. Obviously, she had been in the Puerto Rican rum, her favorite intoxicant.

And where had she heard that little witticism, *The Jerry Springer Show*, Lenore thought sarcastically.

Coming out of her mini flashback, Lenore said, "I'm looking for Michael."

"Why you calling me 'bout it?" Mrs. Tate asked, still being a bitch. "You can't keep track of your *boyfriend*?" She said boyfriend like it was a filthy word. Lenore pictured her wearing an ugly expression.

"I thought maybe Michael had dropped by to see you," Lenore said. He visited his mom a few times a week.

"Well, you thought wrong. I ain't seen Mikey. What's going on here?"

Lenore frowned. "What are you asking?"

"Well, you calling around looking for Mikey. Did y'all have a lover's quarrel? Did he leave you? Is that why you don't know where he is?"

Oh, I bet hearing that Michael dumped me would brighten your day, Lenore thought. Well, she wasn't going to give the bitch the gratification.

"Well, you know one thang," Mrs. Tate said nastily.

"I know many *thangs,*" Lenore stated. "You wanna tell me something new?" She was fed up with this shrew's revolting attitude. And she wanted to cuss her out. For the length of her relationship with Michael, Lenore itched to let Mrs. Tate have it. But because she was Michael's mama, Lenore gave the slut respect she didn't deserve.

"I hope Mikey did leave you," Mrs. Tate spat. "I hope he wised up and got out of that sick relationship with you."

"Goodbye, Mrs. Tate," Lenore said and ended the call. She telephoned Michael's friends and his favorite cousin, but nobody knew anything.

Or so they said. Michael could have put them up to lying.

Calling Michael's employer was pointless, as she knew his work schedule, and he was off that particular day.

It was late. And she wouldn't be able to get to the bottom of things until morning, so, she ate a little food without tasting it, showered, went to bed, tossed and turned, glancing at the clock every few minutes.

And the first thing she did the next morning was phone Circuit City, where Michael worked as an assistant manager. She had him paged. "Michael, what the hell is going on?" she demanded the minute she heard his voice.

"Travis?" he asked questioningly.

Like he needed to ask. He knew her damn voice.

"Lenore," she corrected sharply.

"Yeah, I never got use to it," he said.

"Now answer my damn question," she snapped. "What's going on? Why did you leave me?"

"Travis, this isn't the place to be talking about something like this," he said.

"I want answers," she yelled.

"Somebody could pick up an extension and hear us," he whispered sharply.

"I don't give a shit."

"Well, I do. I don't want everybody in the store knowing my business."

Michael's coworkers didn't know that he was gay. And it really wasn't any of their business.

"Look, you're going to tell me something," Lenore snapped in a lower tone. "I go out of town. Come home and find out that you've packed up and disappeared. I didn't sleep a wink last night. Now, I want to know why you left me?"

He took a deep breath. "Okay, okay," he said, still talking softly. "I can't deal with what you're doing?"

She frowned. "My sex change? Is that what you mean?"

"Yeah. I can't handle it. It was one thing when you dressed up on the weekends and we went to gay bars. But now, you're doing it twenty four seven and taking those pills."

"Michael, 'those pills' are called hormones. And to become female, I have to take them," she said.

"I know. But our neighbors in the complex where we lived, they knew, Lenore."

One minute he called her Travis, and the next it was Lenore. The boy was so confused. And she knew that she was the talk of the apartment complex. She had seen the stares and the whispers.

"I could tell by how they looked at us," Michael said.

"I don't care," she said truthfully.

"I do."

"We could move to another apartment," she suggested.

"Yeah, but they'd pick up on it at the new place," he said. "And with you going through this, there's no way I can stay undercover." His family knew that he was gay, but his coworkers didn't. "My family already had a problem with us, and now, you want to change yourself."

"Michael, this is so unfair," she whined like an injured child.

"Well, hey, I'm sorry." His tone was cavalier. "Also, I've decided to change my life."

Oh, God, was he going to say that he found religion?

"I no longer want to be a part of the gay scene," he revealed. "I'm going straight."

Lenore rolled her eyes. "Michael, you can't go straight anymore than you can go gay."

"I think I can. I mean, if a person decides they want to lose weight, they steer clear of fattening foods, right? Or if someone decides to quit smoking, they fight the urge to grab a cigarette. And after a while, they break the habit."

"You sound stupid," Lenore shot. "Your sexuality is not a bad habit. You will always be gay. You can't change it."

"Well, I don't agree with you. It's all about willpower."

God, people annoyed her thinking they can switch their sexuality on and off like a car ignition. "Michael, all you'll be doing is repressing it," she said peevishly. "And how happy will you be?"

"I met someone," he said, clearly not interested in her opinions.

"A woman?" she said, like she needed to ask. He no longer wanted to be on the gay scene, so he probably found some unsuspecting woman to call his girlfriend.

"Yeah," he said.

"Do I know her?"

"No."

"You sure?" she asked skeptically. In the past, a few of her so-called "friends," heterosexual women tried to bust up she and Michael. He was handsome, gainfully employed and good to Lenore. And Lenore guessed that the women figured that although he was gay, he had to have some straight in him to be involved with a transsexual. And since they knew he was a worthwhile man, they tried to steal him from her.

"You don't know her," Michael said.

She believed him. She could always tell when he was lying. He would stutter and pause. But she wondered about this woman. Her appearance. What did she have that would make Michael dump Lenore for her? Well, she was a real woman. Duh! That was the attraction. By being involved with her, he didn't have to deal with people staring and whispering.

Lenore wondered if Michael's new romantic squeeze knew about his past? She'd bet a thirty-day supply of estrogen tablets that she didn't have a clue. She was sure that Michael hadn't breathed a word to her. Men who went both ways usually kept that info to themselves.

"Look, I'm going to hang up," he said. "Take care of yourself. I wish you luck."

The phone clicked in her ear. How could he do this, live with her for four years and then dump her like she was an old issue of *Newsweek*? All because she was going through a sex change, which shouldn't have come as a bombshell to him.

The whole time they were a duo, she did drag every Friday and Saturday night, dolling up and hitting the gay bars. And Michael always accompanied her. But obviously, he could deal with a weekend drag queen and not a transsexual.

After it ended with Michael, for nights and nights, Lenore couldn't sleep.

Or eat properly. She dropped pounds. Her clothes became baggy and unflattering.

She experienced unexplained itching. Regularly, she smoothed on itch-relief gel. To be on the safe side, she saw a doctor, who told her that she was in perfect health. So, as she suspected, the itching was stress related. She had read that significant changes in one's life could cause itching. At times, she thought she was going insane.

She had bouts of fury, and during those episodes, she banged the walls with her fists. And hurled the dish rack on the floor, turning plates and glasses into shards.

How could Michael hurt her this way?

But he always had issues with his sexuality, masculinity, whatever.

And Lenore supposed he admired her because she was feminine and soft. And without thinking about it, they role-played. She cleaned the apartment, cooked meals and shopped for groceries.

And when the faucet dripped or the heating element in the oven needed replacing, or when their cars broke down, Michael took care of it.

They had assumed rather traditional gender roles.

But despite Michael's manliness, she always feared that he'd dump her for a man-man—a non drag queen.

Lenore had been around the block, and she knew how things went in the transsexual world. Most guys, who were involved with drag queens or pre-op transsexuals, at some point, usually dumped them for a masculine man.

But Michael deserted her for a woman.

That man-stealing bitch, Lenore snapped in her head.

Lenore felt vindictive. She wanted to hurt Michael.

Punch him.

Slap him.

Scratch him.

Give him a black eye.

Stop it, she thought. *You're sounding nutty.* And besides, revenge wasn't her style. She believed in putting unpleasantness behind her and moving forward.

So, on that note, she went on with her life, enjoying her apartment, her favorite TV shows, movies, and novels.

For several months, she had not laid eyes on Michael Tate, but one day, she saw him in the supermarket, cradling a *baby,* swathed in a blue blanket. She caught a glimpse of the caramel-colored infant with soft, jet-black hair.

In front of the dairy case was a stalled shopping cart and a woman grabbing a package of cheddar cheese.

Lenore felt awkward, but she couldn't just walk off without mumbling a word to Michael. That would have been impolite. And she was a gracious southern lady.

So, she put on a smile and said, "Hi, Michael."

"Uh, hey," he said, looking extremely uneasy. He surreptitiously took in her new appearance. Her hair had grown to shoulder length and was styled beautifully. The hormones and electrolysis had made her skin silky smooth. And her makeup was skillfully applied.

And naturally, she was clad in female garb. By then, she had become steeped in the female role, so she was more seasoned and poised. And she knew she looked great. And Michael's expression indicated that he thought so too.

She figured he was edgy because he feared that his woman might have ideas about Lenore and wonder what was his connection to the man dressed as a woman. Although Lenore looked like a woman, some people still wondered about her. *You can't fool 'em all.* Not that she was trying to fool anybody.

"How you doing?" Michael asked Lenore.

"Fine," she replied. Nodding to the squirming lump in the blue blanket, she said, "Who's that?"

Before Michael could answer, the woman piped up. "Michael, who's this?" Her tone was pleasant.

"Uh," Michael said, looking stupid. Thinking on his feet was never one of his attributes, Lenore thought.

"Michael and I used to work together," Lenore lied. She extended her hand to the woman.

"Oh," the woman sang, shaking Lenore's hand. And not seeming to be questioning Lenore's gender. Lenore could tell when people thought something. They'd sneakily check out her hands or feet, which were not giveaways.

"Well, I'm Michael's wife, Bertrice," the woman revealed.

Michael's wife? So, he was now a husband and a father. She wondered if he was having sex with Bertrice while he was living with her. And what the hell kind of a name was Bertrice?

Lenore faked a warm smile. "Hi," she greeted Bertrice.

Bertrice stepped over to Michael, "And this is our son, Michael Jr.," she revealed, grinning abundantly at the child, obviously a proud mama.

"He's adorable," Lenore said truthfully.

"We think so," Bertrice caroled.

"Well, Bertrice, it was nice meeting you," Lenore said graciously. "And Michael, it was good seeing you too. You two take care."

Smiling, Bertrice said, "You do the same."

Lenore seriously doubted if Michael had told Bertrice that he once shacked up with a transsexual. And as much as she resented him for breaking her heart, she wouldn't reveal his past.

It would have been petty and nasty.

Let him live out the life he wanted. That's what she was doing, after all.

But seeing the man she loved, with his wife and child was hard to swallow.

She had wanted to cry, right there on the spot, but fought the desire to do so.

After paying for her items, she entered her car, and sat behind the steering wheel. And sobbed like she was at a dear friend's funeral.

And in a way she was. The life she had had with Michael was dead.

Driving home, she had thought about how she had had it all planned out. She would have a sex change operation, and she and Michael would get married and have a fabulous life. He'd be her loving, supportive husband.

What he had with Bertrice, he could have had with her, even a sweet baby.

They could have adopted. Or gotten a woman to carry a baby for them.

But Michael didn't want to deal with her because she was a transsexual.

So, after seeing Michael and his new family, and being rejected by her so-called friends, Lenore decided to relocate to Charlottesville, and make a new life in new surroundings.

CHAPTER 2

Finally, she pulled into her new apartment complex, gingerly going over a few speed bumps. Maureen and the U-Haul were behind her.

The complex was just a few months old and all the units hadn't been rented. Her new two-bedroom had never been inhabited by another soul. No one else had cooked on the stove, used the fridge, bathed in the tub, or peed in the commode.

Before moving to Charlottesville, she had driven up and looked around and she loved the apartment complex, the vicinity and how the people looked.

She pulled into a space.

On the backseat of her and Maureen's cars were two 32-inch TV sets, two combo VCR/DVD players, stereo equipment, boom boxes, crates containing clothes, shoes, computer equipment, small appliances, CDs, books, DVD's and her vast collection of comic books.

She adored Archie, Jughead, Betty and Veronica.

The U-Haul held her bedroom, living room and dining room furniture.

She kept her fingers crossed that nothing got broken in transit.

She got out of the car, and she and Maureen left the dudes with the truck. They took the stairs up to her new home.

After the move-in was completed, the guys drove the U-Haul back to the rental center and Maureen and Lenore followed in Lenore's car. Maureen's car was parked at Lenore's new digs.

Lenore bought everyone dinner at a pizzeria near her new home.

The pizza parlor was packed. And the food was delicious. They ate two large pizzas with extra mozzarella and the guys and Maureen drank beer. Lenore had a glass of Merlot.

❧ ❧ ❧

Later that night, Lenore was in her new apartment, pooped. Maureen and the moving men had gone home. The driving and all the moving had wiped Lenore out. She had done a little mopping and cleaning, wiping down the refrigerator and the stove, making her new home habitable.

Sure, the place was already clean, but before she could be totally comfortable in her new environment, she had to do a little cleaning, Lenore-style.

Tomorrow morning, she'd tackle that box of dishes and cutlery items and hang some pictures.

Earlier, she had gone to a supermarket and picked up a few things, soap, snack foods, sodas, breakfast items, deli meats and cheese, bananas, apples, crackers and a bottle of wine. After all the activity of the day, she needed a glass of calming wine, her favorite adult beverage. She had had a glass at the restaurant, but she needed another.

And living in a house without food was not an option. Sometimes at night, she woke with a gnawing stomach and she had to eat a little something to quell it.

And she simply liked food in her house. Tomorrow, she'd buy a basketful of groceries.

After taking a leisurely bubble bath and drying off, she rubbed perfumed body lotion into her soft flesh, making it even suppler than it already was.

Her skin had always been baby soft, but the daily estrogen made it even softer.

She tied her hair back with a scrunchy, slipped on her tiger print pajamas, last year's indirect Christmas present from Maureen.

Maureen had given her a gift certificate to a tall girl store that Lenore frequently patronized, and Lenore used it to purchase the pajamas.

And she loved them. They were so silky, made her feel so soft and feminine. Just the thing to relax in.

While sipping her wine, she sat in her bed and watched a DVD of *All About Eve*.

Lenore adored old movies and *All About Eve* was one of her favorites. Eve Harrington and Margo Channing were delightful bitch goddesses.

The dialogue was deliciously phony, filled with wit, bon mots, and one-liners. What real person would even think to say some of the stuff that came tripping off the tongues of those characters?

Hmm. Sharp-tongue queens and transsexuals, Lenore decided after thinking about it briefly. Queens and transsexuals had sassy mouths and nobody could cuss you out like a pissed off queen.

She had seen the movie a zillion times, but tonight, it wasn't holding her attention. Her thoughts drifted to relocating and all that she had to do, and man, was it plenty?

Friends.

She had to make some new ones. She was an equal-opportunity person. She didn't care if her friends were black, white, gay, lesbian, straight, male, transsexual, natural-born woman, middle-aged or old, poor or wealthy. She simply enjoyed the company of nice, trustworthy people. Most of her life, and more so after switching genders, she had been judged unfairly, so she had a rule about giving everyone a chance.

And her new pals would have to have a sense of humor. Humor was a must. To Lenore, humor was like vitamins and minerals. She needed it to survive.

In addition to making new pals, she had to find another gynecologist to prescribe hormones. The thought distressed her. Some doctors refuse to treat transsexuals. Who knew why. Maybe they thought sex changes were wrong, and they weren't going to provide a person with medication to alter their gender.

And there were doctors who didn't give a damn. All they wanted was to get paid. For the price of an office visit, they'd scrawl a transsexual a prescription for hormones and send her on her way, not bothering with an examination or anything.

Lenore avoided such quacks. She wanted a physician who took proper care of his or her patients.

Her gynecologist back home, Dr. Emily Taggart was marvelous. She knew that Lenore was a pre-op t-girl and she treated her with warmth, respect and professionalism.

Prior to meeting Dr. Taggart, through a gender program, Lenore saw this horrible doctor who referred to her as *he* and ridiculed her in front of his staff.

In the waiting room, he'd come out and fetch her, and in front of his patients, he'd refer to her as Miss Cavanaugh. But when they were behind closed doors, he'd call her *he* and *him.* "Don't call me he," she snapped to him.

He smirked. He had irritated her and obviously that had given him pleasure. He was a decrepit white man, and Lenore would bet that when he was a boy, he was probably a bully. "Well, taking hormones doesn't make you a she," he stated.

Frowning, and viewing his ruddy face, plump jowls and forehead covered with liver spots, she said, "If you have such a problem being respectful to people in my situation, why'd you agree to see me?"

Like she needed to ask. The ugly, narrow-minded bastard wanted her money. Well, Lenore refused to put up with such bullshit.

She told him to kiss her ass and left the office. And a few days later, she found Dr. Taggart.

And now, she was once again in the market for a respectful gynecologist.

She sipped her wine. Thank God she didn't have to fret about finding a job, not just yet anyway. She had enough money to pay for her surgery and to sustain her for at least a year and a half.

And she could indirectly thank Kate Turner for that. Poor Kate, Lenore thought, shaking her head, wondering what became of Kate. Kate was a drag queen and she and Lenore used to hang out at the gay bars, dancing and partying.

Like Lenore, Kate wanted to be a full-fledge chick. And Kate looked convincing. She was a sweetheart.

No longer wanting to be a drag queen, Kate decided to become a woman. She began taking estrogen. Had her name legally changed. Got a new driver's license that said f for sex designation.

She worked as a telephone operator. She told her supervisor that she was switching sexes and presented her boss with a letter from a psychiatrist saying that Kate was going to have a sex change, and while preparing for it, she'd have to work and live as a woman.

It was called the real life test.

So, one Monday morning, Kate showed up for work, dressed as a female and wearing makeup.

The previous night, she had phoned Lenore, sounding unsure and scared. "Everything's going to be all right, girl," Lenore said, reassuring Kate.

But everything did not turn out all right.

Lenore shook her head thinking about all the horrible stuff Kate endured. Many a time, she had watched Kate sighing and crying. Lenore had comforted her as best she could.

Kate's co-workers referred to her as *he.* They shunned her. People saw her in the break room and left.

They wouldn't talk to her. Did things to humiliate her.

Female employees complained to the supervisor about her using the women's bathroom. One woman filed a grievance.

But Kate won. The company said that she could use the women's restroom.

Despite winning that battle, she still had to deal with cold shoulders and disrespect.

It all demoralized Kate. Prior to living and working as a woman, she was always cracking jokes and smiling up a storm. But that changed after going to work as a female. "This is a lot harder than I thought it would be," she had told Lenore. "Being a drag queen was more fun." And that was because drag was something she only did on the weekends and in a gay bar, where nobody gave a shit. Living as a woman full-time was a different story.

The workplace abuse continued. Kate could no longer stomach it, so she quit her job and moved away. Lenore hadn't heard from her in years.

But because of what Kate experienced, Lenore decided that she wouldn't transition on her job.

She didn't want to tolerate any bullshit.

As Travis, she worked as a bookkeeper at a supermarket, making out the schedule for the cashiers and baggers, preparing deposits, balancing books and at the end of the week, he took home a little over five hundred bucks for his efforts.

At the time, Travis/Lenore was living with Michael, who paid the rent and the electric bill. Travis/Lenore paid the cable and the phone bills and bought the groceries.

So when Travis/Lenore decided to prepare for her sex change, in addition to working at the supermarket, she worked at Barnes and Nobles part-time. Every Tuesday afternoon, she went to electrolysis and on the weekend, she did drag.

For three years, every Friday, she deposited money in the bank and bought savings bonds. She went in for psychological testing and eventually received a prescription for hormones. When the pills started feminizing her, she resigned from the store.

Later, she had her name legally changed, and got a new driver's license that reflected the female gender.

So life was sweet, but still, she had to deal with disapproving family members, turncoat "friends," and Michael's desertion.

All that was depressing enough. She refused to put herself in a situation where she was scorned and ridiculed by coworkers, which was why she amassed a little fortune, so she could transition in peace.

"That's a very intelligent approach," said Ariel, a pre-op transsexual whom Lenore knew casually. "But that doesn't work for everybody."

"Why do you say that?" Lenore asked graciously.

"Well, some trans women decided to have surgery in their late thirties and older. They tried to live as men, but they just couldn't take it any longer and decided to make the switch."

Lenore nodded.

Ariel said, "Some have children and mortgages and they need a paycheck. Some have worked at jobs for many years. They have seniority and benefits. Paid vacation. Sick leave. They'd be giving up a lot if they resigned from their jobs." Ariel shrugged. "So they have no choice but to make the switch on the job. And in some instances, receive a cold shoulder from co-workers."

Ariel had made a valid point, Lenore conceded. After her surgery, Lenore was certainly going to return to work. She had to. Her savings wouldn't last forever.

And when she resumed the nine-to-five routine, she knew there would be assholes who would give her a hard time. Ah, the life of a transsexual.

CHAPTER 3

A few nights later, in the pitch-black room, Lenore lay in bed. She glanced at the clock on the nightstand. And sighed. It was 3:17 in the morning, and she was wide-awake. Shortly after midnight, she had retired and most of the time she tossed and turned.

She had been in her new home for three days, and she hadn't as yet become totally comfortable with her new surroundings. All the dishes had been put away. Her pictures were on the walls and her books had been placed in her two-tier bookcase.

The fridge and larder were filled with food. So, this was now home, but it would take a while before she was comfortable enough to sleep with ease.

In the dark, she stretched to the nightstand and fumbled for the remote control, found it, and brought the TV to life.

An episode of a sitcom she hated was on. She changed the channel, and stopped on an infomercial about a rotisserie that made chicken, chops and prime rib mouthwatering while removing the health-threatening fat. Who needed another small appliance?

She already had gadgets galore, many that she rarely used. She channel cruised and stopped at *Real Sex.*

Some creep was dumping pork and beans on a nude, giggling woman. *Disgusting*, Lenore thought.

In another scene, a bunch of chuckling naked people put whipped cream, maraschino cherries, chocolate syrup and chunks of pineapple on another smiling woman. They were turning her into a human sundae.

And people called transsexuals' freaks, Lenore thought, flipping the channel.

She was born a male and for some inexplicable reason, she wanted to be female.

So, she was making the switch, and to some people that made her a freak. Okay, then she was a freak.

But this freak read books. Attended college for three semesters. Paid her taxes. Donated money to worthy causes.

She was not molesting children, shoplifting, selling or using illegal drugs. She rolled her eyes when she thought of the injustices of life.

Screw it.

Her thoughts drifted to her loneliness. She had been alone for several months now. She missed what she had had with Michael.

Right now, she'd be sound asleep if a reasonably attractive man was lying next to her.

It would be so wonderful to share her life with someone, someone for her to love and who loved her.

At home, they'd dine by candlelight. They'd go to restaurants. Concerts. To see plays. They'd go on drives. Take vacations. Celebrate Christmas and their birthdays. She had done all that with Michael.

And it would be nice to have a new man in her life.

She wasn't a bad looking girl, and there was a man out there who'd love and cherish her. And even though, she currently had breasts and a penis, there were men who would date her.

But any man that would accept her as she was now would obviously be into she-males and after her surgery, and when she no longer had a penis, he could dump her.

And she'd have to endure the pain of another break-up. Hey, that was a t-girl's life.

She was definitely going to surgery and afterwards, she hoped to meet a man, fall in love. Tie the knot. Have a baby or two. Of course, she wouldn't give birth to the infants. But she and her husband would find a woman to have the babies for them.

She shared her ideas with her nasty sister, Elvira. "You think you have the answer to everything," Elvira said, shaking her head disapprovingly.

"What do you mean?" Lenore had asked.

Elvira was a judgmental bitch, at least to Lenore. She never had a nice word to say to or about Lenore. Was it a coincidence that she shared the name as the evil witch on *The Wizard of Oz*?

Even when they were children and teenagers, Elvira was cruel and insensitive to Lenore.

"You were born a boy," Elvira said, her drab face coiled nastily.

"Really! I didn't know that," Lenore remarked sarcastically.

"You tryna be funny, but I have a point to make."

"Then make it," Lenore said.

"And you decided to become a woman. So you're taking hormones and after you have this operation, you're gonna get somebody to have a child for you."

"Make your point, Elvira," Lenore snapped.

"You're playin' God and it's gonna catch up with you."

Lenore's face was twisted with agitation. "Go to hell, Elvira," she screamed.

One year, Elvira had invited Lenore to a Christmas party she had tossed. The gesture surprised Lenore. She thought Elvira was trying to accept her.

Lenore knew that everyone attending the shindig would be straight and since Elvira's friends knew that Lenore was a transsexual, well, there would be gawking.

And Lenore didn't care. She wanted to be seen. She was pleased with her new breasts and thick shoulder-length hair. And the hormones had made her skin luminous, which made her pretty face even prettier.

The night of the get-together, Lenore applied a perfect makeup, rubbed perfumed body lotion into her flesh and put on a sexy, tight outfit, which gave a hint of her luscious boobs and accentuated her 27-inch waist.

She arrived at the party and immediately felt out of place.

She was the prettiest woman there and some of the women gave her nasty looks.

All evening, some guy had been staring at her. At some point, she went to the bathroom, and when she emerged, he was facing her. "Hi. I'm Gary," he said.

She smiled. "Hello."

He waited. Chuckled. "Um, don't you have a name?"

"Uh, yes, I'm Lenore."

"Hello, Lenore. You're a nice looking lady, you know that" he said, eyeing her intently, like he was starving and she was a steaming platter of roast beef.

"Thanks," she said.

"How tall are you?"

That question. People acted as if she should be put in the Guinness Book of Records as the world's tallest woman, and there was nothing extraordinary about her height. "6'0," she revealed.

He continued to look at her steadfastly, making her feel uneasy. He put his hand behind her head and brought her face to his and passionately kissed her, astonishing her. He was a nice looking guy, but she had no desire to kiss him. She didn't know him. "Why don't we go to my apartment?" he suggested in a husky voice.

Hey, shouldn't he ask her for a date? He was treating her like a pick up? And she didn't know if he even realized that she was a transsexual with a penis.

Some of the people at the party knew her previously, and she didn't know if they had whispered things about her or not. So, she didn't know if Gary was in the dark or knew what was what and didn't care. Some men admired women like her. Whatever the case, she wasn't going off with him.

She had to think of someway to graciously decline his request.

"I want to eat your pussy," he whispered, eyeing her lasciviously.

He doesn't know. How could she extricate herself from this potentially dangerous situation? Lord, if that man realized that she wasn't a real woman, he could become violent and beat the shit out of her.

"Um, I have a boyfriend," she lied. Michael had been out of her life for quite some time by that point.

Gary shrugged. "So?"

"Well, I don't cheat on him."

"Come on, baby," Gary cajoled, stroking her hair. "Be sweet. Show me some love. You'll like it. I promise." He started kissing her again. She tried wriggling free, but it wasn't easy.

A chubby, bespectacled man rounded the corner and Gary, wearing an embarrassed expression, released Lenore. Seizing the moment, she scurried away from him.

Feeling extremely uneasy, she went to her car and drove home.

The next morning, Elvira phoned. "Why didn't you tell anyone you were leaving?"

"I had to get away," Lenore said.

"Why? Were you were uncomfortable with the people?" Elvira stated.

Lenore rolled her eyes. "Elvira, I don't care what people think of me."

"Then, why the hasty exit?"

"That Gary guy," Lenore said.

"Oh, he's a friend of my husband's. What happened? Did he figure out that you're a man? Did he call you names? Well, you know, that's to be expected," she lectured. "Some people don't like what you're doing."

You negative bitch, Lenore thought. "Elvira … Gary came on to me," Lenore revealed. "He tried to get me to go to his apartment. He grabbed me and kissed me."

Suddenly, Elvira's end became as quiet as a classroom of students taking a final exam.

"He grabbed you and kissed you?" Elvira exclaimed furiously.

When push came to shove, she would take Lenore's side. That made Lenore smile. "Yes," Lenore said.

"And what'd you do about it?"

"Um, nothing," Lenore stammered.

"You let him kiss you and get away with it?" Elvira stated.

"Well, I was appalled. It was confusing."

"Oh, you liked it," Elvira blurted.

"What?" Lenore said, shocked.

"Yeah, you liked it."

"I most certainly did not like it," Lenore snapped. The kiss was not repugnant, but she certainly did not like Gary grabbing her and doing what he wanted to do to her. Yes, she was flattered that he was attracted to her. But no, she did not want to be kissing someone she had just met.

"Well, if you didn't like it," Elvira went on, "you would've done something about it."

"Like what?" Lenore said, naïvely.

"Like slapped the shit out of him. And since you didn't do that, you musta loved it."

Elvira was full of it, Lenore thought. For God's sakes, Lenore had only been living as a female for several months. She didn't know anything about dealing with aggressive men. It didn't occur to her to slap Gary.

"Besides, it didn't mean nothin'," Elvira said nastily. "You won't nothing special. That man comes on to everybody. He'll come on to anythang."

That man was not bad looking, and he didn't strike Lenore as the type that would come on to just anything. Lenore believed that he approached her because he was smitten with her.

And Elvira was clearly trying to minimize Lenore's sex appeal. "If Gary drops by here and my husband isn't home," Elvira said. "I don't open the door for him. I wouldn't be alone with him because I know he'd come on to me."

This stupid woman was jealous of a dumb kiss. Unbelievable! Lenore rolled her eyes. She didn't grow up as a girl and go through puberty as one. She didn't have girlfriends and sisters and a mother to counsel her on dealing with guys.

She had no point of reference about handling aggressive men. Instead of feeling envious and threatened, Elvira could have offered her some sisterly advice.

Oh, to hell with Elvira, Lenore thought, banishing that incident from her mind and shifting her thoughts to her surgery.

Sometimes she wondered if she could indeed get a bona fide vagina. Oh, she knew that there were t-girls who had surgery. In dirty magazines, she had seen before and after pictures of transsexuals.

On the Internet, she had found sites with post-op transsexuals showing off their vaginas.

So she knew it could be done. Lenore wondered if those pussies functioned like a real woman's. She wondered if a man could fuck her and would she get any pleasure from it.

She wondered if all that pulling and rearranging could damage some nerve endings.

Having surgery and becoming a total woman would be a dream come true for Lenore.

But was it possible?

CHAPTER 4

Hanging up the phone, Lenore puffed out frustrated air. She reclaimed her seat at the kitchen table, where the phone book lay open, revealing the yellow pages.

She had called five doctors' saying, "I'm a pre-operative transsexual. I just moved to the area and I'm looking for a doctor to prescribe hormones."

That statement always produced immediate silence. She was sure that the docs didn't hear that one too often.

And every receptionist told her that they'd have to speak to the doctor and call her back. And when they did, she was told, in some variation, that the doctor had no experience treating transsexuals, so therefore, they couldn't provide her with the best possible care.

And no one offered a referral.

Treating transsexuals. She was looking for a physician to write her a prescription for hormones, not perform risky surgery. She was down to six pills, which was causing her to feel maximum anxiety. She feared that if she missed taking her pills, even for one day, she'd lose her 42-C boobs, her curves and her hair would fall out.

That was not going to happen, of course. She was feeling crazy insecurity.

She was a member of an online transsexual support group and last night, she posted a message, asking if any of the girls knew of a doctor in the Charlottesville area who would be receptive to seeing her.

Usually, the girls were so helpful providing information about the best place to go for surgery ... voice training ... what doctor to avoid ... where a girl could find clothes for tall women or large-size women shoes.

But no one responded to her message. Obviously, no one knew of a physician in Charlottesville.

She tried another doctor.

Hot damn!

Dr. Bibi Argyle agreed to see her.

♣ ♣ ♣

A few days later, Lenore was sitting across from the gynecologist, an affable white woman, who appeared to be in her early forties.

"I'm very impressed with your appearance," Dr. Argyle stated.

Lenore smiled. "Thank you."

"If I saw you, I wouldn't have thought a thing. And your voice. Did you work with a speech therapist?"

"No," Lenore said. "It's natural. When I was younger, it was even higher."

"I'll bet you took a lot of ribbing for that," the doctor said lightly.

Lenore remembered the jibes. *Sissy. Punk. Faggot.* Back then, she made a conscious effort to make her voice sound deeper. And actually she sounded like a girl trying to sound like a guy.

Lenore was weighed. Her blood pressure taken. She noticed the nurse sneakily checking her out. Transsexuals were forever being placed under the microscope.

Who cared?

Dr. Argyle wrote Lenore a prescription for a year's supply of Premarin, a female hormone.

"Dr. Argyle, as I told you, I recently moved to the area, and I want to meet people similarly situated," Lenore said. "So, could you have some of your transsexual patients phone me? I want to make some friends."

"Sure, no problem," Dr. Argyle said. "I'll have my secretary take care of it. I can have her call some patients and ask them if they'd be willing to talk with you. And if they agree, my receptionist will give you their number."

They had Lenore's phone number on file. She hoped that she'd meet someone worth knowing. It was just terrible being a stranger in a new city.

But some transsexuals didn't want to deal with other transsexuals. Lenore felt that a transsexual needed another transsexual. The girls had to put up with a lot of garbage, family drama, employee problems, jerks in society. And another transsexual could truly understand and feel her pain.

Sadly, some trans women avoided other transsexuals. Some were jealous of those who passed better. Some older t-girls envied those who were younger and prettier.

Some resented those who had thicker hair, bigger boobs, a prettier face, a feminine voice or a boyfriend.

Lenore had met those types and she steered clear of them. Jealous, resentful people didn't make good friends.

Unfortunately, many people oppose transsexuals, so transsexuals should be more supportive of each other.

And there were trans women who wanted to put the transsexual part of their past behind them, and lead "normal" lives. So they avoided other transsexuals. If they thought transsexuals were abnormal. What did they think of themselves?

Lenore's phone buzzed. *Oh, my. A phone call.* Since moving in her new digs, her phone had rung only a few times. Maureen called to say hey and that she missed her. And the state police called begging for a donation. And there were a few wrong numbers, She silenced the chiming.

It was Dr. Argyle's secretary calling to say that Annabelle Morrison, a transsexual patient had agreed to talk to Lenore. She provided Lenore with Annabelle's phone number.

Lenore immediately dialed Annabelle's number. But got her voice mail.

How disappointing. She was so eager to speak to her.

"Hello," greeted a feminine voice that sounded put on. "This is Annabelle Morrison. I'm not home right now, but leave your name, and I'll return your call ASAP. That is, if I like you."

Lenore smiled. Annabelle had a sense of humor.

Good.

Lenore left her name and number. Later that afternoon shortly after five, Annabelle called, explaining that she had just gotten in from work and was anxious to speak with Lenore. Again, Lenore detected that she was forcing herself to sound female. "I just moved to the area," Lenore said. "And I want to meet other girls like me."

"Yeah, that's what Dr. Argyle's secretary said," Annabelle stated.

Lenore wondered if Annabelle was black or white. Not that it mattered. "Well, tell me about yourself?" she requested.

"I'm fifty-one," Annabelle revealed.

Over two decades older than Lenore, but that was no big deal. Lenore enjoyed the company of mature people.

"How old are you?" Annabelle asked.

"Twenty-eight."

Annabelle chuckled. "A baby. I've got children close to your age."

"Uh, have you had your operation?" Lenore probed.

"Yes, ma'am," Annabelle said proudly. "I'm two years old."

Which meant that she had had her operation two years ago. And in a way, a transsexual was reborn after surgery.

"Happy with the results?" Lenore asked, secretly hoping that Annabelle would go into details about her surgery. She wanted to ask if her pussy functioned. But it was too soon to be asking such indelicate questions.

"I have no regrets," Annabelle answered.

Well that was encouraging. "I'll be going to surgery in a few months," Lenore revealed. "I have to find a doctor to perform the operation. I have the money saved up."

"Well, look why don't we get together and talk in person?" Annabelle suggested.

"I'd like that."

"What's your address? I don't have anything planned for tonight. I could swing by. We could have coffee or something."

"Well, I'd like to meet you too, but I'd prefer it if we met someplace, like, uh, a Wendy's, or maybe I-Hop," Lenore said. "It's just that I don't know you. I wouldn't recognize you if I saw you in the supermarket buying a bunch of bananas," she joked. "I don't open my home to complete strangers. I'm simply being cautious."

"I understand," Annabelle said.

She and Lenore agreed to meet at a certain Wendy's the following afternoon at 1:30.

CHAPTER 5

Lenore entered the fast food establishment and heard meat sizzling on the grill. She glanced at her wristwatch. She was about fifteen minutes early for her meeting with Annabelle Morrison.

It was mid afternoon, and a few people were scattered in the lobby, eating burgers, fries and salads. The food aroma reminded Lenore that she hadn't had a crumb that day, so she ordered a Coke and a double cheese with lettuce, tomato and pickle only.

She took her tray of food to the dining area, looking for an empty table.

Off in a corner, she spotted a … um, woman, wearing a blue dress. Because the woman looked like a man in drag, Lenore believed that the person was Annabelle. But Annabelle had said that she'd be wearing a white blouse and lime green pants.

Wearing a warm smile, Lenore walked up to the table. "Hi. Are you Annabelle?"

"Oh, hi, Lenore," Annabelle said pleasantly, sizing Lenore up. "Sit down."

"See you decided to change clothes," Lenore said, placing her tray on the table and sitting in the chair across from Annabelle.

"Well, when I was getting dressed, I was sipping coffee," Annabelle said, watching Lenore wipe off her lipstick with a napkin. "And I spilled some on my blouse. So, I had to put on something else."

"I see," Lenore said, unwrapping her burger. Annabelle was white with deep laugh lines, crow's feet, thinning permed hair and a receding hairline.

Lenore recalled Annabelle saying that she was fifty-one, but she appeared to be a decade older. Either girlfriend had fibbed about her age, or had led a rough life. Maybe, the drama of being a transsexual had taken its toll on her.

With her broad face, thick neck, and large hands, at a mere glance, she looked like a man in drag. But still, she had a right to be who she wanted to be and live a happy life.

"God, you look so authentic," Annabelle praised. "I'm jealous."

"Thanks," Lenore said, a trifle embarrassed. Compliments always made her feel that way. She sprinkled salt on the lettuce and tomato atop her burger.

"Your skin is so soft and clear," Annabelle said. "And your face is sooo believable ... How long have you been on hormones?"

"Over a year," Lenore answered and took a generous bit off her burger. And it was yummy.

Annabelle explained that she had been taking estrogen for almost three years. "So, what do you think of how I look?" she exclaimed, proud of her appearance.

Well, Annabelle's blouse was too small, tight across the shoulders, which emphasized the thickness in her shoulders and back. Something more loosely fitting would have been more flattering, Lenore thought.

And the sleeves weren't long enough, putting her massive wrists on display.

Annabelle Morrison was in dire need of some helpful hints from a transsexual fairy godmother or a full-time drag queen; someone experienced in wearing female clothes.

A lot of neophyte transsexuals were like teenage girls, wearing tons of makeup and the wrong attire.

But teenage girls usually had a mother or big sister to offer some helpful hints. And inexperienced transsexuals needed more seasoned t-girls for pointers and guidance.

Annabelle may have had surgery, but she didn't have it totally together. But she and Lenore had just met, and Lenore didn't want to come off sounding like a know-it-all by criticizing the child's appearance. Maybe if this outing led to a friendship, she could gently offer Annabelle some clothing and makeup tips. It was her wish to help Annabelle, not offend her.

"You look great," Lenore lied.

Annabelle beamed. "Thanks."

People in the adjacent table were cutting their eyes at her. When Lenore took her tray to the table, she saw a woman whisper something to her dining companion, another woman, who surreptitiously glanced over at Annabelle. Surely, Miss Morrison picked up on such things.

Annabelle sipped her soda. "I'm so proud of what the hormones have done." Looking down at her miniature breasts, she said, "They caused my boobs to grow. They aren't as big as I'd like, but they're here."

"Yes, they are," Lenore said.

"And in spots, my hair has thickened. I wish it were longer. I'd like to shake it like the girls in the shampoo commercials." Looking at Lenore's fried potatoes, Annabelle said, "Mind if I have a few?"

"Help yourself, girl." Watching Annabelle remove a few fries from the box, Lenore said, "So, you're happy that you had the surgery?"

"Definitely. But you know, there have been issues."

"Family stuff?" Lenore guessed.

Annabelle nodded. "That, and work."

Annabelle was divorced, but she had been married for over twenty years. And had three adult children. She sighed. "But except for a niece, and my sister, none of my family speaks to me."

Lenore felt sympathetic. She was estranged from some of her family members. She hadn't spoken to her brother since revealing her plans to become female.

Annabelle said, "And my niece and sister are in my corner, but I pay for their support."

Lenore frowned. "What do you mean?"

"I buy them birthday and Christmas presents. More than once, I've helped my niece with tuition and books … I've treated them to restaurant dinners."

"But they don't do anything for you?" Lenore guessed.

Annabelle nodded. "My birthday or Christmas, I don't get a greeting card or a phone call. I guess they figure they should be rewarded for giving the deviant the time of day."

"Annabelle, there's a very simple solution to that, you know."

"Stop buying 'em Christmas and birthday presents?"

Lenore nodded. "Why should you acknowledge them and they don't do it for you?"

"I considered stopping, but … what if I took sick, and needed somebody to help me out? I mean, we don't know what life will toss us."

"Annabelle, if they love you, they'll be there if you have a crisis. And if they don't give a damn about you, they won't be there, despite your gifts and dinners. Sweetie, you can't buy devotion."

Annabelle took a sip of her soda. "Maybe you have a point."

"So how are things at work?"

"Not swell. As I told you, I deliver mail. Two years ago, I moved here from Pennsylvania. I had made the switch at the office there." She shook her head.

"Bad, huh?" Lenore said.

"A nightmare. Many of my coworkers turned on me … Some stop speaking to me. At lunchtime, they stopped asking me to grab a Chick-Fil-A. They stopped inviting me to their backyard cookouts. A co-worker retired, and I wasn't even asked to attend the farewell party." She looked unhappy. "I got tired of it and transferred here."

"Did things improve?" Lenore asked, doubting it. Annabelle looked like a man and society was a tad bit more tolerant of transsexuals who looked believable.

Annabelle sighed. "A little. They have suspicions, and they're cool towards me. I bet it would make some of my co-workers happy if I quit. But it's a government job, so I'm safe."

Wearing a perplexed expression, Annabelle said, "What I don't understand is how do clothes and makeup change a person's attitude towards us? I mean, I'm the same person who took my kids to the amusement park, played Santa Claus with them, and went to PTA meetings. And now they don't want anything to do with me," she said incredulously. "And at my previous place of employment, I'm the same person who went to the hospital to visit sick coworkers. Colleagues came to cookouts I hosted. Came to my house on Christmas and sipped eggnog and ate cookies." Sighing, she said, "Yet, when I became Annabelle, they didn't want anything to do with me."

Lenore shrugged. "Prejudice … What you went through is exactly the reason that I didn't transition at work. Call me a weakling, but I just didn't want to deal with the aggravation." She explained that she had amassed a nest egg before quitting her job.

"You did it the smart way." Annabelle chuckled. "Wish I had done it that way. I could've saved myself a lot of misery." She paused. "Well, look, the day is still young, and you just moved here. Why don't I show you around. Give you a tour of our fair city."

She didn't have anything else to do. "Sounds good to me."

They climbed in their cars and Annabelle followed Lenore to her apartment, where Lenore parked her Taurus.

Yesterday Lenore didn't want Annabelle to know where she lived and now she didn't care. What a difference a day makes.

In Annabelle's vehicle, Lenore received a tour of the city. Annabelle pointed out landmarks, where historical events had transpired.

They drove past the University of Virginia. "Seeing that school reminds me," Annabelle said.

"Of?" Lenore asked.

"I have three kids. Two of them, a son and a daughter are college students. The youngest boy is a welder."

"What are they studying?" Lenore asked.

"My son is majoring in engineering. My daughter sociology."

Lenore frowned. "You said that you're estranged from your children."

Annabelle nodded.

"And your daughter's majoring in sociology?" she said incredulously.

"She's planning on becoming a licensed clinical social worker," Annabelle explained.

"Ha! You'd think she'd have more empathy for your situation."

"Yeah, you'd *think*." She sighed. "But the kids are torn. Their mother hates my guts. In her opinion, I ripped her life to shreds. And she acted so shocked when I told her that the marriage was over and that I was going to change my sex."

"Well, I'd think that would appall the average woman," Lenore said.

Annabelle took a deep breath. "Lenore, she knew. Shortly after we were married, one day she came home early from work, and caught me wearing makeup, panties and a bra."

"How'd she react?" Lenore asked.

"Oh, she became hysterical," Annabelle said at a stoplight. "So I confessed my desire to be female. She said that she didn't want to discuss it ever again. So I lived out my life as a man, and a few years ago, I decided to be who I should have been all along." She paused. "My ex is 52. And she feels that she's too old to make a new life. So to make herself feel better about me supposedly ruining her life, she badmouths me to the kids. And they take her side."

Out of the blue, Annabelle said, "You know, I read that Thomas Jefferson founded the University of Virginia." Evidently she didn't want to dwell on hurtful issues. And Lenore didn't blame her.

Also, Lenore had read that about Jefferson and that Edgar Allan Poe had been a student at the renowned university.

Annabelle was saying something about how fire had destroyed Jefferson's Rotunda.

Who gives a shit, Lenore thought. This field trip was making her drowsy.

She wanted to discuss Annabelle's surgery and sex life. Could Annabelle make love? And if so, did she enjoy it? But Lenore had just met the child, and she didn't feel comfortable enough asking her such personal questions.

They drove to a two-level mall, entered a department store and looked at purses and makeup and jewelry and sniffed fragrances. After Lenore made a few purchases, they dropped in a clothing store that catered to tall women. "Hi," the clerk said, smiling and then frowning, and then rapidly erasing the frown. Her expression suggested that she had ideas about Annabelle.

It wasn't easy being out in public with Annabelle, who got gobs of attention. Even at stoplights, people looked over and gave her knowing stares.

When she and Lenore were walking through the mall, there were many gazes. And Lenore was a little uncomfortable. She was not accustomed to that kind of attention. Sure, she got second-guessed, but it wasn't this often.

And Annabelle seemed uptight. She wouldn't look people in the face. She kept her head lowered to the floor. Which suggested that she was hiding something. But she had a right to be who she wanted to be and Lenore would be her supportive friend.

Lenore asked the clerk if she could try on a pair of pants, a dress and a top.

"Sure," the clerk said and pointed to the fitting room.

A few minutes later, Lenore emerged sporting a tight red tee shirt and a pair of equally tight white jeans. She loved the outfit. It was dressy, and chic, but casual. "What do you think?" she asked Annabelle.

Lenore had a flat stomach and a female's form, which the clothes emphasized.

"Oh, it looks darling," Annabelle sang.

Lenore purchased the outfits, and they left the clothier and went in a bookstore, where Lenore picked up titles by Terry McMillan, E. Lynn Harris, Danielle Steel and Flannery O'Connor, *The Complete Stories.*

Lenore discovered Flannery O'Connor when she was in college. And she loved the southern fictionist, who died too soon.

Several times that afternoon, Lenore had flashed her credit card, but she didn't worry about not being able to pay the bill, as she had a tidy sum saved up.

In the food court, she and Annabelle sipped bottled water. Looking at the ill-fitting dress Annabelle wore, Lenore said, "Annabelle, I want to say something to you, and I don't want you to take offense."

"Go ahead," she said softly.

"I have a feeling that you purchase your clothes from regular stores."

"Yeah, I do."

"Girl, you should shop at a tall store or out of a tall catalog. You're broad and large-boned, and clothes that weren't cut for you emphasize your largeness," she said tactfully.

Eyeing the loose-fitting blouse Lenore wore, Annabelle said, "That does look very flattering on you. And I don't take offense to someone giving me helpful advice."

Since she commented on the girl's clothes, she felt comfortable enough to say, "Tell me about your sex life."

Annabelle chuckled. "What do you want to know?"

"How is sex?" Lenore asked bluntly.

Annabelle shrugged. "Pretty good."

"So your vagina functions?"

"Well, sure," Annabelle exclaimed, like that was the dumbest question she had ever heard.

Lenore shrugged. "Well, it's hard for me to believe that a vagina created from a penis would work like a natural vagina."

"Well, it does," Annabelle said. "I don't get wet like a real woman does. I have to use a lubricant. But it works." She paused. "There's a gentleman I see a few times a month."

"Oh, really?" Lenore said, highly intrigued.

"Yes, ma'am."

But despite Annabelle's encouraging statement, Lenore still had qualms. From Lenore's experience, a lot of transsexuals lied, exaggerated. And having successful surgery was important to her. Outwardly, Lenore looked like a woman. And a working vagina would be the proverbial icing on the cake.

She had so many questions about the surgery.

CHAPTER 6

Later that night, Lenore was sitting up in bed, reading one of the books she had purchased that afternoon. The phone rang. It was Annabelle calling to say that she had enjoyed their outing and that she hoped they became friends.

Lenore appreciated the call.

Annabelle had dealt with some shit. Most of her family had turned their backs on her, and she went through a nasty divorce. According to Annabelle, the judge was more sympathetic to her ex, which was frequently the case.

In the eyes of many, Annabelle was a pervert, who had destroyed a woman's life.

And yeah, any woman whose husband left her to become female got a bum deal.

But people never stopped to consider how nightmarish life had been for a transsexual, who was essentially a woman, masquerading as a man.

Anybody, who lived though that deserved a little compassion too. Didn't they?

Lenore and Annabelle's friendship blossomed. They went out to eat, taking turns picking up the tab. They cooked meals together and dined at each other's homes. They watched movies while sipping Chardonnay. They talked and laughed and were growing closer. Lenore learned that Annabelle had had her surgery done in Thailand. One night, she had lifted her dress and proudly showed Lenore her vagina. "Amazing," Lenore said.

"I'm happy with it," Annabelle said, smoothing down her dress.

Lenore had never had a sexual encounter with a woman and she found the idea revolting. Women were wonderful as friends, but she didn't want to get sexual with one.

The only vaginas she had ever seen were the ones in dirty movies and *Playboy.* And Annabelle's looked similar, authentic. Lenore was jealous. She wished it belonged to her.

"And it functions and everything?" Lenore questioned, still filled with doubts.

"Yes," Annabelle exclaimed. "You've asked me that before. I guess I'm just gonna have to prove to you that it does work, so we can put your mind at ease."

Lenore chuckled. "And how the hell are you gonna prove it?"

"Remember, I told you that there's a guy that I see occasionally," Annabelle said.

Lenore nodded.

"Well, the next time he calls, I'll talk to him about fucking me in front of you," she said, quite casually, like she had suggested they go to Pizza Hut tomorrow afternoon for lunch. "That way, you'll get your proof."

"Oh, okay," Lenore chirped without hesitation. She was eager to have her curiosity satisfied. And she knew watching Annabelle have sex was trashy, but how else could she obtain irrefutable proof that a transsexual's vagina worked? So she'd be a voyeur.

The things transsexuals went through.

CHAPTER 7

It was a bright afternoon, and Lenore was driving down the boulevard, keeping an eye on traffic, making sure she didn't miss her turn. She was on her way to visit Jennifer Ann Hughes, a pre-op transsexual patient of Dr. Argyle's.

Jennifer Ann answered Lenore's request to meet similarly situated people.

While slurping sodas and munching on snacks, a handful of times, Lenore and Jennifer Ann had gabbed on the phone, animatedly sharing colorful stories about their days as drag queens.

Jennifer Ann was a card. She had Lenore on the floor hollering with laughter at some of her antics. At one time, she exposed her breasts to good-looking pizza deliverers and blew them.

Lenore cackled. "You sucked their dicks?"

"Yeah, girl."

"Did they know the deal?"

"Hell no."

"Weren't you afraid that he might start roaming down below? And if he found out, he might get violent?"

"I never worried about anything like that," she said airily.

After becoming fast phone buddies, Lenore and Jennifer Ann decided to meet. Jennifer Ann knew what Lenore looked like, but this visit would be the first time Lenore had laid eyes on Jennifer Ann.

Lenore had suggested that they exchange pictures via email. Jennifer Ann said that she didn't know how to do it. Lenore tried explaining the procedure, but Jennifer Ann couldn't grasp it. So Lenore sent her a picture of herself.

Jennifer Ann had breasts and a penis and she and a man were living together as husband and wife.

There was nothing unusual about that. Lots of trannies did it. For about two minutes, Lenore had done it with Michael.

But Jennifer Ann and her "husband" actually had a ceremony and have a marriage license. "After the wedding, my husband's family hugged me and kissed me and welcomed me into the family," Jennifer Ann bragged. "His mama and I were crying together."

"Where was your family?" Lenore had asked curiously.

"Oh, Miss Thang," Jennifer Ann pooh-poohed, speaking with a southern twang. She was from Tennessee. "Or is it all right if I call you Miss Thang? A lot of t-girls don't like being called that."

"I don't mind," Lenore said truthfully.

"Well, child, my family don't approve of me," Jennifer Ann revealed. "So, no way, would I have had them anywhere near my weddin'. Lord, if any of them were there, you know that part when the preacher asks, 'Can anybody show why these two shouldn't be joined in holy matrimony, speak now, blah, blah? Well, one of them old hillbillies woulda stood up and said, 'Yeah. He's a boy. Nah, honey, I didn't want them fools around."

Lenore chuckled. "What made you pick the name Jennifer Ann?" Actually, she called herself Ann.

"I think Jennifer is a cute name. And Ann goes well with it. So I tell folks that I hate the name, Jennifer, so I call myself by my middle name Ann. A lot of real cunts do stuff like that. I think it adds a dash of authenticity to the fib I'm living," she said jovially.

Fib? She had a dick and was pretending to be a married woman. Fib was a definite understatement.

Lenore became solemn. "Ann, you don't have to live a lie ... You can tell people who you are. And if they have trouble accepting it, that's their problem."

She moaned. "Miss Thang, it ain't that easy. I just want what other people want, to live a simple, quiet life. To take care of my house and my garden, and be happy."

"I feel the same way, but you don't have to lie to have it."

"Wayne's parents would never accept me. They'd turn their backs on him and me if they knew the truth. And I don't wanna put the boy in a position where he's arguing with his people cuz of me."

Bullshit, Lenore thought. Jennifer Ann wanted to be thought of as a bona fide woman. Not a transsexual.

Lenore would never do what Jennifer Ann was doing, but she understood her motivation for lying. Being accepted as a woman without question was wonderful. And it was demoralizing to be judged and looked at differently.

Lenore was curious as hell to see this lady.

Jennifer Ann and Wayne had been "married" for five years, and all that time she had managed to dupe his family. So hell yeah, Lenore wanted to see this queen.

"When do you plan on having surgery?" Lenore had asked during one of their phone chats.

"Girl, I ain't having no surgery," Jennifer Ann said. "I *love* my dick … I love gettin' a good blow job. And I fuck men. I'm a versatile, honey. I can ship it or receive it."

Lots of non-ops, or chicks with dicks, as they were called in the vernacular, screwed men. No way would Lenore fuck a man. Lenore viewed herself as a female, all the way.

She clicked on the left signal, and turned onto a wide street, lined with nice houses and well-preserved lawns. She moved her head back and forth in search of a split-level brick house with a fence.

Jennifer Ann had said that the fence would be opened, giving Lenore access to the driveway. She spotted the house. But instead of parking in the driveway, Lenore turned off the ignition at the curb. When she was dropping her keys in her purse, she saw the front door of the house swing open. And a lady whom she assumed was Jennifer Ann stepped onto the front porch.

The lady was white, 5'11, (she had told Lenore her height), slender, with thick shoulder-length light brown hair. She wore a pair of skin-tight jeans and a baby blue sweatshirt.

Smiling, and waving, and in a incontrovertibly female voice, she said, "I saw you drive up. I thought I'd come out and greet you personally."

Lenore entered the spacious living room filled with gleaming Early American furniture. The inviting house was spotless and smelled fresh.

A vinegary odor filled Lenore's nostrils. "Something sure smells nice," she commented. The aroma brought back memories of Lenore's childhood and being at her paternal grandma, Etta Mae's house. *As The World Turns* would be playing on the floor model TV while grandma sat on the sofa, watching it, while something mouth-watering simmered in a Dutch oven on the stove.

"Oh, I made a crock pot of barbecue," Jennifer Ann explained. "I also made homemade coleslaw. You like b. b. q.?"

Lenore put her hand on her hip. "Girl, I love b. b. q.," she joked, putting down her purse. Looking at a stack of CDs by the stereo, she asked, "Mind if look at your music?"

"Knock yourself out," Jennifer Ann said.

The collection was eclectic. There was Lee Ann Rimes, Macy Gray, Alicia Keyes, Luther Vandross, Beyonce, Loretta Lynn and Patsy Cline, some of everything.

"I love all kinds of music," Jennifer Ann said.

"I see."

Jennifer Ann gave Lenore a tour of her nicely furnished home, and in the bedroom, proudly showed off her vast wardrobe. "I love clothes," she said. And she had excellent taste. Her stuff was simple and tasteful. Pushed back further in the closet were a few ball gowns from her drag queen days.

They got cozy on the edge of the bed and glanced through Jennifer Ann's bulging photo album.

Lenore saw pictures of Jennifer Ann and Wayne, who was a nice looking dude. In one picture, he was flexing his muscles and mugging for the camera.

There were scads of pictures of a smiling Jennifer Ann all dolled up, flanked by overly painted queens, wearing glittering, ostentatious gowns.

One queen was putting a tiara on Jennifer Ann's head. Jennifer Ann explained that she had won a drag competition. "Girl, back then, my stage name was Shasta Hathaway," she revealed. "Everybody loved Miss Shasta."

She pointed out pictures of drag queens that resembled or tried to resemble gorgeous celebrities.

Some of the queens were obviously men. Lenore made a face. "Aren't you afraid to have this scrapbook around?"

Jennifer Ann frowned. "Why? These are my memories."

"But you're living undercover," Lenore said sagely. "And it's obvious that some of those chicks are guys. What if your in-laws saw the pictures?"

"I keep this photo album on my closet shelf, buried under sweaters and blankets," she said, shutting the book. "This is for my eyes only."

Lenore thought that her new acquaintance looked quite believable as a woman, but Lenore would have known.

It takes one to know one.

Jennifer Ann used to perform in drag shows. "Did you use your own voice or lip synch?" Lenore asked.

"Oh, Miss Thang, I ain't no sanger. I mimicked the words."

"Well, put on a show for me, girl," Lenore suggested. "Strut your stuff."

Jennifer Ann did not need asking twice. They went to the living room, and Jennifer Ann lip-synched *Respect* by Aretha Franklin, and *I Will Survive* by Gloria Gaynor. While performing, she skipped around the room, with her hands on her slender, but feminine hips, dramatically pointing her finger at Lenore. She did a commendable job.

"Have you ever done a drag show?" Jennifer Ann huffed after finishing her last number.

Lenore shook her head. "No. I never had the nerve to go on stage and perform in front of a crowd."

"Well, here's your chance," Jennifer Ann said.

"You want me to lip-synch a song?" Lenore stated, incredulously.

"Why the hell not? I did it?"

Lenore looked through the music and selected an oldie by Linda Clifford, *If My Friends Could See Me Now.*

Lenore loved that ditty. She considered it her theme song. Back home, in the late 90's, she was pals with Miss Don, a middle-aged, former drag queen. One night Lenore and Miss Don were listening to music and Lenore heard the Linda Clifford tune and she liked it so much that the next day, she ordered it from Amazon.com.

Also, Jennifer Ann had done, *Respect* and *I Will Survive* and now Lenore was about to perform *If My Friends Could See Me Now.*

Did their selections have symbolic meaning? The songs they picked were about respect, surviving, and wanting friends to see the new her.

While Lenore performed the song, Jennifer Ann clapped and said, "Work it, girl."

They were both clocking thirty, and they were behaving like two teenage girls who had run of the house while mama and daddy were away at work. And who cared? This was the most fun Lenore had had since moving to Charlottesville.

She enjoyed Annabelle's company, but Jennifer Ann was a contemporary. And they both had been on the drag scene and until a few years recently, Annabelle had essentially lived the life of a straight man, so she wouldn't have been able to relate to what Lenore and Jennifer Ann were experiencing.

"You hungry?" Jennifer Ann asked after Lenore had finished her routine.

It had been a while since breakfast. So, sure, she'd love some food. "Why don't we go out for pizza?" Lenore suggested. "I know a great place." She was thinking of the trattoria she ate at the day she moved to the area. "My treat."

"Well, I was thinking we'd have some of the barbecue."

"Ooh, that sounds even better."

They went to the kitchen and while Lenore sat at the table, Jennifer Ann washed her hands, at the sink. "I'm gonna have me two," she said that as if eating two was a big fat no-no. "You want one or two?"

Usually, Lenore would have eaten one, but hey, she was in a partying mood. "Girl, I'll take two," she joked.

Jennifer Ann wrapped four sesame-seeded buns in aluminum foil and placed them in the oven. While they heated, she poured two glasses of ginger ale.

They ate, talked and laughed. When Lenore was taking a bite off the second barbecue, she said, "Girl, this is lip-smackin' delicious."

After she had eaten the last sandwich and with her fingers, picked up pieces of meat and slaw from her plate, she said, "Thanks for a great meal."

Jennifer Ann smiled warmly. "You're certainly welcome."

"I owe you one," Lenore said. "I'm going to skip dinner tonight."

"Oh, you don't have to watch calories. You're so thin."

"And I want to stay that way," Lenore said. "Which is why I'm going to ignore the dinner bell this evening."

"I needa cigarette," Jennifer Ann said. "Mind if I smoke?"

She chuckled. "Girl, this is your house."

"But you're a guest, and I want you to be comfortable."

"Smoke your damn cigarette," Lenore joked. Jennifer Ann disappeared from the kitchen and a short while later, returned with a pack of Marlboros, an ashtray, and a lit cigarette between her lips.

She rejoined Lenore at the table. "I'm so glad I met you," she said and took a puff of her cigarette.

"Same here."

"As you know, I live undercover, and all my other girlfriends are real women, and they don't know what's what ... And it's nice being around someone I can just be myself with."

"Ann, you're stressed out about living a secret life, aren't you?" Lenore said.

Jennifer Ann nodded. "It gets to me sometimes. And sometimes, I wonder, Miss Thang."

"About?"

"I don't think my husband's family has a clue about me."

"I can believe that. You look female. You sound it, and you take a size *eight* shoe." Looking at Jennifer Ann's hands, she said, "And they look fem."

"But sometimes I wonder if they suspect something, and they just aren't saying so. And the joke is on me."

Lenore shrugged. "You could simply be feeling paranoid because you know, you've got a secret."

"A few times, I've caught Alice, my husband's mama, staring at me. Child, one time, Wayne, and I went to a steakhouse with his parents. And this sissified waiter was just a lookin' at Miss Jennifer Ann. He put my ice tea down in front of me, and said, 'Here you are, sir.'"

Lenore made a face. "Asshole!"

"And then he faked a frown and said, 'Long day.' Miss Thang, that nasty sissy did that on purpose."

"Of course." Lenore had had gay men try and embarrass her in public. It was so distressing to be abused by another sexual minority.

Jennifer Ann said, "But nobody said a word. Wayne looked pissed. And if his parents weren't there, he woulda done something. Occasionally stuff like that happens. Now, if Alice or someone in the family has ideas about me, when something like that happens, it reinforces their suspicions."

"Girl, the way to free yourself of the pressures of a secret life is to simply come clean."

"If I did that, I'd lose the love of Wayne's family. I've washed my hands of my own family. For years, they treated me like shit, and I don't want nothin to do with 'em."

"You can't be certain that Wayne's family would reject you."

Jennifer Ann frowned. "Lenore, when girls like us have been on talk shows, Alice said, 'They oughta stay the way the Lord made 'em.'" Jennifer Ann chuckled. "And Pop—that's my father in-law. He thinks *Will and Grace* is sinful … So, telling them about me would ruin my life."

"But they know you," Lenore insisted. "You and Wayne have been married for over five years, and in that time, they've grown to love you." She and Wayne were not really married. But Lenore wasn't going to point that out. "So they may try to understand."

Jennifer Ann didn't agree with Lenore.

"You have every right to live your life openly and honestly. And secrets do have a way of coming out," Lenore said.

"Child, don't say that," Jennifer Ann sounded alarmed. "The truth comin' out has been my biggest fear."

They talked some more. And before ending her visit, Lenore said that she had enjoyed the afternoon. "I hope we have many more like them."

"Me too," Jennifer Ann said, giving Lenore two Tupperware bowls filled with barbecue and coleslaw. Lenore promised to return the bowls. Walking Lenore to the door, Jennifer Ann said, "I want you to meet Wayne and my in-laws. Every Friday night, we all get together and play cards. You should join us sometimes."

"Oh, Ann, I don't think that's such a hot idea," Lenore balked.

Jennifer Ann frowned. "Why not?"

"Girl, what if they thought something of me?"

"They wouldn't. You look genetic," Jennifer Ann said.

"Still, some people have ideas about me. And if your family became suspicious of me, they could ask you questions about me. Now, that would make you more than a wee bit edgy."

"They ain't gonna think nothing of you," she said fiercely.

This girl went back and forth like a yo-yo, Lenore thought. Earlier she expressed concern that her in-laws had ideas about her. But she's willing to expose them to another tranny.

Jennifer Ann said, "And if they did, I'd just tell 'em that they're full of shit. I'd say I knew you when you were a lil girl."

Obviously, Jennifer Ann had no qualms about lying. "We'll see," Lenore said, having no desire to meet Jennifer Ann's 'in-laws.' She didn't want any parts to such subterfuge.

Hey, Jennifer Ann was wrong deceiving those people. Maybe Lenore sounded a little judgmental, but that was how she felt.

CHAPTER 8

"I don't blame her," said Annabelle. She and Lenore were on the phone.

Lenore had told Annabelle about Jennifer Ann. And suggested they all get together one evening and have dinner.

Annabelle was agreeable to that.

"So, you have no problem with Jennifer Ann misleading people?" Lenore stated.

"Not at all. I mean, come on, Lenore, you know how people are. They detest transsexuals."

"Not everybody feels that way. There are people who believe in live and let live."

"That isn't the attitude of most," Annabelle said sharply. "Believe me, I know. So if Jennifer Ann can live her life and her husband's family isn't the wiser, she should go for it."

"I think she should be honest. I don't think it's right to hide things."

"Look, Jennifer Ann doesn't owe them an explanation. Her husband is fine with it. And that's all that matters."

"Annabelle, you sound angry this evening," Lenore said sweetly. "What's wrong?"

Annabelle took a deep breath. "Work. Society. It's all a pain. My co-workers are being shitty … I feel like an Amish girl, who broke a sacred rule and the community is shunning me. No one has said anything to my face. But they let me know they don't like me … In the morning, they greet each other effervescently … 'Oh, hi Joanne. Good morning, Frank.' But no one breathes a word to me."

"That's terrible," Lenore said sympathetically.

Annabelle sighed. "And they avoid saying she when they refer to me ... Stuff like, 'Can you hand this to ...' and then nod at me." She paused "It gets to me. One of the customers on my route, a redneck bitch had some ideas about me. She called the office and asked my supervisor if they knew they had a man dressed as a woman delivering mail."

"You're shitting me," Lenore exclaimed.

"My supervisor told me. I guess the bitch thought, no way would the post office have hired a transsexual, so she figured I had them in the dark and she wanted to flip up the light switch." She moaned unhappily.

People should mind their own damn business, Lenore thought.

"Earlier I talked to my sister, Doreen about the situation, and she wasn't the least bit sympathetic," Annabelle said.

"What'd she say?"

"She asked me, 'Didn't you bother to consider that people were going to be judgmental when you went through this?'" She sighed. "Did I need to hear that?"

"No. You needed to hear some encouraging words," Lenore said.

"Besides, I didn't consider that I'd have to live with this. I thought I'd have the surgery and not look back," Annabelle said. "I didn't realize that people would question who I was and make a stink about it."

Before Lenore put a hormone tablet on her tongue, she knew that people would have ideas about her, and she decided that she'd simply have to grin and bear it.

Annabelle moaned. "But I was wrong. She paused. "And man oh man, you know what makes me nuttier than a bag of fun-size Almond Joys."

"What?"

"They don't even know if what they're saying is true," she shrieked. "I didn't tell them that I'm a transsexual. They *assumed* it. And here they are attacking me because of something they *think* they know."

There was a long silence. For a moment, Lenore wondered if she and Annabelle had been cut off.

She frowned. "Annabelle, you there?"

"Yeah," she said in a bone-weary tone. "You know, periodically, there are stories in the newspaper about unhappy people going on shooting rampages in fast-food joints or the workplace." For a long time, not a word was spoken.

"I'll bet it all started with shit like what I'm going through, what a lot of transsexuals go through—being shunned," Annabelle said, her voice soft and lazy. "Treated like vermin. In some instances, being teased and harassed. And you know, I could see a girl losing it … Snapping. Getting a shotgun and doing a little shoot 'em up, bang bang."

Such talk was making Lenore uneasy. "Annabelle, stop it," she snapped. "You can't talk about going on shooting sprees. You can't allow yourself to even think like that … If you did something so crazy, you'd ruin your life. You'd end up in jail."

"I'd never do something so nutty. I value my freedom. I believe in the commandments. Thou shalt not kill."

"You're not working tomorrow," Lenore said, changing the subject.

"Nope. It's my day off."

"Well, why don't you get your butt over here?" Lenore suggested in a bright tone. "I went to the grocery store today, and bought groceries … Got some Crunch 'n Munch—buy one, get one free. We can eat it and watch a funny movie." She had DVD's of *Look Who's Talking, Sister Act, Some Like It Hot, Mrs. Doubtfire,* to name a few. When she was feeling blue, a lighthearted movie always lifted her spirits.

Annabelle said, "I accept your offer. But forget the Crunch 'n Munch. I'm gonna get a bottle of wine, a big bottle. I'm in the mood to get tipsy."

CHAPTER 9

The following morning, Lenore woke with a vicious headache, thanks to those three glasses of wine she'd had the previous night.

From the kitchen cabinet, where she kept her vitamin supplements, aspirin and hormones, she got two Tylenol and took them with several swallows of Pepsi.

Today, she'd began her search for a surgeon to transform her penis into a vagina.

Annabelle had gone to Thailand, and she was happy with the results. And she was supposed to arrange for that guy to bang her in front of Lenore, so that Lenore could get evidence that a transsexual's vagina did work.

Last night when they were sipping Chardonnay and listening to music, Annabelle said. "I talked to Fred."

"Who the hell is Fred?" Lenore asked.

"My sex buddy," Annabelle said, sounding mellow, courtesy of the *vino*. "I told him about the situation."

Lenore giggled. "What situation?" She knew what Annabelle was referring to.

"That you're a transsexual who wants to know if a transsexual's love box worked. I asked him if he'd give it to me in front of you."

Lenore cracked up. "And what'd he say?"

"'Sure. No problem,'" she quoted Fred.

A time and place was to be announced.

She took a glass of Pepsi to her computer, turned on the machine, and began looking for a doctor who specialized in gender reassignment surgery.

She had a number of names. Thailand wasn't an option. It was too far away. There were doctors in Florida, Canada, Virginia, Wisconsin.

She checked out some of the surgeon's websites. And read about the vagioplasty procedures. And orchiectomies (removing the testicles) and sigmoid this, and penile inversion, and doing this with the scrotum skin.

The procedure in Canada was quite affordable. The surgeon there was Dr. Yves de Maupassant.

Lenore read his credentials, where he had been schooled, etc. He had done thousands of sex change operations. In his guest book, there were

testimonials from happy transsexual patients, who wrote about how the good doctor had saved their lives.

Some patients left their email addresses. Lenore decided to drop them a line and ask about their surgery.

Also, she had to contact the Canadian Medical Association and ascertain if there had been any complaints or malpractice suits against the doctor.

She went to her Hotmail account and penned the doctor a note.

Dear Dr. de Maupassant,

I am interested in having male-to-female surgery. I am 28 years old. Please send me any necessary information.

Thank you,

Lenore Cavanaugh

She sent the message, and immediately heard the AOL guy say, 'You've got mail.'

She returned to her inbox, and discovered a response from the doctor.

She opened the note. It was an automatic response, saying that her message had been received, and offering her a choice of receiving info via snail mail or as an email attachment. 'An attachment will be mailed one day after receipt of your message,' the note said. 'Snail mail will take seven to ten business days.'

Eager to obtain the info, she requested the email attachment.

She looked forward to hearing about the life-changing, irreversible surgery.

CHAPTER 10

"Miss Thang, that food was extra yummy," Jennifer Ann said.

"I agree," Annabelle chimed in. "My compliments to the chef."

Lenore smiled. "I thank you both."

The trio was in Lenore's apartment, at the dinner table. They had just finished a delicious meal of succulent sirloin tip roast, creamy mashed potatoes and zucchini and carrots cooked to perfection. Dessert was a scratch German chocolate cake. Lenore had put out her special occasion tablecloth, the one she used on Thanksgiving and Christmas. "Now, Annie belle," Jennifer Ann said, mispronouncing the child's name yet again. She did that every time and more than once Lenore and Annabelle had corrected her, but it bore no fruit, so they ignored it. "The least you and I can do is bust some suds," Jennifer Ann was saying.

"Sure, no problem," Annabelle said.

"Don't worry about it," Lenore stated. "You're my guests. I'll put everything in the dishwasher in the morning."

"Fine with me," Jennifer Ann said. "I don't feel like getting dishpan hands anyway." To Annabelle, she said, "But let's clear the table. Now, you sit still," she ordered Lenore. "You've done enough today."

Jennifer Ann and Annabelle took the dirty dishes and cutlery to the kitchen and placed it in the sink.

Every Saturday night, for over a month now, the girls had been taking turns having dinner at one another's home.

When they ate at Jennifer's Ann's, her 'husband,' Wayne always came out, talked to them for a little bit, grabbed a plate and went off to another room.

The weekly dinners was Lenore's idea. She thought it would be good for their morale if they were each other's support system.

And Lenore loved cooking.

She was a member of a Yahoo group, and she and another pre-op transsexual regularly exchanged newsy emails and tasty recipes.

Lenore had grown quite fond of Annabelle and Jennifer Ann, and they cared about her as well.

She had introduced Jennifer Ann to Annabelle, and a few times while they were socializing, she had noticed Annabelle eyeing Jennifer Ann wistfully. In fact, more than once, she had looked at Lenore similarly.

Annabelle's expression indicated that she was jealous. Lenore and Jennifer Ann were younger and they passed better than Annabelle.

But Annabelle didn't allow petty jealousy to affect how she treated them. She was sweet to them both.

In the beginning, Jennifer Ann was resistant to Annabelle. "Miss Thang," she told Lenore the day after meeting Annabelle. "Now, you know that I live undercover."

"Yeah," Lenore said.

"Now, it's obvious that Annie belle used to be a boy. Child, a blind man could see it. Now, girl, I can't be runnin' around to no mall or the Old Country Buffet with her. Miss Thang, Wayne and I know people. What if somebody saw me in public with a queen that—well, no, I won't call her a queen cuz she had the operation … But what if somebody saw me with a girl that don't pass too good?"

"So?" Lenore shrugged.

"So?" she shot back, stunned that Lenore didn't see her point. "Well, it could raise some red flags. People would get ideas about me. They would wonder why I was runnin' around with somebody who looked like that."

"Well, more than once, you've invited me to play cards with you and your in-laws. And I get spooked. So you're taking a chance on being seen with me. Someone could make a remark about me."

"That's different and you know it," Jennifer Ann retorted. "You can pass. And even if somebody made a comment about you, I could tell 'em they're crazy. But girl, Annie belle don't leave no room for wonderin'."

"I look at it like this, if you look convincing, you look convincing. And if you're in the company of two dozen obvious trans women, no one is going to think a thing of you."

"Well, there is such a thing as asking for trouble," Jennifer Ann tossed back.

"Look, Annabelle's family isn't supportive of her. And there are assholes in my family who aren't there for me."

"Mine too," Jennifer Ann said.

"And Annabelle's co-workers have been cold to her ... Ann, the last thing she needs is to be rejected by a transsexual. Think back to when you were an effeminate little boy in Tennessee and how other children didn't want to play with you. You told me they called you names and ridiculed you. Think about all the people who have rejected you. Now, don't do that to anybody else," Lenore said, with heart.

"Well, you got a point," Jennifer Ann conceded.

"Look, we're sisters, not by blood. But we are sisters," Lenore said emphatically. "We have to have each other's backs."

"You're right." Jennifer Ann nodded.

Jennifer Ann had always made public appearances with Lenore, going to the mall, the grocery store, to the movies. But if Lenore told her that Annabelle would be tagging along, she'd invent an excuse to beg off.

She went to Annabelle's apartment, and allowed Annabelle to come to her house, but she avoided going out in public with her.

But after her and Lenore's little heart-to-heart, she began making public appearances with Annabelle.

"God, I need a cigarette," Jennifer Ann said, bringing Lenore back to the present. The trio were on their way to the living room.

"You know the rules," Lenore said.

Jennifer Ann went out on the balcony while Annabelle sat on the sofa and Lenore put a *Sounds of the Eighties* CD into the player. She had a collection of 70's and 80's music.

Hall and Oates began belting out Man-eater.

Joining Annabelle on the couch, Lenore said, "I got some info from the surgeon in Canada."

"So when's the big day?" Annabelle asked.

Lenore sighed. "Who knows? First, I have to see the doctor before he'll even consider performing surgery on me. And he may not even think I'm a candidate for surgery."

"Oh, he'll accept you," Annabelle said, reassuringly. She patted Lenore's hand.

"Sure, he will," Jennifer Ann yelled from the balcony, where she was blowing smoke out into the night. "He wants your money."

Lenore chuckled. "Well, if he accepts me, he'll schedule a surgery date. But I have to provide him with three letters of recommendations from three psychiatrists. I don't know why they need to put somebody through all that," Lenore complained.

"Miss Thang, you talkin' about major surgery," Jennifer Ann screamed over the music, holding a lit cigarette between her fingers. "And after you have it, there ain't no going back. Them doctors ain't gone risk no malpractice suit. So they want them letters to cover their butts."

Lenore moaned. "Yeah, I know. But visiting the doctor initially, and seeing a trio of shrinks is just delaying the surgery … And I want a pussy!" she said dramatically.

"Go to the SPCA," Jennifer Ann hollered.

"Ha ha. Miss Jennifer Ann is a stand up comedienne?" Lenore joked.

Annabelle chuckled. She was obviously enjoying Lenore and Jennifer Ann's banter.

Jennifer Ann entered the living room and began swaying to the music. "Y'all can keep that oh surgery. I ain't lettin' no man touch my weinee unless he's about to put it in his mouth."

Annabelle and Lenore laughed.

"That music sounds good," Lenore said and joined Jennifer Ann on the makeshift-dance floor. They jumped around and laughed while Annabelle sat on the sofa, quietly watching, like a shy child at a birthday bash.

"Annabelle, get your ass up here," Jennifer Ann ordered playfully. "And dance with us."

She joined them and giggling, they bounced around to Cindy Lauper's, *Girls Just Want to Have Fun*.

Returning to the couch and puffing, Lenore said, "It's a Saturday night and we're sitting around here like three old biddies. We need to be out, shaking our booties."

Annabelle said, "It's too late to be going out."

Lenore frowned. "Girl, please. It's only a few minutes after nine. Back in my partying days, we didn't hit the clubs 'til about eleven or midnight." Briefly, she remembered the good oh days and the fun times she had had with the queens and gay boys. "We have to find a bar to go to," she stated.

"I've gone to the Hideaway," Annabelle revealed, sitting next to Lenore. "It's nice."

"Is that a gay bar here?" Lenore asked excitedly. She could use a night out.

Annabelle shook her head. "It's for the straight crowd."

Jennifer Ann stopped dancing. Looking at Annabelle, she said, "*You* go to straight bars?"

"Sure," Annabelle replied.

Jennifer Ann shook her head. "Miss Thang, you've got balls."

"Not anymore," Annabelle kidded.

Lenore chuckled.

Annabelle said, "A few guys asked me to dance. Hey, I even asked guys to boogie." She wiggled her shoulders. "This one jerk asked me to dance and when we were on the platform doing our thing, he walked off right in the middle of the song."

Jennifer Ann and Lenore exchanged knowing glances that Annabelle didn't pick up on. Lenore would wager that Annabelle's Fred Astaire probably realized that she wasn't a Ginger Rogers after he got up close and personal.

It was time to give Miss Morrison a crash course in the facts of transsexual nightlife, "I love bars too," Lenore said. "But I don't usually go to straight clubs."

"Me either," Jennifer Ann said.

Annabelle was genuinely confused. "Why?"

"It's a safety issue, girl," Lenore exclaimed. "Trannies in straight clubs can be risky business. We never know what someone may think of us." She shrugged. "They could think that we're a beautiful woman. Or—"

"They could think we're a man," Jennifer Ann said.

Lenore nodded. "And it could lead to violence."

Jennifer Ann said, "And some trannies love hangin' out at the straight clubs, dancin' with the boys, letting 'em by her drinks."

"And if she's ultra convincing, she can get away with it," Lenore said. Back home, she had gone to straight clubs with a few genetic girlfriends and the guys didn't think a thing of her. "Men offered to buy me drinks. They wanted to dance with me. And it was flattering, but I always declined. She paused. "If I had done it and somebody made a comment about me to the guy, he could've flipped out and beat me up. Or worse."

"Back in Tennesse," Jennifer Ann said, "I knew this queen, Miss Percy. She thought she was hot stuff, but she looked okay. She used to go to straight bars, carrying on with the boys. Who didn't know her story. They'd buy her beer. She'd go out to their cars with 'em and give 'em blow jobs and brag to the girls about it." She took a deep breath. "And all the girls told her to be careful. But Miss Percy thought her shit smelled like baby powder. Well, one Saturday night, she went to a straight bar by her lonesome and the next morning, she was found in the Dumpster behind the bar, d-e-a-d," she spelled. "Somebody had shot the child."

"How terrible," Annabelle gasped. "Listening to you two, I realize that I should stay out of straight bars … I wasn't trying to pick up or fool anybody. I just went there to have a little fun."

"Well, a little fun could cost you your life, or at the very least, a bloody nose," Lenore said. "There's a web site called 'Remembering Our Dead.' It's dedicated to the memory of trans people who lost their lives because of hatred … At that site, I read about a transsexual who danced with a man at a straight bar. When he found out she was trans, he killed her."

Jennifer Ann pointed a finger at Annabelle. "So when you get in the mood to shake your ass in a nightclub, go to a queer bar. Ain't no risk in there."

CHAPTER 11

Annabelle had never been to a gay bar. So, Lenore and Jennifer Ann decided to take her to one. They made plans to go on a Saturday night. On the afternoon of the big event, they went to a beauty salon and spent about three hours, getting facials, manicures and pretty hairstyles.

Lenore looked forward to the outing. It had been eons since she had partied. They were going to *Lovers and Friends*, a nightclub that catered to a GLBT (gay/lesbian/bisexual/transgender) crowd. Naturally, heterosexuals were welcome, but they were the minority.

The club was about an hour away from where they all lived. Lenore had gotten the name off the Internet.

They decided to make a night of it. Jennifer Ann's husband, Wayne was off on a fishing trip with his father and brother, and she had told him that she was going to spend Saturday night with Lenore and Annabelle. The girls chipped in, rented a limousine for the night.

The limo was to pick them up at Lenore's apartment at ten o'clock, drop them off at the bar, and then return to the bar at 1:30 to collect them and deliver them back to Lenore's. Annabelle and Jennifer Ann were going to spend the night and the next morning, the trio was going out for breakfast.

Every detail of the evening was Lenore's idea.

They entered the jammed club and paid their cover charges.

The trio looked positively fetching and many eyes were on them. Lenore garnered most of the attention. She was gorgeous and in her heels, she was over 6'0 and her makeup was perfect and her thick shoulder-length hair bounced as she moved.

Annabelle and Jennifer Ann looked great too.

Annabelle's hair was thin, and the stylist talked her into putting in a little weave, which thickened it. The additional hair made her look a little younger. Jennifer Ann and Lenore helped her with her makeup, creating a more dramatic look.

The girls found a place to sit, and a short time later, a sensational looking waiter wearing skin-tight black pants was in front of them, asking them what they wanted.

"How about champagne?" Lenore suggested to the girls.

"I'm game," Jennifer Ann said. "I've never had it."

"I have," Annabelle stated. "Every New Years Eve, my ex and I would have a few bottles. When the kids got older, they joined us." Her expression became melancholy. No doubt remembering all she had sacrificed and lost because of her decision to become Annabelle.

"Well, let's act like tonight's New Years Eve," Lenore said brightly and ordered a bottle of bubbly.

A few minutes later, the waiter returned, carrying a tray holding the champagne and three flutes, which he filled. "Looks like ginger ale," Jennifer Ann remarked.

"But the effect is better," Lenore joked.

As the waiter placed a glass in front of each girl, Lenore got her credit card from her purse. "Lenore, let me help you with that," Annabelle said.

"Me too, Miss Thang," Jennifer Ann offered.

"I'll take care of it," Lenore said. "My treat."

"We'll take turns paying for the rounds," Jennifer Ann stated.

"Let's make a toast." Lenore held her glass aloft. Each girl duplicated her gesture. "To friendship … To joy … To a life that is filled with more celebrations than disappointments."

"Here, here, Miss Thang," Jennifer Ann caroled. They sipped from their flutes. "Ooh, this is nice," Jennifer Ann said, acting as bubbly as the drink she was imbibing.

"That speech was lovely," Annabelle told Lenore. "I'm so glad we're friends." She gave Lenore a little kiss on the cheek.

After they finished one round of champagne, a hot tune came on. "Miss Thang, I love that song," Jennifer Ann exclaimed to Lenore. "Girl, we've got to dance."

"Sure," Lenore said, standing. "Annabelle, come join us."

Annabelle frowned. "Three people dancing together?" Her tone suggested that she thought that was absurd.

"Girl, this is a gay bar," Jennifer Ann yelled. "Look at that." She thrust her head in the direction of the dance floor. Muscle-bound guys were dancing shirtless.

The girls joined the throng of gyrating bodies, swaying to the music, spinning around, giggling like teenyboppers.

After dancing to three songs, they returned to the table and ordered more champagne. After killing it, they went back to the dance floor.

And at a later time, they had a third bottle of champers. By then, all three were buzzing like coeds at a keg party. An oldie by Donna Summers' came on and Annabelle wanted to dance. Jennifer Ann said, "I'm pooped. I'ma sit this one out."

"Well, I'm not tired," Annabelle slurred. "I love it."

You go girl, Lenore thought, going to the dance floor with Annabelle, leaving Jennifer Ann at the table. It was a shame that Annabelle was being disrespected at work and was estranged from her family. She had transitioned so late in life that the male hormones she produced for so many years had made her male appearance almost irreversible. And Lenore felt that was why people were so unkind to her. It was good to see her having fun.

In the middle of their twisting and turning, a man danced over to them, gyrating in front of Lenore. He was about 6'3, with a handsome, hair free face and skin, the color of a Snicker's bar. He and Lenore whirled and twirled while a bewildered looking Annabelle continued to dance.

What the hell is going on, Lenore wondered, amused and dancing.

After the song finished, he followed her and Annabelle to their table. Smiling, he asked, Lenore, "How you doing?" His voice was deep and masculine.

"Fine," she said and reclaimed her seat.

Looking at the empty chair next to her, he asked, "Mind if I sit down?"

"Not at all," she said.

He sat. She was now flanked between this handsome stranger and Annabelle. She introduced him to her friends.

The expression on Jennifer Ann and Annabelle's faces suggested that they thought he was cute. "My name's Trey Fuller," he revealed.

"Nice to meet you, Trey. I'm Lenore Cavanaugh."

Trey said, "Earlier, I saw you sitting over here, and every time I made up my mind to approach you, I lost my nerve. When I saw you and her," he said, nodding to Annabelle, "up there dancing. I just decided to go for it. I hope my forwardness didn't offend you."

"Not at all," she said pleasantly.

"You're a very attractive lady, you know that," he complimented.

Lenore smiled warmly. "Thank you." She wondered if he knew that she was a transsexual. In this place, one could never be certain. In most instances, you could tell the real girls from the drag queens and t-girls.

But not everybody could tell the difference. Earlier in the evening, a couple of lesbians had mistaken Lenore and Jennifer Ann for real women. One wanted to buy Jennifer Ann a drink. "Girl, I'm a t-girl," Jennifer Ann said bluntly, obviously disgusted. She hated it when lesbians approached her.

Looking embarrassed, the woman mutely walked off.

A cute woman in her twenties had invited Lenore for a spin on the dance floor. Lenore explained that she was a transsexual. "You shittin' me? I didn't know," the girl exclaimed. "But we can still dance." She shrugged.

They did. Lesbians had miscalled Lenore before, and it always flattered her when they thought she was a natural-born chick. Validation, baby.

So, she didn't know if Trey knew about her. Additionally, Lenore had received a number of 'Is she or isn't she?' looks. When she emerged from the restroom and was returning to her table, one man stopped her and asked, "What time is it?"

She knew the, 'What time is it,' prank. When people requested the time of a tranny, usually, they wanted to hear her voice to see if it was masculine. She considered asking the guy if she looked like a wristwatch, but answered his question and went about her business.

Focusing on Trey, she said, "I think you should know I'm a transsexual."

"I kinda thought it," he said.

"Am I that obvious?" she spluttered, a bit insulted.

She wished that no one thought a thing, not because she wanted to fool anybody, but because she wanted to be accepted as a woman, unequivocally. But hey, some people had ideas about her. *Get over it.*

"You're not obvious at all," Trey said. "You're gorgeous. But this is a gay club and you're over 6'0 and you look like a supermodel. So, I wondered." He shrugged. "Doesn't matter to me. I'm bisexual." He paused. "Have you had surgery or are you a she-male? Either way, I'd like to get to know you better."

He was attractive and sometimes, she desired male companionship. Smiling warmly, she said, "I'd like to get to know you too. And I'm a pre-op, but I'm definitely going to surgery."

They danced a few songs. She admired the way he moved his body.

After they jumped around to some fast tunes, the lights were dimmed and a slow number followed. He wrapped his arms around her.

In her heels, she was about 6'3, and so was he.

Wonderful, she thought, snuggled up close to him, getting a whiff of his cologne. "I like your cologne," she whispered in his ear.

"Thanks. You smell nice too."

She was wearing Very Irresistible body lotion by Givenchy.

"Your skin is beautiful," he said, caressing her cheek. "So soft."

He stroked her hair. And gently tugged it. She giggled. "It's real, Trey."

He chuckled. "Just wondering. It's gorgeous. And smells nice."

After she started estrogen, her hair became thicker and more lustrous.

"I'd love for you to go home with me," he said seductively. "So I can run my fingers through your gorgeous hair."

"Forget it," she sang sweetly. "I just met you. I need to get to know you before I go home with you."

"Okay, we'll take it slower," he said, sounding disappointed.

Back at the table, he lingered some more, treating her and her friends to a bottle of champagne. And she and Trey danced again.

And when they decided to call it a night, he asked for her phone number, which she scribbled down on a napkin. He also provided his. And although she accepted it, she knew that she'd never phone him.

She was an old-fashioned girl. If a man wanted to talk to her, he could call her.

He escorted her and her girlfriends to the limousine, which was waiting for them. "A limo," he exclaimed, eyeing them all. "One of you rich?"

"Hardly. We just wanted to pamper ourselves," Lenore said, as Annabelle and Jennifer Ann entered the backseat of the car.

"Well, you know how to do it in style," he said appreciatively.

"It was so nice meeting you," she stated in a warm and gracious tone.

"Same here, and I'll call you tomorrow night. Mind if I have a kiss?"

"Sure," she said softly.

He hugged her and gave her a soulful kiss on the lips. At first, she was stunned. She expected a peck on the cheek, not the mind-blowing smooch that he gave her. Which she loved, by the way. That kiss could harden a girl's nipples.

They whispered goodnight.

The limo glided away, and they began their journey back to Lenore's apartment.

Jennifer Ann sat next to the window, puffing a Marlboro and blowing smoke out into the night. Teasingly, she said, "Miss Thang got picked up. He was cute, girl."

"Mm-hmm," Annabelle said. "Tell us about him."

"Well, he's twenty seven and a pharmacist," Lenore said.

"A pharmacist!" Jennifer Ann blurted out. "Oh, Miss Thang, if something comes of this, you may never again have to pay for hormones. He could give you a whole box of 'em."

Annabelle and Lenore giggled.

"He really liked you," Annabelle said. "I could tell by how he was looking at you."

Yeah, Lenore got the impression that he admired her as well.

"I'm jealous," Annabelle said.

"Girl, no one knows what's going to come of this," Lenore said. "I could end up hating the guy. We may discover that we have nothing in common. Besides, you have Fred."

And when was she going to see him sex up Annabelle?

Annabelle made a face in the dimly lit car. "Oh, that's nothing serious. We get together when he can get away from his missus."

"His missus?" Jennifer Ann shrieked, "Miss Thang, you having an affair with a married man? I love it." She chuckled.

Lenore didn't love it, and she had had no idea that Fred was married. That didn't change her desire to see him have sex with Annabelle. She wanted to see if a tranny's vagina worked.

But no way would Lenore mess around with a married man. Some trannies did it, but that was not for Lenore Cavanaugh.

For the sake of his career, or standing in the community, a lot of men lived a double life.

They had a wife and kids, and sneaked around with some dumb transsexual. A lot of trannies thought they were being cute messing around with married men.

But they were being used.

That man had everything, wife, child/children, and the respect of society.

Humph, and there the t-girl was being maligned, disrespected, discriminated against.

Lenore figured if she could be who she was and roll with the punches, any man involved with her could do likewise.

* * *

"Miss Thang, you've got too many hang-ups," Jennifer Ann said a few mornings later when she and Lenore were on the phone, discussing transsexuals having affairs with married men. Of course, Lenore wouldn't have mentioned the subject in front of Annabelle, since Annabelle was a married man's plaything.

"Over the years, I've had sex with many married men," Jennifer Ann said. "I love messing around with a real bitch's husband. That whore's got everythang, so the least I can do is fuck her husband.' She chuckled.

She resents natural-born women, Lenore thought. And what had a natural-born woman ever done to Jennifer Ann, save be what she wanted to be? Lenore bore real women no hard feelings. A real chick was born female and could have children and menstruate and Lenore couldn't. Hey, that's life.

Jennifer Ann was saying, "Seriously, some tranny girls just have to take what they can get."

"Not me!" Lenore yelled. "I want a boyfriend who takes me out. Brings me flowers. Goes on romantic walks with me … I deserve better than being some married man's cheap thrill. And I'm surprised by you, Ann."

"What?" Jennifer Ann said.

"That you'd suggest that a trans woman has to take what she can get. I mean, that isn't what you're doing. You don't work. Wayne takes care of you." And he did so quite well. Jennifer Ann lived in a nice house. Drove a nice car. Had money in her pocket. Her clothes weren't exactly rags. "You haven't settled, and to make sure that you are acknowledged as a woman, you've kept Wayne's family in the dark about your true self."

"I know, Miss Thang, but some girls aren't as lucky as I am."

Well, Lenore Cavanaugh wouldn't settle for less.

CHAPTER 12

It was the night of the much anticipated phone call. The previous evening at the club, Trey said that he'd call her around ten or ten fifteen. "I hope that isn't too late," he had said.

"Not at all," Lenore had replied. "I'm a night owl. I'll be up."

He explained that the drug store where he worked closed at nine. And it took him about fifteen minutes to get home. And then he showered, put on something to relax in. Grabbed a bite and a Heineken to unwind with.

She was sitting up in bed, waiting for the call, wondering what did Trey relax in. Sweat pants? Underwear? Did he wear boxers or briefs?

The phone rang, interrupting her thoughts.

She glanced at the clock on the nightstand. It was 10:12. She silenced the ringing.

She and Trey went through the how are you, did you have a great day routine.

"I told you I'd call," he said. His voice was deep and sexy. And she loved how it sounded.

"And you have. A few minutes earlier than you said, in fact."

"I was eager to hear your sweet voice," he flirted.

"You think I have a sweet voice?" she flirted right back.

"Very much so. Girl, you are a woman. Everything about you."

Ooh, she loved it. Praise was good for the ego. "Well, thank you," she sang.

"I'm not up on what transsexuals do to enhance their appearance," he said. "I know about breast implants."

"Well, mine are real," she said. "But there's facial feminization and voice modification surgery. That's the extreme stuff. The simple stuff is electrolysis and hormones. If anything is simple about altering one's sex."

"So you didn't have any of the extreme stuff done?"

"Uh-uh," she replied truthfully. "Everything is on the up and up. With the help of hormones, I grew my boobs. Electrolysis got rid of my facial hair. You're a pharmacist."

"Yes, ma'am."

"How long have you been doing that?"

"Three years. Wasn't that long ago, I graduated from pharmacy school. So, tell me, pretty lady, how do you earn a paycheck?"

She smiled warmly. She really liked how he talked to her, the way a man spoke to a woman. "Right now, I'm not working," she stated.

"But you have your own apartment and last night, you were riding in a limousine. How're you doing all this?"

"You're wondering if I'm dealing drugs. Or if I'm a paid escort?" she joked.

"Girl, you're crazy. I didn't think you were involved in any shit like that. But if you were an escort, I'm sure you'd be high class, all the way. There's nothing cheap about you."

"Flatterer."

"So, are you an heiress?" he probed.

"Hardly. As a male, for about three and a half years, I worked two jobs. And socked away money. While I was working, I was having electrolysis, and taking hormones. And when my breasts became obvious and my hips curvaceous, I quit my job."

"And became a lady of leisure," he said.

"Eventually, I'll go back to work. My savings won't last forever."

"I'm guessing you handled it the way you did because you didn't want to make a switch on the job."

"Yeah. Transforming on the job was a prescription—deliberate pun—for trouble. There would have been gossip. People refusing to use the correct pronoun. I'm sure that someone would have made an issue out of me using the women's restroom." She sighed. "There's going to be some of that when I rejoin the work force. But when I do, at least, I wouldn't have done it right before everybody's eyes ... And bodily, I'll be one hundred percent female." She took a deep breath. "Maybe, I'm a coward for handling it this way. But I just didn't want to deal with a lot of drama."

And looking back on it, at the grocery store where she had worked, some of her coworkers were quite ignorant. She worked as a man, and did drag on the weekends, so she had arched eyebrows and long nails, and there were rumors that Travis Cavanaugh was gay. And some of her colleagues were aloof to her. So, if she had gone from Travis to Lenore right before their very eyes, she knew those assholes would've stirred up some shit.

"You're not a coward," Trey said, understandingly. "It's not chicken to spare yourself unnecessary bullshit. You simply made your life easier."

"Right now, my life is in limbo," she said. "I don't have a surgery date. So, I'm not working because I don't want to get involved in a job, and then have to request time off to have surgery and recuperate."

"Makes sense. Just be grateful you have money set aside."

There was a pause. "Trey, I'm curious about something you said."

"What?"

"You told me you're bisexual. Now, I'm not judging you. But I don't understand bisexuality. I mean, I can appreciate same sex desires. God knows, I can understand a person wanting to alter their gender. But I don't get a person's attraction to both genders."

He chuckled lightly. "I don't really get it myself. It's just who I am. I think the biggest reason why happiness eludes a lot of people is because they spend too much time analyzing everything instead of just accepting what is what, and going with it."

She nodded emphatically. She agreed with that.

Trey said, "I'm attracted to men and to women. I admire handsome and beautiful faces. I enjoy breasts. I enjoy pussies. I enjoy ass."

An equal opportunity fucker, she thought, giggling.

"Did I say something amusing?" he asked.

"I noticed that you didn't comment on penises," she said.

He chuckled. "I have no problem with penises. I like penises."

"Trey, you really have it together," she said.

He sighed. "M-m, not entirely. I have idiosyncrasies."

"Oh?" she stated.

"I enjoy having sex with men. But I don't kiss men. Can't deal with facial hair."

"Well, not all men have facial hair. So do you kiss clean shaven men?"

"No ma'am," he replied. "I only kiss women … and I consider you to be a woman, and I'd love to get my lips on yours," he said seductively.

She giggled like a schoolgirl flirting with a cute boy in her biology class. "I'm curious about something," she said. "How does a bisexual handle a relationship?"

"I don't understand what you're asking."

"Do you have an understanding with the people you're involved with. When you're dating a man or a woman, do they know about your desires for the opposite sex? And do you have some kind of an agreement with them, that you can see other people on the side?"

"For starters, I don't date men … I have sexual encounters with men, yes. But I don't do the dinner, walks on the moonlit beach thing with dudes."

"But you do date women?" she said.

"Absolutely."

"Do the women know about your bisexuality?" she asked.

"No. A lot of them just couldn't grasp it. Guys I get off with know that I'm into women as well as men. And they can deal with it. They know it's a reality … And I view you as a woman, but because of your background, I figured you could deal with the truth."

"So, I wonder when you're involved with a woman, do you step out on her with men?" Lenore asked.

"Absolutely not. When I'm involved with a woman, I'm devoted to her."

"So you curb your desire to be with men?" she said, curious.

"Lenore, I don't desire men 24/7. But if I'm in a relationship with a woman, and I encounter a man whom I dig, I don't act on it. It's that simple. When I'm in a relationship, I don't cheat on her. Hey, if I was totally heterosexual that would be my attitude … If I feel the need to cheat, the relationship isn't working for me. I don't care if a person is heterosexual, bisexual, gay, when you're in a relationship, sex with other people is a no-no. At least, in my book."

Lenore wondered if Trey was full of shit. She believed him when he said that he swung both ways. But she had misgivings about his claim that he was one hundred percent loyal when he was involved with a woman.

She wondered if he had sex with guys while seeing a woman. Many husbands, boyfriends and fiancés did it.

For about three hours, they chatted. At some point, she heard a splashing sound. Frowning, she asked, "What the hell is that?"

"Me, taking care of nature."

"You're peeing while I'm on the phone?" she exclaimed. Giggled. "How rude!"

While they conversed, she sipped two goblets of wine. He ordered a pizza from a delivery place and said he wished she was there to share it with him.

That would be nice, she thought. They talked about music, pop novels. He said he read *The Washington Post* and *The New York Times* for national news. He enjoyed the details and the sophisticated writing.

She told him that one day she wanted to visit Paris and Hawaii. "That's my dream," she said.

"Sounds achievable," he replied. "Maybe I can go with you."

That made her smile warmly.

At one something in the morning, they whispered goodnight. What she had shared with Trey was nothing more than a wonderfully lengthy phone conversation, but Lenore now knew why Cinderella merrily danced around the room when she came home from the ball. Spending time with a prince was delightful.

CHAPTER 13

"Miss Thang, there's got to be a fly in the ointment," Jennifer Ann said, pulling the skin off a chicken breast and putting it in her mouth. She and Lenore were in a park, sitting at a picnic table, eating a bucket of KFC they had picked up.

Earlier, Lenore had phoned Jennifer Ann and suggested they grab some chicken and take it to the park.

The sun was shining, and the park was overflowing with people, pushing squealing kids in swings. Couples in love were taking hand-in-hand strolls.

"That boy sounds too perfect," Jennifer Ann remarked. "Like he doesn't have a pimple on his ass."

Lenore chuckled. "But I think he's sincere."

"Yeah, but I have issues with that stuff about when he's with a woman, he doesn't cheat."

"I wonder about it too," Lenore said, breaking a chicken wing in two. She loved KFC's wings. They were so flavorful and tender. "As I said, we're in the talking stages, but girl, he would be the perfect man for me. He knows my situation and he's okay with it. And he's *tall*." She wiggled her shoulders.

"Hello!" Jennifer Ann snapped a finger. "I don't want no boy shorter than I am."

After they finished all but two pieces of the poultry, Jennifer Ann tossed their trash in a nearby garbage can. They went to the ladies room, where Lenore was swept by that familiar feeling of wrongdoing. She looked like a woman, and for the most part, she was accepted as one. But every time, she entered a women's restroom, she felt like she was doing something that she shouldn't be doing. Maybe she felt that way because she still had a penis.

But looking as she did, she'd create a commotion if she used the men's room, something she'd never considered doing.

While Jennifer Ann was in a stall tinkling, Lenore was at the basin, washing her hands, which was what Jennifer Ann did after she emerged from the stall. She and Lenore returned to the park, and sat side-by-side in swings.

"You know, Trey's got two children," Lenore revealed, swaying gently. Jennifer Ann did likewise. When they had talked the previous evening, Lenore had learned that Trey had two young children whom he saw every weekend. "And he doesn't want anymore. So if anything comes of this, a baby won't be an issue."

"Why did he and his wife bust up?" Jennifer Ann asked.

"He said she had a daddy complex. That she was looking for someone to take care of her, financially and emotionally."

"Hmm. I wonder if he's stingy. Now, you don't want a boy that won't spend no money on you."

"He said the breakup wasn't about money," Lenore said. "But that she was child-like and needed someone to watch out for her, make all the decisions. Besides, I want someone I can trust and love. I can earn my own money."

"Well, that's all good and fine, but you want a boy that will buy you gifts."

"On special occasions, I want to be acknowledged," Lenore said. "When we go to dinner, I prefer a man to pick up the tab." She had a little peeve about that. "But I can work for my own money. And help with the bills."

"Well, I like being taken care of," Jennifer Ann gushed. "It makes me feel like a total woman to have a man support me … I like staying at home, sitting on my butt, while my husband works."

Jennifer Ann was a homemaker and Wayne earned a paycheck. They lived a very traditional man/woman life.

"I wonder," Jennifer Ann said. "If Trey really broke up with his wife because she was so needy. Or if the breakup was because he liked men."

"That crossed my mind too. But he said when he's involved with a woman, he doesn't cheat."

"People say a lot of things that aren't necessarily true," Jennifer Ann said.

They had driven to the park in Lenore's car. And Lenore drove Jennifer Ann home. When she was approaching Jennifer Ann's house, she saw Alice, Jennifer

Ann's 'mother-in-law,' standing on the front porch, holding a brown paper bag.

"Oh, there's Alice," Jennifer Ann exclaimed.

Lenore parked at the curb. Alice turned at the sound of the car and waved.

"Miss Thang, come on in," Jennifer Ann said to Lenore.

They got out of the car and walked up to the front porch. "So, there you are," said Alice, smiling pleasantly at Jennifer Ann. Alice was a commonplace looking white woman, of average height, in her early fifties. "I saw your car in the driveway. I thought you were inside ignoring the door," she joked.

"Now, you know I wouldn't ignore you, Alice. You remember my friend, Lenore?"

Alice nodded and smiled. "Hey Lenore. How are you?"

"Fine," Lenore replied, while Jennifer Ann was unlocking the door.

Lenore had conversed with Alice periodically and found her to be a likeable woman.

However, Lenore felt uncomfortable in her presence. Jennifer Ann was lying to the woman about who she really was. And because Lenore had to be conscientious of everything she said, she preferred not to be around that kind of deceit.

And when in the company of her 'in-laws,' Jennifer Ann did not refer to Lenore as Miss Thang. In fact, in the presence of Wayne's family, her speech wasn't as colorful.

In the house, Jennifer Ann asked Alice what was in the bag she was carrying.

"Tomatoes, peppers, cucumbers and zucchini from my garden. There's plenty here," Alice answered. "Why don't you give Lenore some?"

"I will."

In the kitchen, Lenore and Alice sat at the table while Jennifer Ann poured ginger ale into three glasses. Alice asked what they had done that afternoon. "Oh, we got some chicken from KFC," Jennifer Ann said. "Went to the park. Just sat and talked." She needlessly elevated her voice. She sounded like a woman, naturally. But when she was around people that didn't know her situation—waitresses, store clerks, she made her voice go higher. It was amazing that she could accomplish it.

Lenore felt quite comfortable with her feminine voice and felt no need to try and make it sound higher.

"That's nice," Alice said. Smiling extravagantly at Lenore, Alice said, "Did Ann tell you her good news?"

"What?" Lenore asked. Did Jennifer Ann hit the lottery? Win a giant screen TV?

Eyeing Jennifer Ann, Alice said, "You didn't tell her?"

Jennifer Ann looked sheepish. "I haven't gotten around to it," she mumbled.

Frowning, Lenore asked, "What's going on?"

"It's your news," Alice told Jennifer Ann. "You tell her."

"I'm pregnant," Jennifer Ann blurted, in a voice that was shrill and antsy.

"Why you sounding nervous about it?" Alice stated. "It's wonderful news."

Jennifer Ann smiled stupidly.

"Um, that's nice," Lenore managed to get out. She could not believe that Jennifer Ann had told this sweet woman such a gigantic lie.

"Isn't it, though?" Alice exclaimed. "I'm going to be a grandma once again," she sang joyously. Patting Jennifer Ann's hand, she said, "She's not too far along, just a few weeks. I was beginning to wonder if Wayne and Ann would ever give us a grandchild."

They aren't, Lenore thought.

* * *

Driving home, Lenore wondered how in the world did Jennifer Ann expect to pull off this pregnancy scam?

She shook her head. It just didn't make any damn sense for Jennifer Ann to be lying to those people. It was wrong.

But it wasn't her problem. She had her own issues.

CHAPTER 14

Later that evening, Lenore was sitting at the kitchen table enjoying a salad with chicken strips and some of the veggies that Jennifer Ann had given her. When she was pouring a little more homemade vinaigrette onto the mixed vegetables, the phone rang.

She answered it. "Miss Thang, I bet you mad with me," Jennifer Ann said.

"Why would you say that?" Lenore stated.

"Because of that little lie I told Alice."

Lenore chuckled. "Little lie? You told Alice that you're pregnant and that's not possible because genetically you're a male."

"Oh, you just don't understand," Jennifer Ann spat irritably.

"No, I don't. And it's not important for me to understand. It's not my life." She stabbed a forkful of salad and put it in her mouth.

"Miss Thang, listen, five minutes after Wayne and I got married, Alice—"

You and Wayne aren't married, Lenore thought. *Two men cannot get married in the state of Virginia.* And although, Lenore saw Jennifer Ann as a woman, that isn't how the lawmakers of the commonwealth of Virginia would see it.

Jennifer Ann was saying, "started harassing us, 'When y'all gonna have a baby?' When y'all gonna have a baby?'"

"In her eyes, you and Wayne are a traditional couple," Lenore said. "So she assumed that you were going to have children."

"Well, I kept telling her that Wayne and I wanted some time together before we had a child. But that didn't shut her up. I got sick of hearing it," Jennifer Ann said.

"So to hush her, you told her that you're pregnant?" Lenore rolled her eyes.

"Exactly," Jennifer Ann said.

"Well, when women are with child, they tend to develop a big belly ... So, how do you intend to pull this off? On the soaps, women who lie about being pregnant wear pregnancy pillows. Maybe, you're going to wear one of those," she said sarcastically. "Where would you find such a thing, by the way?"

"God, you are so judgmental," Jennifer Ann said wearily.

Still being acerbic, Lenore said, "And are you actually going to have this baby? What are you going to do—steal an infant from a hospital nursery and pass it off as yours."

"Oh, Miss Thang don't be ridiculous," Jennifer Ann snapped. "Though your idea isn't half-bad," she kidded.

"Ann, this situation isn't remotely funny."

"For your information, in a few weeks, I'm gonna say that I lost the baby, and that the doctor told me that I can't carry a child full term."

"Oh, my God," Lenore exclaimed, rolling her eyes.

"Well, that happened to my Aunt Tammy, so I know it's true. And it'll get Alice off my back."

"Know what I think," Lenore said.

"No, but I'm sure you're gonna tell me."

"I think you take perverse pleasure in deceiving people. Maybe you resent them because they're accepted, and you know that you never will be. So you get your kicks out of making fools out of them."

"Miss Thang, you can kiss my ass," Jennifer Ann exploded. "Everything you've said is so off the mark. I'd like to know why you care so much any damn way? Considering, it ain't none of your fuckin' business."

"Well, I'm entitled to my opinions. And you made it my *fuckin'* business when you involved me in it. I don't like lying to people."

"So what are you sayin'? You gonna blab to Alice?"

"You know, I'd never do that," Lenore said.

"Look, I love Wayne's family. They are *my* family. They've been good to me, and I want their acceptance. And if I have to fudge things a little, so be it. I ain't doin' nothin' to nobody, except living out my life the way I want to." She took a breath. "All my life, I was belittled, criticized, and it would start all over again if I told people I'm a transsexual. I ain't doin' it." She slammed down the phone.

Secrets always come out, Lenore thought and in time, so would Jennifer Ann's. The question was when and how.

CHAPTER 15

Lenore pulled her car into a parking space and turned off the ignition. She vacated the auto, locked the door, and entered the lobby of the five story brick building, joining a few people on the elevator and riding up to the fourth floor.

She was on her way to see Dr. Eleanor Castle, a psychiatrist. Before she could get the doctor in Montreal to perform her surgery, she needed three letters from three different head doctors. She hoped Dr. Castle would provide a letter of recommendation.

Lenore had obtained Dr. Castle's name from the Internet and the doctor counseled transgender patients.

Lenore got off at the fourth floor and briefly searched for suite 419, Dr. Castle's office, which she entered, and was relieved to discover that no other patients were in the waiting room.

The sooner she got out of there, the better.

She informed the receptionist of her arrival. She didn't have to fill out any paperwork. She had taken care of that online. "Dr. Castle will be with you in a few minutes," the receptionist said. "You can have a seat."

Lenore sat and flipped through an old issue of *Family Circle.*

The sound of a door squeaking open grabbed Lenore's attention. "Are you Lenore?" Dr. Castle asked, smiling warmly.

She nodded.

"I'm Dr. Castle," she said, extending her hand, which Lenore graciously accepted. The doctor appeared to be Jewish, in her early fifties, with long brown hair, streaked with gray, dull and in need of a deep conditioner. She wore it parted in the middle. Her face was *sans* makeup.

Dr. Castle's expression suggested that she was impressed with Lenore's appearance. Her eyes went from Lenore's attractive face to her feet. "Let's go to my office," she said pleasantly.

When they were in the office, the doctor closed the door. "Have a seat," she said, pointing to the loveseat facing her desk.

Sinking into the soft cushions, Lenore noticed that the office was serviceable, nothing ostentatious or ritzy. There was a crammed bookcase, framed diplomas on the wall. On her desk were framed pictures and a mug containing pencils and pens.

From behind her desk, Dr. Castle said—"I am impressed with your appearance. I would've never thought you were anything but a woman. Even your voice wouldn't have made me think anything."

"Thank you," Lenore said.

"Would you like a Coke, orange juice, spring water, coffee, tea?" she asked.

What are you, a flight attendant, Lenore thought. "I'm fine, thank you," she said.

Dr. Castle said, "So, you want to have sex reassignment surgery?"

"Yes," Lenore stated.

"Do you have a doctor in mind?"

"A surgeon in Canada," Lenore answered.

"Canada? Well, there are a number of eminently qualified doctors in the U.S. who could help you. Why go out of the country?"

"Money."

"So the surgery is cheaper in Canada?"

Lenore nodded. She was sure that the doctor was aware of this. After all, she worked with trannies.

Many transsexuals traveled outside of the United States to have surgery. Some girls said they would have never amassed the funds if they did it on U.S. soil. And since the doctors overseas regularly performed SRS (sex reassignment surgery), Lenore felt they had perfected the procedure.

Lenore explained that she checked out the surgeon's credentials, had spoken with some of his patients and was confident that she would be in capable hands.

"How long have you been on hormones?" Dr. Castle asked.

"A little over a year."

"They have certainly served you well," the doctor said.

Lenore smiled warmly.

"How old are you?" she asked.

"Twenty eight."

"How does your family feel about what you're going to do? Or what you've done so far?"

"They don't like it," Lenore replied.

"So, you've had spats with them about it?"

Lenore chuckled. "Spats? Try, knock down, drag outs."

"Does their rejection bother you?" the doctor wanted to know.

"A little."

"Please explain."

"I wish I were on better terms with my family, but I'm not. I have my own life to live, and I'm going to live it. And I don't care what my family thinks. If they don't want to be bothered with me because of who I am, that is their loss."

The doctor's facial expression suggested that she thought Lenore had a healthy attitude about it. And Lenore was not feeding the woman a bunch of bullshit. She was not living for her family. Actually, she never felt connected to them. She had nothing in common with them. They didn't like the same things she liked. Lenore enjoyed reading books and she wanted to travel. Her family thought books were a waste of time. Traveling and broadening their horizons was not a priority to them.

"What are you hoping this surgery will accomplish for you?" Dr. Castle queried.

"Bring me peace."

"You see having a vagina as making you peaceful?"

"Yes, I do," Lenore said.

"Can you elucidate?"

Lenore sighed. "Well, right now, I have breasts and a penis. And when I have surgery, I'll be whole, and that will make me comfortable, put me at ease."

The doctor said, "So, you're not at ease with the way you are physically, right now."

"Not really," she said.

"But you seemed poised and confident."

"For the most part, I'm comfortable with myself. I don't feel ill at ease in public," Lenore said. "Again, for the most part."

The doctor frowned. "For the most part?"

"Well, when I go in the ladies restroom, I feel funny, like I'm entering a place that I don't feel I should go in."

"Why do you think you feel that way?" the doctor asked.

Lenore scowled. "Maybe, a part of me feels like someone will tell me that I'm not supposed to be there."

"Has that ever happened?" Dr. Castle asked.

"No. But there are people who have ideas about me."

"You mean, there are people who question your gender?"

"Yes," Lenore rejoined.

"I wouldn't see why. Do you think perhaps because you know what is what that maybe you think others have suspicions about it?"

"See, you're asking me that because you wouldn't have questioned my gender. But there are people who do question it," Lenore said. "I have been called sir by nasty grocery clerks. In the apartment complex where I live, I think a few neighbors have suspicions about me."

"And how do you feel about people having thoughts about you?" the doctor inquired.

Lenore shrugged. "It's just something that I have to deal with, and that will probably be the case for the rest of my life."

"Okay," the psychiatrist said in a tone that suggested that at that very instant a bright idea had popped in her mind. "You do realize that people's questions about you won't stop because you have a vagina. I mean, you won't be walking around naked."

"And even if I did walk around naked, some people would still think I'm a transsexual," Lenore retorted. "They would make an issue of my height. People are enlightened about this subject. They know that people can and do have sex changes."

"You have a good head on your shoulders," the doctor said.

"I think so," Lenore replied.

"You view things realistically. Do you see yourself as a woman?" she asked. "I mean, as trite as it sounds, many transsexuals say that they feel like a woman trapped inside a man's body."

Lenore chuckled. "I've heard that one. It's as old as reruns of *I Love Lucy.*"

"How do you feel about it?"

"I don't see myself as a woman trapped in a man's body. My mother gave birth to a baby boy. And I … that baby boy wanted to be a girl." She shrugged. "Why? That's a real mystery. So, I've stopped trying to figure it out. I'm just me, Lenore."

"How do you feel about your penis?" the doctor asked.

Lenore chuckled. "I want it gone. That should answer your question."

"But how do you view it?"

"Women don't have penises," Lenore stated.

"Do you hate your penis?"

Okay, Lenore wanted this woman to give her a letter saying that she was a good candidate for sex change surgery. So, to boost her chances of getting what she wanted, she could lie and say she hated her penis. But she refused to misrepresent her feelings about anything. "No, I don't hate my penis ... My penis gives me pleasure."

"So, you have a sex life?" the doctor asked.

"I have in the past, but right now, I don't." That could possibly change with Trey, she thought. That remained to be seen. "But I masturbate."

"So you have erections?"

"Yes."

"And the hormones haven't interfered with you getting erections?" the doctor wanted to know.

"Not at all."

"How often do you masturbate?" came from Dr. Castle.

"Once or twice a week," Lenore answered.

"And you realize that you won't be able to stimulate yourself after you have surgery," the doctor said.

"Perhaps, I can do it with my new equipment," Lenore retorted.

Dr. Castle took a swig from the bottle of spring water that was sitting on her desk. "Well, after surgery, some transsexual patients say there is a reduction in sensation; that they can't orgasm."

"That's a chance I'm prepared to take," Lenore said.

"So orgasms and sexual sensation is not important to you?" the doctor said.

"Well, I'd like to have sexual sensations," Lenore said. "I'd like to climax. Sex is a thrilling experience. It is how couples express their affection for each other."

"Just one of the ways couples express their love," retorted the doctor.

"A very essential way ... One day, I hope to marry, and make love with my husband."

Dr. Castle asked, "Do you think being a transsexual will interfere with your chances of finding a husband?"

"Some men will definitely have a problem with me, yes. No doubt about it," Lenore said. "But I'm reasonably attractive."

"That you are," the doctor said.

"And I'm articulate and intelligent. I'm honest, reliable. I'll make some man a great wife. But I know, because of what I am, finding a husband won't be as simple as one, two, three."

"Trust me," the doctor said. "It's difficult for any woman to find a husband."

There was a pause. "So, you don't think you will have any emotional problems after surgery ... when your penis is gone?"

"No. For me, surgery would be reason to bring out the party hats and the bottles of bubbly," Lenore joked.

The doctor smiled.

"Seriously," Lenore said. "For me, having this surgery is as simple as coloring my hair or painting my nails. My genitals don't match who I am, so they must go."

"But when you color your hair or nails, and if you decide you don't like it, you can always recolor it or remove the polish." She shrugged. "But with this surgery, there is no going back. It is irreversible. And there are some transsexuals who have had surgery and then decided that they wanted to go back to being men. They had lost their families, and society still questioned who they were, and they wanted to return to their original gender."

Lenore shook her head emphatically. "Not me. The person sitting before you is who I am. I want to be put in a coffin this way and a vagina will make me whole ... My life is not going to be perfect after I have surgery. People will still have ideas about me. I will have to find employment. My co-workers will probably gossip ... Some of them will shun me. But I will be okay." She took a deep breath. She wanted to put an end to this discussion. And she did not look forward to going through this with the other two shrinks. But it was inescapable.

"Our time is almost up," the doctor said.

Thank God, Lenore thought. "So," she said, "Will you write the letter of recommendation?"

"I'll have to see you a few more times before I can answer that question," Dr. Castle replied.

Moneygrubber, Lenore snapped inwardly. She went to the receptionist's desk and scheduled another appointment

Driving home, she reconsidered her opinion about Dr. Castle. Maybe, she wasn't solely motivated by money. Perhaps, the good doctor figured that she couldn't decide from one conversation that Lenore should have the surgery. And she needed to see her a few more times before she made that determination.

Lenore had to be patient. But she wanted that damn surgery.

CHAPTER 16

At home, Lenore soaked in a hot bubble bath. When the water became lukewarm, she drained some of it and added more hot.

Before immersing herself in the delightful bath, she had changed the bedclothes, putting on fresh sheets and pillowcases. She loved the smell of clean bedding. And she changed her sheets every other day.

In addition to bathing, she washed and conditioned her hair, set it on large rollers. Dried it under the hair dryer.

She brushed it out, rendering it full, bouncy glistening and soft. Standing before the bathroom mirror, she tossed her head back and forth like those chicks in the shampoo commercials and managed to giggle.

She was dressed in one of her favorite lounging outfits, a floor-length silk peignoir, a light peach color, soft and silky. Ooh, she adored it. She had found it in a catalog specializing in garments for tall women. And it reminded her of something a screen siren would have donned in an old movie.

And with her just styled hair, and clad in the robe, she could pass for a screen siren.

Many transsexuals had the glamour girl thing going on. Many had it without trying to achieve it. A little makeup and a hairstyle could bring it out. But being tall and gorgeous could get a t-girl read. Countless times, Lenore heard—"She looks too good to be a real woman."

What rubbish. There were plenty of real women who prettied up all the time.

Some real women thought Lenore spent hours and hours in front of the mirror getting dolled up. And it usually took her about thirty minutes if that, to bathe, apply a face and rub on some perfumed body lotion.

To avoid getting unwanted attention or raising people's suspicions, or just to blend in, some trannies shunned cosmetics and perfume. Some didn't even style their hair.

Forget that. Lenore liked looking pretty and feminine and she was not going to forgo cosmetics and enchanting fragrances, so that people wouldn't scrutinize her.

She went through a lot of heartache and yearning to become Lenore, and by God, she was going to celebrate her femininity, her softness; her womanhood.

It was only four-thirty in the afternoon, and she was dressed like she was ready to call it a night.

But who cared? She was in for the rest of the day. She had no desire to leave the apartment. The session with Dr. Castle had left her emotionally drained.

So, she was going to sip wine and watch TV or a movie. When she grew bored with that, she'd read.

All snug and cozy on her queen-size bed, she thought about her visit with Dr. Castle, which had put her in a reflective frame of mind. And that was a good thing, she supposed. She needed to ponder her choices and motivations, though she had no misgivings about wanting to have surgery.

She thought about real women. God, they had it so much easier. They took so much for granted. Sometimes when Lenore was in an eatery or the grocery store, she'd watch a real woman having a meal or putting eggs in her shopping cart, just being herself.

Not concerned with what some person may be thinking of her. If a passerby looked at her and whispered something to his or her friend, Miss Natural-born woman would think they were praising or ridiculing her earrings or shoes.

A transsexual would think they were questioning her gender.

Real women didn't worry about sick people in society humiliating them. Or beating them up or killing them.

But there were troubled souls in society who'd do bodily injury or murder a transsexual, just for being a transsexual.

Normal women didn't have to worry about some suspicious person furtively looking at her hands or feet. Or neck in search of an Adam's apple. Normal women didn't have to deal with people inventing an excuse to get in her face, so they could search for a five o'clock shadow.

Normal women didn't have people engage her in conversation just to hear her voice.

And who could forget the gazers? They have suspicions about a transsexual, so they stare her down. Staring is their indirect way of saying, 'I know about you.' The transsexual is supposed to react with a hand caught in the cookie jar expression. She is supposed to quickly avert her face. And that will confirm the gazers suspicions.

Naturally, Lenore had been stared at, and not once, out of shame, had she moved her eyes in another direction. Not once had she turned away with a guilty look. She wasn't committing a crime, so, why should she behave as though she was? The gazers could go straight to hell.

Lenore passed well, and people could stare and inspect her all they wanted, but they couldn't say unequivocally that she wasn't born female.

And besides, if some fool is gazing at a transsexual and she rapidly wheeled her face away, how the hell does that prove that she is a transsexual?

Let's be real. Some stranger staring at a person could very well be a maniac, and the transsexual could have shifted her eyes out of fear.

And why oh why was Lenore even pondering this bullshit?

And when she complained about the things transsexuals went through, she got the sense that some people felt no compassion for her. They felt that she had brought it on herself.

Truthfully, she didn't want their compassion. It was Lenore's cross to bear. And she'd bear it.

The phone chimed, yanking her out of her thoughts. Looking at the phone, she wondered if Jennifer Ann or Annabelle was calling. She hoped no one wanted to come by for a visit. She could handle a phone chat, but she wasn't in the mood for any face-to-face conversations. She silenced the ringing.

"Hello," she said in a tone devoid of brightness.

"Hey, pretty lady," Trey said.

She smiled warmly. "Hey yourself." Hearing his baritone helped to elevate her spirits.

"How you doing?" he asked.

This man did not need to hear about her woes. "Wonderfully," she said.

"Well, you didn't sound *wonderfully* when you picked up the phone."

"You're very perceptive. When you called, I was deep in thought."

"Thinking about something unpleasant?" he asked.

"Just thinking," she said, evasively.

"Well, you need to take your mind off it."

"Maybe this phone call will do that," she said.

"What cha you doing tonight?" he asked.

They had had three lengthy phone discussions, and he had sent her two lovely email greeting cards and some jokes he had found online. Now, he wanted to ask her out. She had no desire to hit the town. But she wanted to see where this situation with Trey would go. The man was gorgeous, a pharmacist, fun-loving and he knew her situation. And he was bisexual. He could take her current, 'as is' physical condition or after she had surgery.

So, Trey was most definitely a catch. So when he asked her out, of course, she'd say yes. "Nothing's on my calendar," she announced brightly.

"Have you had dinner?"

"No. And I'd love to go out to dinner with you."

"Actually, I thought we'd eat in," he said. "I want you all to myself. You like Chinese food?"

Since she had no desire to leave her comfy apartment, eating in was better than going out. "I adore Chinese food," she said.

"Good. What are your favorites?"

"Um, shrimp lo mein. Egg rolls. Spare ribs with plum sauce."

"Forget the ribs," he said. "But you'll get the other stuff. This evening, you're gonna get the best Chinese cuisine you've ever tasted. I'll see you in about a half-hour."

Hmm. Obviously, he was going to go to a Chinese restaurant that didn't sell good spare ribs. She remembered that she didn't have on any makeup.

Luckily, she had washed her hair, so it looked and smelled great. A little makeup would further enhance her appearance.

She went to the bathroom, and unzipped her makeup pouch, placing foundation, rouge, an eyelash curler, eye shadow, mascara and lipstick on the vanity. As she was painting her face, she thought about Trey and how much she really liked him. He was intelligent, educated. Had a sense of humor.

She giggled when she thought about how they had engaged in phone sex. "I'm naked," Trey had said out of the blue one night.

The announcement had just about made Lenore tumble off the bed. "Oh, really," she said.

"Yes," he replied. "What are you wearing?"

"A robe," she had revealed.

"Take it off," he ordered.

Well, Lenore Cavanaugh did not like being ordered around, but she'd make an exception this instance because she was titillated by this unusual phone chat. She opened her robe. But didn't remove it.

"Are you naked?" Trey said.

"Um, yes," Lenore said, suppressing the urge to cackle. Laughing could offend the man. So, she covered her grinning lips.

"Play with your nipples," Trey instructed.

Lenore put her fingers on her nipples and rubbed them.

"Gently pull on them," Trey suggested.

She did as he said.

"I'll bet they're hard," Trey said.

"Yes, they are."

"I wish I was there with you," he said throatily. "I'd give those nipples a good sucking. I bet you'd like that."

"I'm sure I would."

"You know, my cock is in my hand."

Again, Lenore wanted to laugh. "Oh," she said.

"And it's hard as a fire log. You should see it. Do you suck cock?"

Her eyes got big. *I don't believe this guy,* she thought. "I've been known to," she said.

"Do you lick balls?"

"Um, yes," she replied. She could not believe this conversation. It was appalling. But delightfully so.

"I'd love for you to lick my balls," he said.

I bet you would. She heard him huffing and moaning and saying, ooh … and … ah. She knew what he had done. He told her to hold on and she figured he went to clean up the gooey mess.

Coming out of her flashback, she wondered if sex with Trey would be as good as phone sex had been.

CHAPTER 17

"What's all this?" Lenore said when Trey entered her living room, toting two plastic grocery sacks.

"I just came from the supermarket," he said. "Where shall I put these?"

"Follow me." They went to the kitchen and he put the bags down on the counter.

Frowning, she said, "I thought you were going to bring over Chinese food."

"I'm going to *cook* shrimp lo mein," he announced.

Her eyes lit up. "You make Chinese food?"

He nodded. "I love the stuff. A while back, I took a class in Chinese cooking," he explained, digging in the bag and removing a carton of fresh bean sprouts, egg roll wrappers; a plastic bag of shrimp, bottles of sesame oil and soy sauce, and yock-a-mein noodles. "It's nice to see you," he said, eyeing her solemnly.

She smiled sweetly. "Good to see you too."

"You look fabulous," he said, admiring her in her floor-length silk robe. "Do you always hang around the house looking so glamorous?"

"Actually, I decided to call it a day early. So, I put on my robe. I admit to putting on some makeup, so that I could look attractive for my gentleman caller," she flirted.

He took her in his arms and said, "Well, your gentleman caller appreciates the gesture." He kissed her passionately. And she loved it. His lips were full and sensuous, his chin smooth and hair free. In fact, his candy bar brown face was sans hair. And his signature after-shave, a wonderful scent, filled her nostrils.

She wanted to linger in his strong arms. In his embrace, her issues—getting letters from shrinks, going into surgery—didn't seem so overwhelming.

Lenore was strong. She could deal with whatever came her way. But Trey's presence made everything easier to handle.

When they separated, she said, "I have wine. Want a glass to sip while you cook?"

He nodded. She a goblet from the wine rack, filled it with Chardonnay and handed it to him.

He sipped. "Good stuff." He mentioned a local wine merchant that had a great selection.

They chatted while he was at the sink, pulling the shell off the shrimp, making a slit down its back, rinsing off the black vein and tossing the shrimp in a bowl.

"Can I do anything to help?" she asked, feeling useless standing there doing nothing.

"You can finish cleaning these if you like," he said, referring to the shrimp.

She had never cleaned shrimp before, but she had watched him do it, so she mimicked his actions. While she did the shrimp, he chopped Chinese cabbage, onions, and julienne carrots.

Lenore loved preparing meals. And doing it with Trey was even more fun. "You obviously enjoy cooking," she said.

"Very much. I find it relaxing."

Yet again, Lenore thought about what a great catch Trey was. There were his fantastic attributes and the man liked to cook.

She knew plenty of women, real and transsexual who would love to get their paws on that giant chocolate kiss. And here he was in her kitchen, making shrimp lo mein. Trey was one of those rare dudes, treating her like a woman.

A lot of men would sex up a tranny in a heartbeat. But many of them wouldn't date her or cook for her.

Once upon a time, Lenore met an arrogant bastard who came right out and told her that he'd have sex with her, but he wouldn't date her. Humph! Like she'd have sex with such an asshole.

But Trey was cool. He was treating her the way she wanted to be treated.

When she saw that the meal was almost done, she spread out a tablecloth and put out two candles. They dined by candlelight. "This food is fabulous," she said, twirling shrimp lo mein around her fork. It wasn't as greasy and salty as the take-out joints.

Smiling, he said, "You like it, huh?"

"That's why I said it was fabulous," she joked, splashing a little more soy sauce on her pasta.

"Smart ass," he retorted. His tone became serious. "When I called, you sounded kind of down."

"Yeah. But I feel better now. That's because of the great company."

He smiled. "Wanna talk about what was bothering you? I'm not dippin' in your business. It's just that if you want to talk, I'm a good listener."

She sighed. "Well, before the surgeon will even consider doing my surgery, I have to present him with three letters from three different psychiatrists … This morning, I saw shrink number one …" She sighed. "I was hoping she'd give me the letter, but she wants to see me a few more times before she'll even *consider* writing it."

"And that upset you," he said.

She nodded.

"She'll write it. Anybody can tell by how you look, talk, and act that you were meant to be a woman. But hey, sex reassignment is serious stuff." Dipping an egg roll in some duck sauce, he added, "And the doctor probably can't get an accurate read on you from just one interview. So she probably wants to see you a few more times to determine if there are any inconsistencies or contradictions in things you've told her."

That was the conclusion that Lenore had come to. "Well, she won't find any inconsistencies. I was totally honest with her, and I'm not fickle. I want the surgery."

After dinner, they took their plates and glasses to the sink. "What's your pick?" Trey said. "Wash or dry?"

She wrinkled her nose. "Forget it. I'll take care of it in the a.m."

"Leaving dishes overnight. You wouldn't get away with that in my mama's house," he joked. "My mother wouldn't go to bed with dirty dishes in the sink."

"Is she scared the health department will make a surprise inspection?"

"Ha ha," Trey said. "You're a real smart aleck, you know that."

"I've been told that," she said, going to the living room. He was behind her.

Sitting on the sofa, she said, "So, what's next? TV? A movie? I have a stash of flicks."

"What about music?" he said.

She pointed to her stack of CD's. He looked through them, put on the old *Waiting to Exhale* soundtrack. Chaka Kahn began soulfully belting out *My Funny Valentine.*

"I love that song," Trey said, joining Lenore on the couch. He took her in his arms and held her while Chaka serenaded them. "Johnny Mathis also has a nice version," Trey said.

Lenore loved this backdrop, listening to music while snuggled in Trey's strong, powerful arms. She had heard *Funny Valentine* a thousand times and could never grow weary of it.

Trey kissed her forehead. His lips moved to her mouth, and they kissed passionately. He gently bit her chin, and transferred his hungry mouth to her neck, kissing it.

Ooh, Lord, she thought. It had been so long since she had been in a scene like this. She couldn't remember the last time, and right now, she didn't want to try and remember. She only wanted to concentrate on kissing Trey.

She could feel his hot breath on her face. He pushed his fingers through her hair, and with a low, passion-filled voice, he praised the smell of it.

He unleashed the silk robe that she wore, exposing her breasts. "Oh, wow," he moaned, his voice low and sexy. He cupped her left breast and greedily put the nipple in his mouth, causing her to gasp.

He sucked her nipple, licked it, kissed her entire breast, and not wanting her look-alike to feel neglected, he moved his insatiable mouth to it.

Oh, it was true, Lenore thought. There was such a thing as heaven on earth. She was there right now. *Oh, God,* she thought, tensing when she felt her private appendage responding, straining against the panties she wore.

Trey had always thought of her as an enchanting woman.

She had intrigued and excited him, but this enchanting woman had a penis. And sure, he knew that, but it was one thing for him to be told that she was a pre-op transsexual and quite another for him to actually see what she had. It may shatter his illusion of her.

She'd feel considerably better if she had a vagina. She wanted to engage in man/woman sex, not man/she-male sex. Suddenly, she was ambivalent about this scenario. She loved the making out, the sensations. But she didn't like that other part of her. Her penis.

She turned her face away.

Frowning, Trey said, "You're tensing up. What's wrong?"

"Just a little embarrassed," she admitted, sheepishly.

"About what?"

"Down below."

"It's no problem," he said. "I'm cool with it."

But she wasn't cool with it. She was embarrassed and she wanted to flee this situation. "Well, what about protection?" she questioned. "We said we'd get tested before we did anything."

And getting tested and waiting for the results could put this off a little longer.

"I have condoms," he said. "Look, I don't want you to do anything that you don't want to do. But I want you," he stated. The bulge straining against his pants offered incontestable proof of that. "And I'm okay with what's what. You're unique and I like that."

Girl, go for it, said her inner voice.

They rose from the sofa and went to the bedroom, and undressed. Trey's body was muscular and hard. All of it. His arms, stomach and protruding cock. From the back pocket of the black jeans he wore, he pulled out a condom. "There's K-Y in the bathroom," Lenore said. "In the cabinet, under the sink."

He went and got it.

There was more kissing, When they had phone sex, she remembered Trey said that he enjoyed getting his balls licked. So while performing fellatio on him, she did that. And his moans told her that he liked it.

And after making love to her breast yet again, he sucked the head of her penis, licking it like it was a lollipop and masturbating the shaft while sucking her. Ooh, she loved it.

"Get on your knees," he said.

She did so and he pulled her ass cheeks apart and spread lubricant on her asshole. And slowly, he entered her ass. She wasn't that crazy about anal sex. She could live without it, in fact. But at this particular point, she had no other option.

To please a man they admired, women frequently did things they weren't that wild about.

For a long time, Lenore lay next to Trey, listening to him sleeping.

Quietly, and naked, she slipped out of bed and in the dark, went to the kitchen and poured a glass of Pepsi.

Drinking it, she wondered if her sexual encounter with Trey would color his view of her. Would he now see her as some freaky half-and-half that he did X-rated things with?

He had assured her that he accepted her as she was. And looked at her as a woman. But she just wasn't sure.

After finishing the soda, she returned to bed and glanced at the clock on the night table. It was a few minutes after midnight. She nudged Trey. "Huh? he mumbled sleepily.

"It's late," she said. "You staying the night or what?"

"If it's okay with you," he mumbled.

"Sure, no problem," she whispered, very much liking the idea of Trey spending the night.

She gave him a kiss. Rolled on her side, her sleeping position. He wrapped his arms around her and while still drowsy, he stroked her boobs. She could feel his warm breath on her naked back. A few minutes later, they were both in dreamland.

CHAPTER 18

"Miss Thang got plugged," Jennifer Ann said, teasing Lenore.

"Oh, shut up," Lenore said, amused by the ribbing.

It was a Saturday night, and the girls were at Annabelle's kitchen table, having dinner. Annabelle had made enchiladas. Lenore contributed a salad tossed with steamed shrimp and Jennifer Ann provided a Better Than Sex cake. "Now, I love this cake," Jennifer Ann had said, licking chocolate off her fingers. "But it damn sure ain't better than fuckin'."

"Maybe better than lousy sex," Annabelle joked. "A good meal is certainly better than a lousy lay."

"Now speaking of sex," Jennifer Ann said to Lenore. "Tell us about Trey?"

"What do you want to know?" Lenore asked.

"Does he have a big dick?" Jennifer Ann bluntly questioned.

Annabelle cackled. "You're a mess!"

"I didn't measure it," Lenore exclaimed, putting a thick slice of cake on her plate.

"You ain't got to measure it to tell if it's big," Jennifer Ann said. "Now, does the boy have a big—"

"I don't kiss and tell," Lenore said.

"Some people claim that black men have enormous dicks," Jennifer Ann said. "Now, I've been with black and white guys. And I've seen black guys with dicks no bigger than a cocktail wiener. And I've seen white dudes with dicks as long and thick as a keilbasa sausage."

Annabelle said, "So, when will you see Trey again?" She sipped decaffeinated coffee from her favorite mug that said—*A good friend knows how you take your coffee. A great friend adds booze.* She bought it when she and Lenore were browsing in a Hallmark card and gift store.

Lenore shrugged. "Who knows? We've talked on the phone since that special night. But he hasn't said anything about us seeing each other."

"When his dick gets hard, he'll be calling you," Jennifer Ann said.

"Well, I'm not going to be a booty call for Trey," Lenore said. "I want more."

Annabelle said, "I think he sees you as more than someone to have sex with. After all, he cooked for you. He likes you."

"And he was understanding," Lenore said.

"About?" Annabelle said.

Lenore sighed. "My penis."

Jennifer Ann frowned. "What about it?"

"Girls, I look like a woman."

They nodded. Lenore said, "And Trey developed a fondness for the woman I am. But I was afraid that his feelings would change when he saw me naked."

"But he knows your situation," Annabelle said and took another sip of coffee.

"I just felt self-conscious in front of him naked. But he said it didn't matter," Lenore said. "And I was relieved about that." She sighed. "I will be one happy woman when I have that surgery. No more feeling self-conscious about the lower region."

Annabelle said, "Surgery will relieve you of some of the stress. You'll know that you're female."

"Well, people ain't gone see you naked," Jennifer Ann said. "I mean, we do wear clothes in public."

"But mentally surgery made me feel better," Annabelle said. "I just knew that that part of me was no longer there."

"Lately, my penis has been the subject of much discussion," Lenore said.

"Oh?" Annabelle said, going to the kitchen. She held up her coffee mug. "I'm going to get a refill. You girls want one?"

They declined her offer.

"I told the psychiatrist that I masturbated," Lenore said.

"Oh, Miss Thang, you think that was smart?" Jennifer Ann said, concerned.

Annabelle said, "I mean, you want the doctor to write you a letter recommending surgery, so maybe you shouldn't have told her that you use your penis for sexual pleasure."

"I considered lying," Lenore said, "telling her that I hated my penis. Which is bull. When I get horny, I masturbate. Okay." Her tone sounded defensive.

"You sound apologetic," Annabelle said.

Lenore sighed. "It's confusing. I want a sex change operation. I want to be a woman. Women don't have penises."

"Some women don't," Jennifer Ann kidded.

Lenore said, "Now, here I am deriving pleasure from my penis. And I want to get rid of it. When I look in the mirror and I see my boobs and my penis, I think this picture isn't right. This has got to go. But there I am, using it to get off."

"You're human, girl," Annabelle said. "And you get horny and sometimes you use your penis to get rid of the horniness."

"And after your surgery," Jennifer Ann said. "You'll do it the new way. You'll rub that clit and stroke them pussy lips."

Annabelle asked, "Are you having second thoughts about going to surgery?"

Lenore shook her head. "No, ma'am. I want that operation, but change is scary." She chuckled. "Our penises can cause us so much conflict."

"Y'all's penis cause y'all so much conflict," Jennifer Ann said. "I ain't nevah had no problem with mine. I'ma she-male and proud of it."

"If you were proud of being a she-male, you wouldn't lead your husband's family to think you're female," Lenore retorted.

"Bitch, you know why I'm doing that," Jennifer Ann exclaimed. "I don't want people looking at me differently. But I love my pecker."

"I have an idea," Lenore said brightly. "Let's go to Lovers and Friends and have a little champagne and do some dancing."

"Sounds good to me," Jennifer Ann exclaimed.

"We're not dressed," Annabelle objected. They were wearing casual attire.

"They don't have a dress code," Lenore said. "Come on. Let's go for about an hour."

They grabbed their purses and in Lenore's car, went to the club. After their night out, Lenore drove them back to Annabelle's apartment, where Jennifer Ann's vehicle was parked. It had been a fun evening.

CHAPTER 19

"So, Anna tells me that you want to know if her pussy works like a real woman's," said the man.

"Yes, that's right," Lenore said from Annabelle's Lazy-boy chair. She was facing Fred and Annabelle, who were perched on the sofa.

It was the big night. Lenore was going to see with her very own eyes a transsexual having sex.

Lenore knew what she was about to do was seedy.

Also, this little peep show wouldn't be like watching a porn movie with sexy stars, getting it on. There was nothing sexy about Annabelle Morrison or Fred whatever his last name was.

Fred was in his late fifties, about the size of John Goodman from the *Roseanne* show, with gray hair styled in a crew cut. He drove a school bus for the public school system.

"So where shall we do this?" he asked eagerly.

"Bedroom," Annabelle said, rising from the couch.

Following Annabelle and Fred to the bedroom, Lenore thought, *It isn't too late to back out. You could tell Annabelle that you aren't comfortable with it, that you had a change of heart.*

But she wanted to know if a transsexual could have intercourse. Her surgery was not dependent upon proof of that. So, what was the point of this nasty situation?

She just wanted to see. Fred and Annabelle started kissing, hot and heavily. Fred's big hands roamed Annabelle's small breasts, and soon they were tearing off each other's clothes, tossing them on the floor.

Oh, my God, Lenore exclaimed inwardly when she saw them in the buff. Their bodies were as white as milk. Fred's stomach was as big and round as a beach ball and white hair covered his chest.

Leering at Lenore while pulling on his semi erect penis, Fred asked, "Wanna join us?"

Hell, no, Lenore thought. She didn't do threesomes. And if she did, no way would she do it with these two. And Annabelle's expression showed that she wanted Fred all to herself. *Honey, you can have him*, Lenore thought. "No, you're Annabelle's man," she said sweetly.

Annabelle got on her knees and inserted Fred's manhood into her mouth. *Oh, Lord,* Lenore thought.

And after she had blown Fred to total hardness, they moved to the bed. Annabelle put her head on two pillows, and Fred got on his knees and made love to her breasts, causing her to moan with pleasure. "Put your face in it," she yelled, in her falsetto voice.

He licked her vagina while she played with her nipples. "Ooh, that feels so good, Freddy boy. Fuck me," she demanded.

She stretched to the nightstand and got the lube. "I'm ready for you baby," she yelled.

Lenore could not believe that they were carrying on this way, as if she weren't in the room. For that matter, she could not believe that she was in the room.

Annabelle squeezed some of the grease in her hand and slathered it on Fred's dick. He gingerly entered her and they got a rhythm going. "Fuck me good," she yelped. "Fuck me good."

Annabelle was putting on, Lenore thought, watching Fred hammer away at her. After watching the scenario for a few minutes, Lenore decided that she had seen enough and tiptoed out of the room.

She had her proof. And she was jealous of Annabelle for having a vagina.

If she had a vagina, she'd be able to express her desire for Trey the way she wanted to and not use her ass as a substitute vagina.

"Baby, one day, you'll have your operation," Trey said, a few evenings after the episode at Annabelle's. Lenore talked about how much she wanted to have surgery. Of course, she didn't tell him that she had watched Annabelle and Fred have sex.

She didn't have gobs of experience with men, but she knew that no woman should tell a man that she did something so freaky. It would only lead to him asking her to do things that she might find disagreeable.

She sighed. "Yeah. One day."

"And when you have it, I'm going to put a job on you," he joked.

"Trey, I don't want to have surgery to screw as frequently as a hooker."

"I know. You want to be a whole woman. But hey, sex is a part of life," he said.

That evening, he had arrived with the ingredients to make Moo Shu Pork, which was yummy. "You know if you ever grow tired of filling prescriptions, you could open a Chinese eatery," she kidded.

After dinner, he took off his shoes and said that he wanted to spend the night.

Smiling gently, she said, "I'd like that."

"I'm gonna hit the shower. Wanna join me?" he suggested, smiling suggestively.

She agreed, but she was in no mood to get fucked in the butt.

They had taken AIDS tests and they both were clean. Lenore knew that would be the case with her, as she had been celibate since breaking up with Michael.

In the shower, he soaped her up, and bathed her, lathering her boobs, lifting them up and washing underneath them. He told her to turn around and washed her back. "Bend over," he whispered in a guttural tone, sounding turned on. And his erect dick gave further proof that he was aroused.

She did as he asked.

He washed her buttocks, pulled her ass apart and washed the inside of it. He told her to spread her ass cheeks and allow the warm water to trickle down her back and into her ass. And while that happened, he sucked her nipples, and went down on her. "Ooh," she moaned.

The bathroom had become as hot and as steamy as a sauna.

She lathered his entire body, and helped him rinse off.

While the bearably hot water cascaded down their bodies, she got on her knees and put his rock hard cock in her mouth, licking and sucking it. Her objective was to get him off, so she could avoid getting penetrated. Some guys were quite happy with a blow job. And although he came from her oral attention, when they were in bed, he was hammering away in her.

One day, he'd enter her the normal way.

CHAPTER 20

From her mailbox, Lenore extracted an envelope from Dr. Eleanor Castle. Excitedly, she tore it open and it was *the* letter.

Via a few typewritten paragraphs, Dr. Castle said that she had spoken with Lenore Cavanaugh extensively, and that Ms. Cavanaugh had no unrealistic expectations about the surgery and that surgery would be beneficial to her life and peace of mind. And that in Dr. Castle's opinion, Lenore Cavanaugh was a good candidate for sex reassignment surgery.

You got that right, doc, Lenore thought. One letter down. Two more to go.

She phoned Jennifer Ann and shared her great news. "Oh, I'm so happy for you, Miss Thang," Jennifer Ann said.

"Let's go to Applebees and have lunch," Lenore proposed.

"Miss Thang, you got a letter from a shrink, not the damn surgery," Jennifer Ann joked. "I don't think that letter is cause for celebration."

"Girl, I've been worrying about this damn letter for weeks." She proudly waved it, like she had been broke for months and it was a refund check from the IRS. "And now I have it and I want to do something fun."

"Then, we'll go to lunch," Jennifer Ann agreed. "I'll pay. You wanna pick me up or you want me to drive over?"

"I'll come get you," Lenore said. She liked providing the transportation, so she could leave when she wanted to. Waiting was not one of her virtues.

She collected Jennifer Ann, and en route to the restaurant, they listened to loud music while Jennifer Ann blew cigarette smoke out the window. They passed a construction site. "Ooh, Miss Thang, look at them boys," she gushed in an ooh, ah tone.

It was a hot day and the construction workers were hammering and toting lumber, shirtless. A few of them were muscular and looked like models from *Playgirl.*

"Pull in there a minute, girl," Jennifer Ann said, all agog.

Lenore frowned. "For what?"

"Just do it," Jennifer Ann demanded playfully. "I feel naughty."

Lenore figured that Jennifer Ann was going to flirt with the guys. So, she pulled onto the construction site, driving over gravel; the car slightly bounced and made a crunching sound as the tires went over the loose blend of pebbles and rocks. Jennifer Ann shoved her hands under her blouse.

Lenore wondered if she was itching.

They were coming up on a handful of cute guys. "Toot the horn, Miss Thang," she told Lenore.

Lenore did so. A gorgeous black dude and a couple of equally good-looking white ones turned to look. Jennifer Ann twisted her body to face them. "Hey boys," she yelled, grinning profusely. She yanked up her blouse, exposing her bare back to Lenore and her boobs to the guys. Evidently, when she shoved her hand under her blouse, she was unhooking her bra. "All right. Yeah, baby," the men cheered like she was a stripper at a gentleman's club.

Lenore cackled. "Oh, my God." She drove off, keeping her eyes straight ahead. She was too embarrassed to look at the guys.

"That was fun," Jennifer Ann said, smiling up a storm. "Girl, I'm so proud of these boobies. And I love showin' 'em off."

"You are wild," Lenore chuckled, shaking her head in disbelief.

At a stoplight, Lenore remembered Jennifer Ann's lie about being pregnant. "So, how's the mommy-to-be?" she asked sarcastically. "Experiencing any unusual cravings?"

Jennifer Ann chuckled. "Oh, fuck you. Girl, I lost the baby." She burst out laughing.

"You told Wayne's mama you had a miscarriage?" Lenore said.

"Yeah, child. She felt sorry for me. She was crying and carryin' on. She held me in her arms. Gave me a Tupperware bowl of homemade vegetable soup."

Lenore shook her head, thinking that the deception was wrong.

As if reading Lenore's mind, Jennifer Ann said, "I told you once, and I'm gonna repeat myself."

"I know, I know," Lenore said, not wanting to hear the excuses. "Alice wanted a grandchild and she had been harassing you about getting pregnant. You had to silence her by telling her you were with child."

"And later on, I'm going to tell her that the doctor said I can't carry a baby to term. And finally, she'll get the hell off my damn back."

One of these days, all those lies are going to catch up with you, Lenore said inwardly.

CHAPTER 21

Lenore and Trey continued to see each other. They spent many evenings, lounging around her apartment, talking, listening to music. Or watching movies and TV, playing Scrabble. When he came over, he always made Chinese food, even preparing the spare ribs with plum sauce that was too much trouble the first time he had cooked for her. And the ribs were tender and scrumptious, the meat fell off the bone.

Lenore loved spending time with Trey. But she was beginning to reassess their relationship. Something about it didn't feel right to her.

And she had to discuss it with her girls. She called them and suggested an expedition to the mall. They needed to analyze this Trey thing.

At an appointed time, they met on the parking lot of their favorite mall. They shopped, going from store to store, buying clothes, makeup, earrings. Lenore picked up a few paperbacks and Jennifer Ann bought some romances. Annabelle got a couple of titles by Tom Clancy and Stephen King. It was a weekday afternoon, so the mall wasn't that busy, a moderate amount of people were scattered here and there.

As usual, people were eyeballing Annabelle suspiciously. Occasionally, Lenore and Jennifer Ann got a 'Is she or isn't she?' glimpse. But Annabelle lived with the looks.

At the food court, Annabelle and Lenore got bottles of water. Lenore poured some over a cup of ice she had also requested. She hated drinking from a bottle. Jennifer Ann got a Chick-Fil-A with extra pickles, which was given to her in a plastic cup. "Them two pickles they put on it ain't enough for me," she said, placing more pickles on her sandwich. "I'm a pic-a-holic."

Looking at Lenore, Jennifer Ann said, "Miss Thang, something's bothering you. I could sense it on the phone when you said we should get together."

"Me too," Annabelle said.

"So tell your sisters what's wrong." Jennifer Ann took a bite of her sandwich.

Lenore sighed. "Trey."

"You two have a fight?" Annabelle inquired.

Lenore shook her head. "It's just that I told you how he comes to the house and—"

"Makes Chinese food," Jennifer Ann said.

Jennifer Ann had an annoying habit of cutting people off and finishing their sentence. "Yeah," Lenore said, hiding her irritation. "And we listen to music. Watch movies."

"And fuck," Jennifer Ann said.

"I'd prefer to say we make love," Lenore corrected. "But that's the extent of it."

Annabelle scowled. "I'm not following you. Now, Trey cooks for you and the two of you have enjoyable evenings together ... So, what's your complaint?"

"We never leave the apartment," Lenore revealed.

Shrugging, Annabelle said, "So, Trey's a homebody."

"Miss Thang, the boy's a couch potato," Jennifer Ann said, but her expression indicated that that was not her true take on the matter.

Annabelle was naïve regarding the ways of the transsexual world. But Jennifer Ann had been around, so she knew better.

Lenore frowned. "Oh, girl, why don't you come off it?" she whined to Jennifer Ann. "You're just sparing my feelings. Trey's problem is not about being a couch potato or a homebody. And you know it."

"Why you need me to say what you already suspect is the issue?" Jennifer Ann said.

"What are you two talking about?" Annabelle questioned, innocently.

Jennifer Ann said to Annabelle—"Trey doesn't want to go out in public with her because she's a transsexual." With her eyes on Lenore, she said, "There. Happy?"

"That's what I think," Lenore said.

"Oh, gosh, that never crossed my mind," Annabelle said. She was such a baby, Lenore thought. For many years, she had lived the life of a straight man, and she just didn't know what went on in the world of t-women.

Even though, she was having an affair with a married man. Maybe, she felt that was the best she could do. "I figured that because he was coming over and cooking for you that he greatly admired you," Annabelle said.

"I think he does greatly admire me," Lenore stated. "But he doesn't want to go out with me."

"You think he'd be embarrassed?" Annabelle said.

Lenore nodded.

"I don't understand why," Annabelle commented. "I mean, you're beautiful. Most people accept you as a woman."

Eyeing Annabelle, Jennifer Ann stated, "But Miss Thang, some men can deal with us behind closed doors. But they don't want to take us out in public."

"I knew there had to be something wrong with that guy," Lenore snapped. And sipped her water, taking a few ice cubes in her mouth and sucking them. "I mean, he's gorgeous. He loves to cook. He likes to laugh. He treats me well. He has no problem with my pre-op status."

"So, how are you going to handle this?" Annabelle asked.

Lenore sighed. "I don't know. I don't want to lose Trey."

"I wouldn't want to lose him either," Jennifer Ann said.

"Me either" came from Annabelle.

Lenore moaned. "But if he doesn't want to go out in public with me, we have no future." Her voice sounded depressed and weary. "A relationship is about going to dinner, to movies, to concerts, taking vacations. And if Trey doesn't want to do those things with me, what the hell do we have?"

"You should talk to him about it," Annabelle offered.

"Yeah, Miss Thang," Jennifer Ann added.

They were right, Lenore thought. She and Trey had to talk.

CHAPTER 22

But she didn't want to get into a shouting match.

A few evenings later, he called, and after they went through the how-are-you, how-was-your-day bit, he asked, "What are your plans for this evening? I'd like to come by and see you." He always called before coming over and he always said that.

"What kind of Chinese food do you want to prepare this evening?" she teased.

"You getting bored with my Chinese cuisine?" he joked.

"Never. I love it. But all we ever do is stay cooped up in this apartment, eating, and watching movies."

"What's wrong with that? It's a quiet evening."

"And they're nice. But sometimes I'd like to go out, to a restaurant, or a movie," she said.

"Hey, I like having you all to myself. Your apartment is our love nest."

She rolled her eyes. "Well, I'm beginning to feel like a married man's something on the side." She frowned. Until that very moment, it never occurred to her that Trey might be married with kids.

He had told her that he was a divorced father of two. Maybe he was a married father of two. Other women had told Lenore appalling stories about how married men lied about being single, making unsuspecting women mistresses without their consent.

"Well, I don't have a wife," he stated. "We'll have to hit the town sometimes. I'll give you a call in a few days," he said shortly, sounding irked.

She wanted to ask him if he still wanted to come over. But she supposed he didn't want to be around her that evening. Oh, well. "Okay. Talk to you soon."

❧ ❧ ❧

The next day, Lenore was sitting on Jennifer Ann's couch, watching her biting her fingernails and pacing. Her thoughts were obviously elsewhere.

"Girl, what's got you so agitated?" Lenore asked.

Jennifer Ann sighed. "I don't know. Wayne's parents have been acting peculiar lately."

"Peculiar how?" Lenore stated.

"It all started after I told them that I lost the baby."

"The baby that never existed," Lenore said dryly.

"Well, since I told them. They've been acting odd," Jennifer Ann said.

Lenore inquired, "How?"

"Well, Alice, Wayne's mama used to visit a few times a week, and we'd talk and have soda. Or we'd go to the grocery store or to the mall. And once a week, we'd all get together and play cards. But since, I told them that lie about losing the baby, they haven't be coming around as much."

Lenore gazed at Jennifer Ann. She honestly didn't know what to make of it.

"I wonder if they see me as some kind of a failure because I lost Wayne's baby, and they don't want to be around me." She took a deep breath. "Look, I know that I was never pregnant, and that getting pregnant isn't even possible. I'm just trying to figure out what has caused Alice and Pop to act weird."

"Ann, they may not know what to say to you," Lenore said. "They may feel uncomfortable with you because you lost the baby." She giggled.

"Miss Thang, this is not amusing. We talking about my life here."

"Ann, I'm not laughing at you," Lenore said sincerely. "But come on, you're a transsexual, and your in-laws don't have a clue. You told them that you lost a baby. The whole scenario is odd and a little amusing."

"Well, I'm not amused that Pop and Alice are acting funny towards me."

"Look, for all you know their attitude may not even be about you. They could be having money problems. One of them could have had an affair. Pop could be having problems with erections. Who the hell knows? And because you've been lying, you're feeling paranoid."

She sighed. "Yeah, I guess it could be something else. I hope it is."

She didn't look too comforted by Lenore's input on the situation.

CHAPTER 23

Lenore was curled up on her bed, sipping white wine and watching *Girlfriends.* Tracy Ross Ellis was positively stunning, she thought, viewing the show. Lenore wished she had those cheekbones and that bone structure.

In addition to enjoying *Girlfriends,* Lenore adored *The Golden Girls, Sex And The City, Designing Women* and *Living Single.* She bought DVD's of *The Golden Girls,* although she realized the show could be found regularly on the Lifetime network, she wanted to watch Dorothy, Blanche, Rose and Sophia when she was in the mood for them.

She loved shows with women characters supporting each other. The phone rang. Without bothering to look at the caller I.D., she silenced the chiming.

"Hey, pretty lady," Trey greeted effervescently. A few days had passed since their little talk about going out in public. It was good to hear his voice.

"Hey, handsome man," she sang, being Miss Cute.

After they chatted about this and that for a few minutes, he said in a chipper tone, "You said you want us to hit the town."

"Yes, I think it would be nice if we went out sometimes."

"Why don't we do it this coming Saturday night?" he said.

Saturday night was when she got together with Annabelle and Jennifer Ann for food and chitchat. This coming Saturday was her turn to host the soiree. But hey, she'd be willing to sacrifice the occasion for a night out with her boyfriend. She knew the girls would understand. "What do you have in mind?"

"How about *Lovers and Friends*?" Trey stated. "We could go dancing. Have some drinks."

Lenore raised her upper lip. "*Lovers and Friends*?" she said with zero enthusiasm.

But Trey didn't catch it. "Yeah, the place we met."

"And you want us to go there for a date?" Her tone was devoid of enthusi asm.

"Sure, why not? It's a nice place."

Ain't this some shit. He wanted to take her to a gay bar. Now, she had no problem with gay bars. She had had some great times in them.

But she'd like to visit a nice straight club. Maybe one that featured live entertainment, singing, stand-up comedy. She didn't have a problem visiting straight clubs with a man.

"Trey, come on," Lenore complained. "You can do better than a gay bar."

He sighed. "What's your problem with a gay bar?"

She pictured him frowning. "I was hoping we'd do something more mainstream. I mean, why didn't you suggest a straight club?" *I bet that's where you'd have offered to take a real woman.*

"I didn't think you'd be comfortable in one," he said.

"I have no problem going to straight clubs with a guy. And why even suggest a bar? We could go see a play … or a concert. Or the circus, which is in town." And she hadn't been to the circus since she was a kid and it would be fun to re-experience that. She took a deep breath. "Trey, the whole time we've been together, we haven't done anything socially. We haven't gone to the mall or out to eat. You said you loved Walter Mosley novels. We haven't gone browsing in Barnes and Nobles. You haven't introduced me to any of your friends. I mean, what's up with that? Call me paranoid, but I get the distinct impression that you don't want to be seen with me and you don't want anybody to know that you're involved with me."

Trey sighed powerfully. "Look," he snapped. "I don't need this. I can't get this shit from a real bitch. So, just cut it out, okay?"

Lenore could not believe her ears. "Trey, I may not be a real *bitch*, as you so eloquently put it. And obviously, you don't see me as a woman, but let me tell you something—"

"Look, I've told you more than once, that I look at you as a female."

"Yeah, but a few seconds ago, you said, and I quote—'I can get this shit off a real bitch—"

"Actually, I said, from a real bitch," he barked.

She rolled her eyes. "Oh, spare me your nitpicking."

"Well, hey, if you're gonna quote me, tell it right."

Her eyes caught the sight of the TV, and she found the sound distracting. She grabbed the remote off the nightstand and clicked the off button.

"Okay, you said that you can get this shit *from* a real bitch," Lenore said. "Now that comment suggests to me that deep down inside, you don't view me as a woman." She took a deep breath. "But you know something, Trey, it doesn't bother me that you don't see me as a real woman—"

"Look, why don't you calm down? All this drama ain't necessary."

"Oh, I'm quite calm. You know Trey, I have chosen to live out my life as a female … And I want to be treated as such. When I'm involved with a man, I want him to take me to dinner … I want him to go to the mall with me. I want him to take me on vacations and to introduce me to his friends … And if I'm not good enough to go out in public with, I'm not good enough to have sex with." She paused. "If you're unwilling to accommodate me, I don't want you in my life. And speaking of life, have a good one." She graciously put down the phone.

Instantaneously, it rang back. The caller I.D revealed Trey's number. She ignored the incessant ringing. So, he hung up and called back, but she still didn't answer. And on two separate occasions, he let the phone ring over thirty times. But still, she didn't pick up, and the nonstop ringing was causing her to shake with fury.

Oh, God, he pissed her off, trying to *force* her into talking to him. With trembling, rage-filled fingers, she unplugged the bedroom and kitchen phones, resisting the urge to yank the damn things out of the walls.

She'd bet Trey felt that if he went out with her, and someone read her as a tranny, they'd view him as gay. Now, by his own admission, he was bisexual. But obviously, that was his little secret. And he felt being seen with her was a threat to it.

Well, fuck Trey Fuller.

The following afternoon, a warm, sunny day, Lenore and Jennifer Ann were having lunch, at a hotel restaurant. They were sitting outside on the patio under umbrellas.

The smiling waitress placed a cheeseburger on a Kaiser roll, French fries and pickle spear in front of Jennifer Ann. Lenore received a Chinese chicken salad. Trey had made it a few times and his was delicious. She wanted to try the restaurant's. After receiving their food, they smiled their thanks.

After a few minutes of discussing this 'n that, the conversation drifted to Trey. Lenore poured out last night's phone chat. "You told him, didn't you, girl?" Jennifer Ann said. "And I love it. If the boy don't want to go out with you, I wouldn't be bothered with him either."

Lenore sighed. She had cooled off since the showdown. "I hate dropping him. He's educated, handsome, attentive."

Dipping a French fry in ketchup, Jennifer Ann said, "Yeah, he has good traits galore."

"But his refusal to treat me as he would a real woman is unacceptable," Lenore said. She stabbed a forkful of salad, making sure to get a mandarin orange. Lenore gave this salad three stars, and Trey's got five.

Jennifer Ann wiggled her shoulders playfully. "Sounding just a tad big-headed, ain't you, Miss Thang?"

Lenore sighed. "Ann, it's not about me being egotistical … It's an issue of pride, girl. It's about being treated with respect … Eleanor Roosevelt said, 'No one can make you feel inferior without your consent.' No man is going to come to my house, fuck me, but never step outside the four walls with me … I already have self-esteem issues."

"Show me a transsexual who doesn't?" Jennifer Ann stated.

"How can a girl in our situation have good self-esteem when frequently her family doesn't approve of her, when society doesn't approve? So, yeah, I have low self-esteem, and probably always will." She took a deep breath. "But allowing Trey to treat me as something to be ashamed of would only exacerbate my self-esteem issues." She sipped her sparkling water. "I will not stand for a man treating me differently." Her tone was emphatic.

"Well, a lot of transsexuals are involved with men who won't be seen in public with 'em. Behind closed doors, he'll fuck the shit out of her, but he won't be seen in the daylight with her. And some trannies accept it. They don't think they can do any better," Jennifer Ann said.

"Humph," Lenore replied. "Well, they need an injection of self-esteem. Any boyfriend of mine will treat me with respect and if he refuses to do so, it's adios homeboy."

CHAPTER 24

Lenore sat in the passenger's seat of Trey's Volvo. He was driving. They were on their way to the mall. After a few days had passed, he finally got her on the phone.

She definitely had no interest in talking to Trey, so every time the phone rang, she checked the caller I.D., and if Trey's number appeared, she didn't pick up the phone. Once there was a number that she didn't recognize, so she took the call. It was Trey, calling from his cousin's house, he explained.

"Look, we need to talk," he said.

"I have nothing to say to you," Lenore stated.

"Well, if you don't wanna talk, cool. Then just listen to what I have to say. Can you at least give me that?"

"The floor's yours."

"I'm sorry about the gay bar suggestion," he said. "And I can appreciate that you want to be treated like any other woman."

"Glad to hear it."

"Also, I'm sorry about the real bitch comment. Lenore, I admire you, and I do want to keep seeing you. So, that comment was made in anger."

"Trey, that comment annoyed me, but I wasn't hurt by it. I have breasts and a penis, and you've seen me naked, so how can you look at me as a woman?"

"Well, when I'm in your presence, I feel like I'm in the company of a woman. And I've cooked for you, given you flowers, sent you email greeting cards. I wouldn't have done those things for a guy." He paused. "With guys, it's purely physical. I court and woo the ladies." He took a deep breath. "Now, I've never dated anyone like you and I have to get used to the public appearances thing. I have an idea."

"What?" she asked.

"Let's go to the mall? I need some new shirts and cologne. Why don't you go with me? I'll buy you something."

She agreed to tag along.

To avoid a pothole, Trey suddenly swerved the car, bringing Lenore back to the present. They reached the mall. Trey pulled into a parking space. They entered the mall, joining the throng of shoppers. And many sets of eyes were on them.

Lenore was tall, and striking, and her makeup and hair looked marvelous. She was dressed casually, but chic, so naturally, she got attention from men and women. Additionally, she was in the company of a tall, handsome, chocolate-colored man. One would think that Trey could figure out the nature of the stares. But he appeared tense.

At some point, he walked ahead of Lenore. And when she caught up to him, he lagged behind her.

Fuck this, she thought. "Trey," she said calmly. "You don't have to put yourself through this. Goodbye," she said, feeling hurt and about the size of a peanut. She had been in this mall many times and she knew there were some pay phones in a corner by the bathrooms. She headed in that direction.

Trey stopped her. "What's going on?" he asked, feigning innocence.

"You know what's going on. This isn't going to work."

"Well, let me drive you home," he said.

And since he didn't challenge her 'this isn't going to work' comment, evidently, he silently agreed that a Lenore/Trey match wasn't feasible.

"I can get a cab," she said.

"Lenore, I can give you a ride."

"That's not necessary," she snapped, wanting to get the hell away from this guy. Yeah, behind closed doors, he was a transsexual's dream man. But he flunked the real life test. Tears filled her eyes.

He noticed it too.

"Lenore, look, I—" he said soothingly, wearing a remorseful expression.

"Have a good life, Trey." She walked off from him and went to the phone and ordered a cab.

CHAPTER 25

It was a Saturday night, and Lenore, Jennifer Ann and Annabelle were in Ruby Tuesday's having dinner. It was Annabelle's birthday. Actually, her birthday was a few days ago, but she had worked that day. So Lenore had suggested to Jennifer Ann that they chip in and treat Annabelle to dinner that coming Saturday night, skipping their usual at-home dinner party.

So, they were in Ruby's, eating and drinking and having a blast. And a few people looked over at Annabelle, and whispered things to their dining companions.

But in Lenore's opinion, they all could straight to hell. They weren't picking up the tab for this event, so who cared what they thought?

She had heard horror stories about obvious transsexuals visiting restaurants, and wait people refusing to serve them, and customers complaining about their presence. And in some instances, the manager asked them to leave.

Imagine!

To avoid such disrespectful treatment, some trannies only patronized trans-friendly restaurants.

Lenore had no problem with such businesses. But she'd eat any place she damn well chose to.

That was her right. That was any transsexual's right. And Lenore had never been denied service at an eatery, or been mistreated by the staff. Most people accepted her as female. But if someone ever refused her service because they suspected she was a t-girl, there would be a lawsuit, and the dining establishment would be renamed, *Lenore's*.

"Oh, my God," Jennifer Ann blurted, about to sip her strawberry daiquiri.

Annabelle and Lenore looked confused.

"Now, I only saw the boy once, but he was good looking. And I don't forget a good looking boy," Jennifer Ann said.

"What the heck are you talking about?" Annabelle asked.

Lenore said, "I'd like to know that too."

"Over there," Jennifer Ann said, thrusting her head forward.

Lenore turned and saw Trey, off in a corner, looking handsome and gazing into the eyes of an attractive woman sitting across from him at a table. And he didn't appear uncomfortable about being seen with her. Actually, he looked rather proud. And he should be. She was lovely.

"That's Trey, ain't it?" Jennifer Ann questioned.

Lenore nodded, feeling hurt.

Annabelle touched Lenore's hand. "Sweetie, if you want to leave, we can—"

"Annabelle, this is your birthday celebration, and I'm not going to ruin it for you. Now, we're going to enjoy ourselves," Lenore said.

"But I don't want you to be uncomfortable," Annabelle countered.

"Me either, Miss Thang," Jennifer Ann remarked. "We can go someplace else."

"I'll be okay," Lenore told them. With her eyes in the direction of Trey's table, Jennifer Ann said, "You know, Lenore, that bitch reminds me of you. Of course, you're prettier. But y'all have a similar look; the skin color and the hair."

"I agree," Annabelle said. "Obviously, he goes for a certain type."

Glancing at the woman, Lenore saw their point. Her skin was the color of apple juice and she had shoulder length dark auburn hair. She and Lenore could pass for sisters. But what's-her-name was real, and society wouldn't question who she was. *Life was so unfair.* "Well, he's bisexual," she said snippily. "Wonder what kind of man he goes for?"

Jennifer Ann said, "Miss Thang, why don't we switch seats?"

Lenore frowned. "Why?"

"Well, I have a bird's eye view of Trey. You take my seat, and you'll have that view."

"I don't want to watch Trey having a grand old time with another woman?"

"Oh, girl, you need to get bitchy," said Jennifer Ann. "Now, you're a spurned woman and you have a right to get nasty."

"I'm not stirring up a scene," Lenore said.

"You can stir up something without breathing a word," Jennifer Ann said. "Now, eventually, Trey is going to take his eyes off that whore, and he's bound to look over here and spot you. That is, if you take this seat. And the sight of you is gonna make his ass extremely uncomfortable. Now, at the very least, he deserves that for hurtin' you. Come on, child, swap seats with me."

"And you do look great tonight," Annabelle said. "Let the jerk see what he won't ever get to touch again."

Lenore switched chairs with Jennifer Ann.

"You know, Miss Thang," Jennifer Ann said, "You ought to march over there and tell that girl—'Excuse me, honey. Did you know that Trey has a soft spot for she-males. He loves girls who have titties and a dick. He showers with 'em, child.'"

"She'll probably lose her dinner," Annabelle joked.

Jennifer Ann burst out laughing, much louder than necessary, bringing eyes to their table. And her goal was to grab Trey's attention. And sure enough, he glanced in their direction and did a double take when he spotted Lenore.

Rolling her eyes, Lenore chuckled. "You were right," she said to Jennifer Ann. "He does look extremely uncomfortable." Which made her feel good.

"He's probably scared you're gonna charge over there and make a scene. I hope he pisses his pants," Jennifer Ann sipped her daiquiri.

"Bastard," Lenore said.

"Miss Thang, if you go over there and stir up some shit, it'll make you feel better," Jennifer Ann encouraged. "I'll go with you. We can read oh Trey-Trey's ass."

"I'll pass," Lenore stated.

"You're no fun," Jennifer Ann pouted.

Lenore said, "Girl, that woman has never done anything to me. And I'm not going to mess with her."

Once again, Trey glanced over at Lenore. She wished she were on a date with some drop dead gorgeous guy. That would show Trey.

Stroking his hairless chin and watching her, he wore a solemn expression. Was it her imagination or did his expression look yearningly?

He didn't seem as enchanted by his date as he had earlier. In fact, his date's eyes followed his and when she saw Lenore, a lopsided smile appeared on her face. Perhaps, she was annoyed because Lenore had managed to take some of Trey's precious attention from her. Lenore smiled gently at the woman, thinking, *You can have him.*

After bidding Annabelle and Jennifer Ann goodnight, Lenore went home, bathed, put on moisturizer, a floor length silk robe and poured a glass of white wine. Which always relaxed her.

Sipping the beverage, she thought about Trey. She was angry with him, but she didn't hate him. She did not think Trey was a bad person. In fact, she believed he was essentially a good person. But he had never been involved with someone like her and she felt that he got entangled in a situation that he didn't know how to handle.

He dated women, so he would have no problem going out with a real woman. He didn't date men. He simply had sexual encounters with them, so things were fairly cut and dried with him until he met Lenore, a woman with a difference.

And he tried to do right by her when he offered the mall excursion, but he quickly learned that it was just too much for him to deal with, so he was probably relieved when she said screw it.

But Lenore believed that from every negative situation, one should learn something.

She had told the girls—"When I meet another man, I'm going to ask him how he feels about going out in public with me."

"That's a good idea," Annabelle had said.

"And before there is any sexual contact, there are going to be a few dates, to a restaurant, a museum," she said.

The next man would have to prove to her that he was okay with her before they became intimate. Trey had been her first boyfriend as Lenore. When she was with Michael, she had been a weekend drag queen, and Mikey couldn't handle it when she became female, twenty-four hours a day.

When she met Trey, she was lonely and eager for companionship, and he visited her apartment, cooking for her and making love to her and that became their routine and at some point it hit her that they had nothing else.

But the next romantic trip, she would date a guy before she let him hang out at her apartment.

She went to her computer, and checked her emails. It had been a while since she had done so. And as usual, the quantity was voluminous. Mostly nonsense, teen sluts offering a good time, ads promising men with small cocks that they could grow bigger and better ones in twenty-four hours.

Lenore rolled her eyes, and check-marked the messages that she was going to send to the cyber Dumpster.

Clicking away, she stopped when she spotted the name, J. Cavanaugh.

She had a brother named Jimmy. But this must be a coincidence. Jimmy didn't know her email address.

And why would he contact her? They hadn't spoken in years. Jimmy couldn't deal with Lenore's decision to change her sex. And every time they had seen each other, he'd shake his head at her disapprovingly, calling her Travis, refusing to use the proper pronoun.

Just thinking about it now pissed her off. It was her choice to call herself Lenore. *Her* choice. Yet, Jimmy took it upon himself to refer to her as Travis. Who the hell did he think he was to disregard her wishes?

One Christmas Eve, she dropped by her parent's house, toting their gifts, and Jimmy was there, smelling like he had been soaked in rum for two hours. "This shit is wrong," he slurred to Lenore, looking at her dressed in a lovely Christmas ensemble, red blouse, black, pleated, swingy skirt, and black suede pumps. She looked positively fetching, very Christmassy, if she must say so herself.

And Jimmy's eyes told her that he thought she looked great, but of course, he wouldn't dare allow such praise to come off his rum saturated lips.

"Wrong, Jimmy?" she said.

"Yeah," he said, getting in her face, offering her an unwanted whiff of his potent rummy breath. They were in the kitchen.

"And what's so wrong with it?" she demanded, not backing down.

"Like you need to ask. You weren't born no woman, and if the man upstairs wanted—"

Mom was leaning against the sink, silently viewing the spectacle, but nodding. Obviously, she agreed with the ravings of her drunken son. And Lenore didn't give a shit what either of them thought.

"Yeah, yeah," Lenore said, her face twisted with anger. "If God wanted me to be female, he'd have made me one."

"Got that right!"

"I've heard it all before. And what are you so damn upset about?" It wasn't like she and Jimmy had ever been close. They had never shot basketball together or hung out and talked about pussy. As boys, Jimmy was macho and into girls. Travis/Lenore was soft, fem. And when Jimmy's friends visited the house and Travis/Lenore entered the room, Jimmy seemed embarrassed.

"Cuz of the shit you're doing," he snarled like an irate German Shepherd, "people are talking about me. They're saying my brother's a faggot."

"Let 'em."

"They joking with me about being gay. You're being selfish," he said drunkenly. "This isn't just about you, you know. This shit affects other people. Mama, daddy, the whole fuckin' family."

He suggested that she stop taking those fuckin' hormones, and go back to being what God meant for her to be—a man.

It was amazing how family members of transsexuals always accused the girls of being self-centered by pursuing their happiness and ignoring their critics. Moms, dads, brothers and sisters wanted trannies to forget about changing her sex because the new her humiliated them, put them in an awkward position. But wasn't their request that a transsexual forgo her desires because it embarrassed family members a tad self-centered?

There were transsexuals who didn't like their sibling's spouses or boyfriends or girlfriends. Lenore wondered if the siblings would divorce or dump their loved one to please the transsexual.

Highly doubtful.

Lenore and Jimmy hadn't said boo in years. Brother or no brother, Lenore could not be bothered with his negative attitude.

And now, she sat in front of her computer, staring at an unopened email from J. Cavanaugh.

She opened it.

Hey, Lenore read. *Long time since we've talked. What u been up to? Well, I was thinking about u. I got your email address from sis. I know I acted like a fool about your situation, and I'd like to discuss it. So, drop me a line, or call me. Love, Jimmy.*

What is this about, Lenore wondered.

"The only way you're going to find out is to contact him," Annabelle said, pouring maple syrup over two orange/pecan waffles. Lenore and Annabelle had met for breakfast at Eggs-ceptional, a local eatery that specialized in breakfast foods.

In front of Lenore was a delightful Swiss cheese omelet, two link sausages, a popover, and chunky applesauce sprinkled with cinnamon. "I don't know if I want to contact him," she admitted, savoring her breakfast.

Annabelle frowned. “Why not?”

Lenore shrugged. “We haven’t spoken in over a year. I can’t imagine why he’d contact me after all this time.”

“You said that he had a heated reaction to your announcement that you were going to change your sex,” Annabelle said and sipped her steaming decaffeinated coffee.

Lenore laughed without glee. “That’s putting it gently.”

“Well, after all this time, maybe he’s had a change of heart. And wants to hug and be friends again.”

Lenore supposed she’d like that … Jimmy was her brother, after all, and she’d like to be on good terms with her family members. But he had said vile things to her, and even after all this time, it still hurt.

And she wasn’t too sure that Jimmy’s desire to connect with her was about wanting to kiss and makeup. She sighed. “Frankly, I wonder if he wants something,” Cautiously, she sipped her piping hot coffee.

“Like?”

“Think twenties, fifties and hundreds. Maybe, he wants to hit me up for a loan.”

Annabelle shrugged.

Lenore wasn’t sure if she’d get in touch with Jimmy or not. But she didn’t want to hold a grudge for the rest of her life. She’d have to think about it a bit longer.

CHAPTER 26

The room was pitch black. Lenore was in bed, sleeping peacefully. But all good things must come to an end. A series of raps jolted her awake. *What the?* she thought, scowling in the dark. Sighing, she lifted her head half way from the pillow and squinted at the clock on the bedside table.

It was 1:49. In the morning. Who would be knocking on her door at this hour?

Fire. She wondered if the place was in flames and a concerned neighbor had come to alert her. But she didn't see any flames or smell any smoke.

Another round of urgent knocks came. She got out of bed, put on her silk robe, which she had gotten off the Queen Ann chair next to her bed.

Quietly, in the dark, she went to the living room door—the only door in the apartment, actually—and glanced through the peephole and frowned when she saw Jennifer Ann standing in the hallway. Quickly, Lenore opened the door. "Ann, what in hell is going on?"

"All right, if I come in?" Jennifer Ann asked, in a voice that sounded weak and pathetic.

Lenore stepped aside so she could enter. She noticed that Jennifer Ann had been crying her eyes out. The child's nose was as red as ketchup and her eyes were watery and bloodshot.

Lenore closed the door and clicked on the lamp. Jennifer Ann wearily sat down on the sofa.

"What's going on?" Lenore asked.

Jennifer Ann broke into a new set of tears and cried into trembling hands.

Lenore sat next to her and patted her back. "Girl, what's wrong?" she said soothingly. "Did you and Wayne have a fight about something?"

Jennifer Ann shook her head. "Oh, Lord, oh Lord. I wish that was it." She sighed miserably. "Oh, child. Way-Wayne is dead."

Lenore could feel her eyes grow twice their usual size. She patted Jennifer Ann's shoulder. "Oh, my God."

"My baby's dead," Jennifer Ann wailed.

For a long time, not a word was spoken. God, this was shocking, Lenore thought. She did not know Wayne. Of course, when visiting Jennifer Ann, she had met him. And usually, he only said a few words to her, and then he'd disappear to another part of the house, and play computer games or watch television.

And briefly, Lenore had wondered if he disliked her and she uttered her sentiments to Jennifer Ann, who said that Wayne was shy and didn't have much to say.

And now, he was dead. "What happened?" Lenore asked.

"Car wreck," Jennifer Ann said in a barely audible tone. She took a deep breath. "Some motherfucker was drunk, Miss Thang. And he ran into Wayne," she snapped, saliva flew from her mouth. "Now, Wayne's gone." She broke down and cried again.

Lenore wrapped her arms around Jennifer Ann, who wailed and wailed. When she was a little composed, Lenore said, "Want a soda? Some water?"

"Soda," Jennifer Ann said.

Lenore went to the kitchen, and poured two glasses of 7-Up, which she took along with two coasters back to the living room. She handed one of each to Jennifer Ann and resumed her position on the couch next to her. They sipped their sodas.

"How are Wayne's parents holding up?" Like she needed to ask. Surely, they were heartbroken. Children were not supposed to pre-decease their parents. That opposed life's natural order.

And to think of it, why wasn't Jennifer Ann with Wayne's parents, her "in-laws"? They should all be together, consoling each other.

"Miss Thang, I don't even wanna talk about them people," Jennifer Ann snarled, her expression angry.

What was that about, Lenore wondered?

Jennifer Ann took a deep breath. "Lenore, look, I'm in trouble," she said piteously. "I don't have any place to go. I don't have but six dollars and some change on me right now."

Lenore frowned. "You have your house … But then too, because of what's happened, it would probably be hard to stay there tonight."

"That ain't it," Jennifer Ann spat.

Frowning, Lenore said, "Um, Ann, what's going on?"

"Wayne's daddy threw me out of the house. I walked over here."

Lenore was totally confused. "Ann, how can Wayne's father throw you out of your house?"

Jennifer Ann took a deep breath. "Miss Thang, I don't want to talk about this shit right now. I just can't deal with it."

"Okay," Lenore said sympathetically. "I don't have but one bed. But you can share it with me or you can use the couch, if you'd prefer."

From the kitchen cabinet, Lenore shook two pills out of a bottle, returned to the living room and extended the tablets to Jennifer Ann. "Take these."

"What is it?"

"Sominez," Lenore explained. "They'll help you sleep."

Jennifer Ann took the tablets with a gulp of 7-up.

"Let's lay down. We'll talk in the morning," Lenore said.

They went to the bedroom. Lenore removed her robe, returned it to the chair and got into bed. Jennifer Ann stripped down to her bra and panties. Save that lump in her underwear, her body looked totally feminine. Like Lenore, she had curves and no muscles.

Lenore rolled on her side and Jennifer Ann lay beside her. Throughout the night, Jennifer Ann tossed and turned and quietly wept and Lenore patted her back, wondering why Wayne's parents tossed Jennifer Ann out of her own house.

The next morning, Lenore was in the kitchen, making bacon, pancakes, and hash browns. She doubted if Jennifer Ann would have much of an appetite.

But if she were hungry, the food would be there.

Prior to starting breakfast, Lenore collected the morning paper and a two paragraph story about Wayne's death and the car accident was in the local section. The paramedics unsuccessfully tried to save Wayne. And the drunk driver was in jail.

It was all so tragic. Wayne wasn't even thirty and now he was gone.

When Lenore was placing strips of crispy bacon on a plate covered with sheets of paper towel, the phone chimed. Rapidly, she snatched it up. She had left Jennifer Ann, sleeping.

"Have you seen the morning paper?" Annabelle inquired.

"I have," Lenore said.

"Some guy, Wayne Hughes was killed in a car accident. Now, Ann's last name is Hughes, so I wonder if that was her husband."

"It was."

Annabelle sighed. "Oh, God. "We've got to do something. We have to go see her."

"She's here with me. Right now, she's sleeping," Lenore explained.

"Um, why is she with you?" Annabelle asked, sounding confused. "I mean, she should be with her in-laws. I can understand why she wouldn't want to stay at her house, but at a time like this, she should be with her family, Wayne's family."

"All that crossed my mind as well," Lenore said, flipping a griddlecake. "I don't know exactly what's going on. Last night, she was pretty messed up and didn't want to talk."

Annabelle sighed. "Well, I have to work today. But I'll drop by your house after work to see Ann. That is, if she's still there. But I'll eventually talk to her."

They said goodbye.

When the meal was almost ready, Jennifer Ann appeared in the kitchen, wearing the clothes she had on last night. "What cha doing?" she asked, looking at the feast Lenore was preparing.

"Breakfast," Lenore said. "I thought you might want something to eat."

Jennifer Ann smiled faintly. "Lenore, you're so sweet."

"Why don't you pour yourself some coffee? There's juice in the fridge."

Jennifer Ann got a cup from the cabinet and filled it with steaming coffee and a little milk.

At the kitchen table, Lenore and Jennifer Ann ate in silence. Sudden widowhood hadn't affected Jennifer Ann's appetite. Girlfriend ate with gusto, Lenore observed.

Jennifer Ann sighed. "I can't believe this. Wayne is dead. And Wayne's family ..." She shook her head. "What sweethearts," she said sarcastically.

Lenore was eager to hear what happened, not out of nosiness, but curiosity. But she didn't want to come off like a busybody, so she kept mum.

Jennifer Ann said, "The police came to the house to tell me about the accident. They needed me to go downtown to identify the body. I didn't want to do it alone."

"Of course not," Lenore said.

"So, I called Wayne's parents, and they went with me to the morgue." Her eyes filled with fresh tears, which slid down her cheeks. She wiped them away with her fingertips. And in a choked voice, said, "We identified Wayne's body … and drove back to my house. Or what I thought was my house." She sighed. "Miss Thang, Pop did a Jekyl and Hyde on me. He had never been overly friendly to me, but he was always pleasant. But pleasant isn't the word I'd use to describe his behavior last night … He was evil and nasty."

Lenore simply listened.

Jennifer Ann's expression became distant, far away. She began revealing verbatim what happened with her 'father-in-law.'

"Ann," Pop said snidely. "I want you to get the hell out of this house."

"What?" Jennifer asked, with tears in her eyes, looking totally confused.

"You heard me. You aren't wanted here," Pop said.

"Pop, what's wrong?" she asked.

"Don't call me pop," he snarled.

"Why are you acting this way towards me? I just lost my husband."

Pop looked as though he was about to vomit. "Your husband?"

Not catching how he uttered the word, husband, Jennifer Ann said, "I'm in a lot of pain. I don't need this." Her voice was emotional and shaky.

"I know the truth," Pop bellowed. "I know that you're a man masquerading as a goddamn woman."

She moved her lips to speak.

"And don't deny it," Pop snapped.

"Well, I do deny it. It's ridiculous, Pop."

"I said, don't call me, pop. You ain't nothing to me." He took a deep breath. "In the beginning, you had me fooled. But after a while, I started to get suspicious. I don't know. You look like a woman; you sound like one, but for some reason, I began to think I wasn't dealing with a woman. Alice told me that I was wrong."

"You are wrong," Jennifer Ann yelled.

"And then you told us that you were pregnant. I thought, 'Okay, maybe I am wrong … But then you had a *miscarriage* … I felt a scam was being pulled."

"I did have a miscarriage," Jennifer Ann said.

"Stop your damn lying," he shouted. "Now, after you said that you had a miscarriage, I had you investigated."

"Investigated? What the hell are you talkin' about?"

"I hired an agency to do a background check on you," he disclosed. "And your name used to be Richmond Peoples." He told her where she had attended high school, the year she had graduated. He named the judge who granted her name change.

She was appalled that this man had gone to such lengths to prove his point.

"I saw the name change affidavit," he revealed. One would think that Pop would have been proud of how he had unmasked Jennifer Ann, but he simply stated the facts. No smugness. He just told what he knew.

Because Pop had done his homework, Jennifer Ann figured that it was pointless to continue lying, so, she said, "Okay, you know. But why didn't you say anything?" A few weeks had passed since she had said that she had had a miscarriage.

"Because I love Wayne … and I hated that he was gay … that he was involved with something like you," he replied in a nasty, sharp whisper. "I didn't want to mention what I knew. I didn't want to talk about it. So, Alice and I decided to just play along with it … Playing along with it was easier than discussing the sick shit." He released a long sigh. "But Wayne's dead now, and I don't have to hide my feelings anymore. I want you out of this house."

"This is my house," Jennifer Ann said. "You can't throw me out of my own house."

"This is Wayne's house."

"This is Wayne and my home. My name is on the deed," Jennifer Ann said.

"And I want you to sign it over to me."

Jennifer Ann was frowning up a storm. She could not believe her ears. "I won't do that."

"You listen to me, *pal*," Pop hollered. "You ain't got a legal leg to stand on. The state of Virginia won't recognize a marriage between two men. Now, you get the hell out of my son's house."

"You can't toss me out of my own house," Jennifer Ann said, refusing to back down. "Just who do you think you are?"

"I want you gone," Pop demanded.

"I'm not leaving. This is my house."

Pop put his hand behind his back and pulled out a gun, evidently from the back of his pants. Pointing it at her, he barked, "You better get the hell out of here, or I'll send you straight to the devil where you belong."

"Look, you're being unreasonable. I'll talk to you when you're calmer," she said, feeling defeated, but not planning on giving up. "I'll go someplace else."

"That's a brilliant idea," he said.

She got her purse.

"Want to give me the car keys?" he said.

"The car keys? What for?" she asked.

"The car is in Wayne's name. It ain't yours. So hand over the keys," Pop said.

"Pop, that is my car. Wayne bought it for me."

"I told you not to call me, pop. And that car ain't yours. Wayne's money paid for it, and you ain't gettin' it. Now, you give me them keys."

"Fuck you," she said. And proceeded to exit the house.

He cocked the pistol. "Now, you give me them damn car keys," he demanded, sounding like an angry carjacker.

"Look, it's night, and I'm going to a friend's. I need a way there."

"Thumb. Walk. I don't give a shit. But you ain't using that car."

Jennifer Ann said, in a fatigued tone, "You know, if it's in you to shoot me, go ahead and do it. Wayne's dead and I don't know if I want to go on. But I ain't giving you the keys to my car, and on second thought, I ain't leaving this house."

"I'm not playing with you, boy," Pop yelled, veins popping out of his neck.

"You ain't hurting me by calling me boy," Jennifer Ann said. "You've known me no way except for the way I am now. So, you called me boy to be nasty. But I'm not leaving. If anybody is leaving, it's you. So, get the hell out."

He took a deep breath. "Look, if you don't get out of this house and give me them car keys, I will shoot you," he threatened. "Now, you've sponged off my son long enough. Sitting on your faggot ass while he was out working. And you ain't takin' nothing else that belongs to him."

"Look, Wayne took care of me because he wanted to," Jennifer Ann snapped. "And I'm not going anywhere." Her tone was resolute. "So, if you're gonna shoot me, do it."

Pop took a deep breath. "Look, if you don't get out of here, I'll call the police. And tell them the whole story."

"What story?"

"That you're not a woman. That you're playing the grieving widow. They'll kick your ass out of here. I'm sure of that."

Anger had painted Jennifer Ann's face red and tears filled her eyes. Furiously, she unzipped her purse and grabbed the car keys. "Here!" She threw them on the floor. "Now, you be sure of one goddamn thang, you cold-hearted son-of-a-bitch, I'ma fight you on this."

She stormed out of the house and walked to Lenore's.

Jennifer Ann emerged from her word-for-word flashback, wiping tears from her cheeks. It was a gripping story that had kept Lenore spellbound.

"Wow," Lenore said. "I can't believe that he pulled a gun on you. And you challenged him to shoot you. Girl, you're a brave one. Now, the mystery has been solved."

"What are you talking about?"

"A few weeks ago, after your miscarriage," Lenore said and tapped her fingertips together creating quotation marks. "You said that your in-laws were acting odd towards you."

Jennifer Ann nodded. "And that's because they knew I was a transsexual."

"Yeah. Pop had you investigated."

"Son-of-a-bitch! Delving into my business. Well, he ain't gettin' my house. I'm gonna hire a lawyer," she said firmly. "Wayne and I shared that house, Miss Thang. My name is on the deed, and now that Wayne's gone, that house is mine. And his money-grubbin' daddy ain't takin' it from me. I'll fight the asshole."

Lenore placed her hand over Jennifer Ann's. "I don't think you have a legal leg to stand on."

"Look, Wayne and I were married," Jennifer Ann exclaimed. "We have a marriage license. That house belongs to me. Wayne would have wanted me to have it."

"I'm sure you're right, but—"

"Pop can't just toss me out and then demand that I sign it over to him."

"Ann, I'm not a lawyer. But you have a penis, and in the eyes of the law, you're a man. And two men can't marry in this state. And I'm confident that if this went to court, Pop would win."

Jennifer Ann sighed. "Well, I'm gonna take my chances."

Lenore sighed. "Wayne supported you, right?"

Jennifer Ann nodded.

"He claimed you on his taxes, state and federal?" she speculated. "And you two probably filed a joint return."

Jennifer Ann nodded. "The refund checks were made payable to both of us."

"Again, legally, you're not a woman. If you had surgery, Wayne claiming you on his taxes would've been legal."

Extremely agitated, she jumped up from the table. "Miss Thang, like you said, you ain't no lawyer. So how can you sit there talking like one?"

"Ann," Lenore said calmly. "It's common sense. In the eyes of the law, you aren't female. You didn't have a sex change operation. So, you aren't entitled to anything. Wayne's father is in a favorable position … If you had had sex change surgery, everything would automatically go to you."

"Well, I'm still gonna challenge him" Jennifer Ann hurled. "If he wants to go to court, then that's what we'll do."

"Your marriage is not valid," Lenore said.

"I have a license," she said rapidly. "Which was signed by a witness. The girl, who signed it can be brought in to testify on my behalf."

"Ann, your witness thought you were a woman. Hell, everybody that attended the wedding was under the impression that you and Wayne were a traditional man/woman couple tying the knot. They didn't realize that you were a woman with a difference … So, the court probably won't recognize your marriage."

"I'll deny being a transsexual. I look like a real woman."

"Oh, Ann," Lenore said with a sigh. "If you denied what you are, the judge is going to order you to take a physical."

"Oh, Lord. Oh, Lord," Jennifer Ann gasped. "So everything … my house … my car, you're telling me that Pop can just take it?"

Moaning, Lenore nodded.

"That just doesn't sound right, Miss Thang." She took a deep breath. "I grew up in a dump, girl. And no love was in that house … I always fantasized about having a nice home. I shared that fantasy with Wayne. Together, we picked out that house. Oh, some other people had lived there before us. But it was ours … I got a copy of *Better Homes and Gardens,* and got decorating ideas from it." She sighed. "Wayne and I went to the furniture store and bought furniture, stuff for the living room, the bedroom, the den, the kitchen." She sighed. "My kitchen. Everything in that kitchen, the pots, the plates, the spice rack, the glasses; that's my stuff. My belongings." Tears rolled down her cheeks. "Wayne was the one who worked, and yes, he paid for it … but that house and its contents was something he worked to provide for the both of us …" She snarled. "And now, Pop, that son-of-a-bitch can just take it from me. Just like that." She snapped her fingers. "Lord, Lord, where's the justice in that? Where's the fairness?"

"There isn't any," Lenore said.

"Wayne accepted me and loved me. So, how can Pop do this?" She cried into trembling hands.

Lenore took Jennifer Ann into her arms. Jennifer Ann cried against her chest. "Sweetie, in the eyes of the law, you and Wayne were never married," Lenore said, with tears in her eyes. It was just devastating to see Jennifer Ann in such distress. "Also, in the eyes of the law, you committed fraud when you applied for a marriage license and had a ceremony." She paused. "And if you refuse to sign over the house to Pop and he takes this damn thing to court, it's quite possible that the Internal Revenue Service and the state of Virginia will file fraud charges against you. Ann, you could end up in the state penitentiary." She took a deep breath. "You have a penis, so they would put your ass in jail with those men … Now, imagine, *you* in a correctional facility for men."

Jennifer Ann looked horrified. She released a piteous sigh. "Wayne's dead, Miss Thang, and I'm all alone. I ain't got nobody." She sounded broken.

"That isn't true," Lenore said. "You have yourself. And you have me. And Annabelle. You're not by yourself, child."

Jennifer Ann broke down and cried like she was at the funeral of a loved one.

CHAPTER 27

In Lenore's vehicle, she and Jennifer Ann drove to Jennifer Ann's former home to collect her clothes. "I wonder if that old bastard will refuse to give them to me?" Jennifer Ann said.

"Why would he want your clothes?" Lenore inquired, halted at a red light.

"He took my damn house," she spat. "He took my car. Wayne bought most of my clothes. So, why wouldn't Pop keep 'em? And give 'em to charity. Throw 'em away. Burn 'em. Who knows?"

Lenore truly hated going there. She had no desire to deal with Pop's anger. But she would be supportive of Jennifer Ann. They reached the house and Lenore parked at the curb and was relieved to see that the only auto in the driveway was Jennifer Ann's or what used to be Jennifer Ann's car.

After all, Pop had taken it from her. They vacated Lenore's Taurus, and going to the front door, they spotted five bulging trash bags and a few boxes of canned vegetables on the porch.

Canned vegetables, Lenore thought, frowning. Why was trash and canned vegetables on the porch? "What's all this?" Jennifer Ann mumbled, peeking inside one of the bags and then another. "They're my clothes," she revealed. "I guess he figured I'd be coming for them, so he put them out here."

"What's in the boxes?" Lenore inquired.

Jennifer Ann lifted the box tops. "My shoes, blow dryer and picture album. He has no right doing this." She shook her head.

Taped to the door was a hand written note that said, 'For anyone who wants to extend their condolences to the family. Please come to 616 Rockwell Lane, the residence of Alice and Robert Hughes.'

Lenore said, "I assume Robert is Pop's real name?"

Jennifer Ann nodded. Sighed. "Miss Thang, this situation is so messed up." She paused. "He didn't bother to put any pictures of Wayne in the boxes. And I want some pictures of Wayne. There are some framed ones in the house." From her purse, she removed her house key and inserted it in the lock. But it didn't budge. "Shit. He changed the fuckin' locks. That son of a bitch." Looking at the bags and boxes, she said, "Let's put this stuff in your car."

They cleared the bags and crates off the porch and put them on the backseat of Lenore's car. When they were down to the last packages, a middle-aged black woman, crossing the lawn of the house across the street, waved and yelled, "Ann."

When she and Jennifer Ann were facing one another, Jennifer Ann said, "Hey, Lula." Looking at Lenore, she said, "Lenore, this is one of my neighbors, Lula Fauntleroy. Lula, this is Lenore Cavanaugh, a friend of mine."

Lula and Lenore exchanged hellos.

Wearing a compassionate expression, Lula said, "Ann, I read about the accident in the paper. Baby, I'm so sorry."

"Thanks, Lula," Jennifer Ann and Lula hugged.

"Wayne was a fine young man," Lula said. She reminisced about when her husband, Charles' back had gone out, how Wayne took care of their yard and wouldn't accept a penny for his troubles. "Now, what's going on?" Lula asked.

"What cha talking about?" Jennifer Ann questioned.

"Well, I bought a pineapple upside down cake over to your house. I saw a sign on the door saying that people should come to your in-laws to pay their respects."

"Yeah," Jennifer Ann said, bitterly.

"And I went to your in-laws, and you weren't there. I found that odd," Lula said. "Now, Ann, I'm not prying, but I wonder, what's going on?"

And she probably saw Jennifer Ann's belongings boxed up on the porch, Lenore thought.

"I, uh, had a falling out with Wayne's parents," Jennifer Ann prevaricated.

Lula frowned. "That's unfortunate. But at a time like this, all of you should put your differences aside."

"Lula, look, I don't want to discuss it," Jennifer Ann said, scarcely keeping annoyance out of her tone. Although Lenore thought that Lula was intruding in private matters, her questions were perfectly understandable. "Thanks for your sympathy," Jennifer Ann said, walked off from Lula and climbed in Lenore's car.

❦ ❦ ❦

Driving home to her apartment, with Jennifer Ann sitting quietly in the passenger's seat, staring out the window, Lenore recalled Jennifer Ann's comment about this situation being messed up.

Ain't that the truth. Certainly friends and coworkers of Wayne's were dropping by his parent's house to extend their sympathies, undoubtedly carrying flowers, food and sympathy. And Jennifer Ann, his widow, was no where to be seen.

Now surely, that appeared strange to people. And Lenore wondered how Pop was explaining Jennifer Ann's absence. Judging from Lula's confusion, he wasn't revealing the truth.

And Lenore truly felt sorry that Jennifer Ann had lost her beloved Wayne, and Lenore would never say this to Jennifer Ann, but she was in this messed up situation because she had handled it in a messed up way from the word go.

She and Wayne should have had a will drawn up that said in the event of either of their deaths, the house, cars and etc would go to the other.

Sure, Pop could have challenged the will, but Jennifer Ann would have been in a better position than she was in now. She could have gotten backing from the GLBT (gay, lesbian, bisexual, and transgender) community.

But because her marriage was invalid, her position was fragile. She had committed fraud and Pop could use that against her.

❦ ❦ ❦

Later that evening, Annabelle dropped by Lenore's apartment to see Jennifer Ann. She hugged her, told her that if she needed anything, all she had to do was ask.

"You two are the best," Jennifer Ann said to Annabelle and Lenore. "It's been a rough day."

She went to Lenore's bed to rest.

Lenore poured herself and Annabelle glasses of sparkling water, which they sipped while eating Pepperidge Farm cookies at the kitchen table.

"Ann should be with Wayne's family," Annabelle said and sipped her water.

"They don't consider her part of the family," Lenore said and bit into a chocolate pirouette cookie.

"Well, their attitude stinks," Annabelle snapped.

Lenore nodded.

"And her own family should be comforting her at a time like this," Annabelle stated.

Lenore sipped her water. "You're right. But they aren't even aware of where she is. They don't even know about Wayne or the role he played in her life." Lenore recalled that Jennifer Ann had told her that her family did not attend her make-believe wedding. "And Ann's family should know where she's living and what she's going through. They should be here consoling her."

People enraged Lenore, disapproving of someone because of their choices.

After Annabelle left, Lenore took a bath, put on a silk robe, and while eating popcorn, curled up on the couch and viewed a DVD of *Imitation of Life,* the one with Lana Turner. Lenore loved the glamour of yesteryear's Hollywood.

Jennifer Ann was still sleeping.

Watching the film, Lenore thought about Sarah Jane, the black girl who abandoned her unmistakably black mother, and lived out her life as a white girl. Back then, there was an advantage to being white.

Lenore always thought that, in a way, the movie's plot line paralleled the lives of some transsexuals. To live as a woman, many transsexuals relinquished their families.

Sarah Jane led a white boy to believe that she was Caucasian and when he learned the truth, he kicked her ass. Many transsexuals have led men to believe they were real women, and when he found out otherwise, he kicked her ass.

Sarah Jane ran off and became a stripper, which was a form of selling sex. Many transsexuals go into the sex for sell business, becoming dancers, phone sex operators, hookers.

Lenore was shaken out of her thoughts when Jennifer Ann appeared in front of her, wearing a pink cotton robe. Well, at least, Pop had given her, her clothes. The bags and boxes that he had packed them in were in the spare bedroom. "Hey," Jennifer Ann whispered in the semi dark room. The only light on was the flickering TV screen.

"Hey, yourself," Lenore said. "Hope you had a good rest."

It was after midnight and she had laid down about seven that evening.

"Yeah, I did," Jennifer Ann said, joining Lenore on the sofa, watching the rest of the movie with her. Jennifer Ann had seen it before.

After the show was over, Lenore turned off the TV and clicked on the end table lamp. Jennifer Ann looked rested. That haggard look was gone.

Jennifer Ann grabbed a handful of popcorn from the bowl on the coffee table, saying, "I'll be out of your hair in a few days."

"I don't mind your being here," Lenore stated truthfully. "Besides, where will you go?"

"Well, I don't have my house to go back too," Jennifer Ann said resentfully. "But I'll get an apartment."

"Apartments costs money. You don't have a job."

"I'll find one. And I have a couple thousand dollars saved up."

Lenore frowned. "Last night, you said that you were down to six dollars and some coins."

"That's all I had on me. But I have a savings account. Wayne gave me the check and I took care of the bills. I opened a savings account in my name only and dropped money in it every week. Just in case he left me, I wouldn't be left with nothin."

Lenore smiled. "Smart girl."

Jennifer Ann chuckled bitterly. "When I considered him leaving me, I always thought it would be for a real woman. Or even, a masculine man. I never thought he'd leave me like this."

Lenore patted her hand.

"So in a few days, I'll get my own place and start my job search," Jennifer Ann said.

"There's no rush. There's enough room here for the two of us. Just take your time and adjust to everything that's happened to you."

"Lenore, you're gonna think I'm nuts. I'm angry with myself for even feeling this way."

Lenore eyed her curiously.

"I'm pissed off with Wayne."

Lenore frowned. "Why?"

"For dying. For leaving me. I think, why didn't he get out of the path of that drunk driver?" She sighed.

"You're understandably angry," Lenore said. "Your life has been ripped to shreds."

"And I've wondered if losing Wayne is my punishment for lying to people about who I am … Miss Thang, lately, I've been wonderin' about a lot of shit. So many transsexuals ain't happy. And I wonder if that's because what we're doing ain't right … That God sent us on a specific journey, and we decided to take a detour and go another way. And maybe because we went against what God decided for us, we're suffering for it."

Lenore made a face. "A lot of us are suffering because of prejudice in society and people's narrow-mindedness. A lot of us are suffering because of our own inability to make the best of our lives ... I believe that your life is what you make it. I'm reasonably happy, and I firmly believe that you can be trans and happy. But you have to make the best of what is what." She paused. "Wayne's death was an accident, not your punishment for being a t-girl."

Wayne's obituary and picture appeared in the newspaper, and Jennifer Ann's name wasn't even mentioned. The obit said that his parents and brothers and sisters survived him.

"Those motherfuckers are acting like I never existed," Jennifer Ann spat.

And Lenore knew that Jennifer Ann had not been consulted about Wayne's burial, about what suit he should wear, etc. His family totally excluded her from everything, treated her as if she wasn't alive.

The death notice revealed the time and place of the funeral. "I'm going to it," Jennifer Ann said excitedly.

"Do you think that's a good idea?" Lenore said. "I mean, Pop may make a scene."

"I don't give a shit," Jennifer Ann said, sounding out of breath. "Wayne was a part of my life for five years. I'm going to that funeral and Pop can kiss my ass."

CHAPTER 28

"What the hell are you doing here?" Pop demanded of Jennifer Ann. Pop was dressed in a black suit.

Jennifer Ann wore a black dress with low black heels. Lenore had nothing in black, so she wore a purple two piece outfit. Jennifer Ann had insisted on attending the funeral, and Lenore didn't blame her. She had every right to say her final goodbye to Wayne.

Figuring that Jennifer Ann's presence would lead to a hideous confrontation with Wayne's family, Lenore decided to accompany her to the church. And sure enough, the minute they stepped inside, and Pop caught sight of them, he charged up to Jennifer Ann, being rude and blustering.

Curiously, he eyed Lenore, furtively looking at her features. No doubt asking himself if she was a transsexual. Because of the recent turn of events, she'd bet that he was scrutinizing all of Jennifer Ann's girlfriends.

"What do you think I'm doing here?" Jennifer Ann said saucily. "I'm here to pay my respects."

"Well, you turn right back around," Pop snapped. "You're not wanted here."

"I don't give a damn what you want. Wayne is in that coffin up there," she said, nodding to the front of the church. "And I'm gonna say goodbye to him. You can take MY house. You can take MY car. But you will not deny me the right to say goodbye to MY husband."

"You'd better leave," Pop snarled. He seemed to become even angrier when Jennifer Ann called Wayne her husband, Lenore observed.

Alice appeared next to Pop. "Robert, stop this," she ordered in a sharp whisper, looking back to make sure that no one heard her. "This isn't the place for it. Now, like it or not, she loved our son. She has a right to say goodbye to him."

"*She*?" he spat nastily, spittle literally flew from his mouth. "Try he."

"Shush," Alice said, "before someone hears you."

Evidently, they hadn't revealed to people that Wayne had been involved with a transsexual, Lenore thought.

Alice said to Jennifer Ann. "Now, come on up and sit with us." She took Jennifer Ann's hand.

"I'll sit in one of the pews," Lenore said.

"Don't you want to look at the body?" Jennifer Ann asked, sounding truly pitiful.

En route to the coffin, people rose from the pews and approached Jennifer Ann, hugging her, squeezing her hand, telling her that if she needed them, she shouldn't hesitate to contact them.

They were Jennifer Ann's mainstream friends; 'normal' people, who were unaware that she was a transsexual. *How would they react if they knew the truth?* Lenore wondered.

Together, Lenore and Jennifer Ann went to the casket, which was surrounded by roses and lilies and chrysanthemums. Wayne was dressed in a dark blue suit, looking serene. "Oh, Lord," Jennifer Ann cried out, eyeing the corpse.

"Oh, Lord. Oh, Lord!" She turned to Lenore and whispered piteously, "He looks like he's sleepin'." She sounded like a lost child.

Tears sprang to Lenore's eyes.

Jennifer Ann bent down and kissed Wayne's cheek. "Bye baby." She joined Alice in a pew at the front of the church. The crowd was a mixture of white and black folks.

Lenore went searching for a place to sit, found an empty seat, next to a middle-aged black couple.

The service was sedate, dignified and people gave lovely eulogies. Jennifer Ann stood and haltingly revealed to all that Wayne was a special man who brought joy and happiness to her life, and that she would miss him terribly.

Lenore and Jennifer Ann climbed in Lenore's car and followed the procession to the cemetery, where the pallbearers lowered Wayne's coffin into the earth.

Wayne's family wept and Jennifer Ann sobbed.

After the burial, Jennifer Ann and Lenore headed to Lenore's car. Everyone else was going to Alice and Pop's, but Jennifer Ann understandably decided to beg off.

En route to the car, Lenore heard a female voice call, "Ann."

Jennifer Ann and Lenore turned to find Alice walking towards them. Jennifer Ann didn't speak. She solemnly eyed her 'mother-in-law.' Lenore wondered if Alice was going to tell Jennifer Ann precisely what she thought of the deceitful lie that she had lived, if Alice was going to castigate Jennifer Ann for leading her to think that she was pregnant.

Sure, she could have done it all in church. But in church, her treatment of Jennifer Ann had been respectful and exemplary. But they were no longer in God's house, and perhaps Alice was going to let Jennifer Ann have it.

"Excuse me," Lenore said and proceeded to the driver's door.

"You don't have to leave," Alice said. "I don't mind if you hear what I have to say." She paused. "Considering what you heard my husband say in church, I assume you know that Ann isn't a woman."

"Actually, I'm a transsexual too," Lenore said.

Alice chuckled without glee. "I didn't know. You both had me fooled."

Jennifer Ann said, "It was never Lenore's intent to fool you. In fact, she suggested I open up to you and Pop."

"If you had told us, I woulda tried to understand. I'm not an ignorant woman," Alice said.

"Alice, I've been in the room with you when transsexuals were on talk shows, and you said that they should stay the way God made 'em," Jennifer Ann said. "So, how can you say that you would've tried to understand?"

"Ann, looking at somebody on a talk show, and dealing with a person in real life are two different things. Wayne is my son, and I love him, and his happiness was important to me. And if being with you made him happy, I woulda tried to accept you … And I believe I would have. After all, I got to know you, and I grew to care for the person you led me to believe that you were." She paused. "I could have grown to care for the person that you are, but you didn't give me that chance."

Alice sighed. "I don't know if you were amused by deceiving us or if you were ashamed of your situation … But you are doing yourself a disservice by lying to people. You are underestimating people. I truly believe that deep down inside you are a good person." She took a deep breath. "And I don't agree with what Robert has done, taking your house and your car. But he's angry, and he wants to punish you, and right or wrong, that's what he's doing." She paused. "And I'm not going against my husband." She went in her roomy handbag and removed a bulging manila envelope, which she handed to Jennifer Ann.

"What is it?" Jennifer Ann asked, accepting the envelope.

"The insurance company on Wayne's job sent me a check. He was working there before he met you, and he never got around to changing the beneficiary. I was the beneficiary. The check was for twenty five thousand dollars. I cashed it. The money is in the envelope." She sighed. "I had a feeling that you'd show up here today, so I brought it … I would have written you a check, but Robert would have been livid if he realized what I had done. You were with Wayne for five years, and I know my son. He would not have wanted you to end up with nothing. Also, there are some pictures of him."

Jennifer Ann's eyes filled with tears. "Thank you, Alice."

Alice smiled sadly. "Be happy." She hugged Jennifer Ann and walked off.

Lenore and Jennifer Ann entered Lenore's car, and for several minutes, they rode in silence.

From behind the steering wheel, Lenore said, "That was decent of Alice."

Jennifer Ann nodded. "But you know, Miss Thang," she said, her voice practically a whisper, looking down at the envelope, which lay in her lap, "I'd give up every dime of this money, if I could have Wayne back."

"I know you would," Lenore said.

"Could you stop at the bank, so I can deposit this money in my account?"

"Sure," Lenore replied.

At a stoplight, Jennifer Ann said, "Miss Thang, I want to thank you for everything you've done. I don't know if I could have handled this by myself."

"You're my sister, girl," Lenore said and squeezed Jennifer Ann's hand.

Jennifer Ann and Lenore were in the kitchen, preparing Swiss cheese/mushroom omelets, crispy bacon, popovers and mimosas. Lenore had suggested that Jennifer Ann make the popovers, but she said that she had never heard of them. So, Lenore handed her a cookbook, and told her to follow the instructions.

They were expecting Annabelle for breakfast.

And when she arrived, they ate, sipped mimosas and talked. Jennifer Ann said, "My attitude has always been that this is my life, my business."

"I agree," Annabelle said.

"Here, here," Lenore added, holding up her champagne flute in a toast.

"And I still feel that way," Jennifer Ann said. "The world does not need to know that I'm a transsexual. But I've decided that when other people are in my life, that they do have a right to know. A close friend should know … Your boyfriend's parents should know." She took a deep breath. "I mean, I lied to Wayne's family, and they are probably being evasive to other people about me."

Annabelle sipped her mimosa. "What do you mean?"

"Wayne and I had friends that didn't know the situation."

Lenore said, "Yeah, yesterday, at the church, I noticed some of them extending their condolences to you."

Jennifer Ann said, "And you know, they had to wonder why I wasn't at Alice's house, receiving mourners. And I'm sure that Alice didn't tell them anything." She paused. "So because I was living a lie, I put Wayne's family in a position that they had to tell lies too."

Annabelle and Lenore simply listened.

Jennifer Ann shrugged. "But their pride was hurt. And I did that to them, and I'm sorry for it." She sighed. "So, in the future, if I get involved with a boy, and he introduces me to his family, I'm gonna tell 'em my story. Anybody I call a friend is gonna know what's what, and if they don't like me, fuck 'em."

"Like Mary J. Blige said in that song," Lenore said, "And for those of you who don't like it, you can hate it or love it."

Jennifer Ann sighed.

"What, honey?" Annabelle said.

"I've been doing a lot of thinking lately, asking myself, why was I lying? And a part of it was because I wanted to be accepted as a woman without question."

"We all want that," Lenore said.

Annabelle nodded.

"And a part of it was shame," Jennifer Ann said. "I was ashamed to let people know that I was different. But in the future, I'm gonna be honest with people I'm close to." Switching topics and assuming a brighter tone, she said, "Let's see what's on the boob tube." She sashayed to the set, leaving Annabelle and Lenore at the table.

"That was a marvelous breakfast," Annabelle said to Lenore. "Thanks."

"You're welcome, my dear," Lenore said.

"Oh, my God," Jennifer Ann shouted from the living room.

"What?" Lenore called.

"Maury Povich is doing one of those, 'Is she or isn't she' shows."

Lenore rolled her eyes.

From time-to-time, *Maury* brought out a mixture of real women and transsexuals, prancing around in swimsuits, evening gowns, and he'd asked the audience the burning question, who's the real woman? And at the end of the show, the person would reveal if they were biologically, male or female.

The audience was always conflicted about who was what.

But usually they guessed correctly. But there was always an undetectable t-girl in the throng. And everybody thought she was a real chick, and at the end of the show, she'd reveal she was a t-girl, shocking the audience.

Usually, it was some Oriental child, about 5'3, if that.

Lenore and Annabelle went to the living room and sat in front of the TV. "I don't know why these women subject themselves to this nonsense," Lenore said disapprovingly.

"The spotlight, girl," Jennifer Ann said with her eyes on the screen.

"They're turning themselves into a side show," Lenore argued. No way would she participate in such a spectacle.

Annabelle said, "I wonder where they found them and who came up with the show idea."

"Probably some producer went to a nightclub patronized by trannies," Lenore theorized, "and he or she was looking at the girls, wondering, is she or isn't she real. And then Mr. or Miss Producer presented their *marvelous* idea to the show … And since they've done these shows many times, the audience loves them." She rolled her eyes.

Jennifer Ann said, "And to get fifteen minutes of fame, some dizzy queens jumped at the chance to be on TV."

"Well, they're making a fool of themselves," Annabelle said. "And that kind of exhibition doesn't really help us."

"Why do you say that?" Lenore asked, sipping her mimosa.

"Okay, I know I look like a man done up as a woman," Annabelle said.

"Oh, Miss Thang, you do not," Jennifer Ann lied.

"Annabelle, you look fine," Lenore added.

They both knew that Annabelle did not looking convincing, but of course, they wouldn't tell her that.

"Oh, you girls are being sweet," Annabelle said. "But I know I'm no pin-up girl."

"None of us are," Lenore stated, being modest. She knew damn well that she looked good enough to participate in the *America's Next Top Model* competition.

"But you girls look like women," Annabelle said. "But because of your height, you've been read as men or sex changes."

Lenore and Jennifer Ann nodded.

Annabelle stated, "And where would people have gotten the idea that you were a sex change? Now, if a t-girl looked like a guy, I can see somebody saying,

'That's a man.' But if she looks and sounds like a woman, why would anybody think she was a man? And where would they come up with the word, transsexual?" She nodded to the TV. "Those damn shows."

Lenore's mind regressed to the time when she was in a department store. Her breasts had developed to a good size and she was proud of them. She pranced around bra-less, bouncing all over the place, grabbing the attention of men, who eyed her assets appreciatively. Her hair had grown quite a bit, and she wore makeup. She looked damn good.

A middle-aged black clerk in the ladies department had been eyeing her, observing people admiring her. The clerk scurried up to Lenore and said, "Oh, I saw somebody like you on a TV talk show. *He* said that *he* growed his breasts by taking ho-mone pills. Is that what you did?"

Lenore was stunned by this woman's nerve. That wrinkled bitch just wanted Lenore to know that she knew her story.

Annabelle was right. Talk shows have made it difficult for a trans woman to move about in society unnoticed.

It was a pain.

CHAPTER 29

"Miss Thang, I have an idea," Jennifer Ann said to Lenore.

"What?" Lenore asked.

"Well, I've been staying here for almost three weeks. And we've been getting along great. Why don't we try the roommate thing?"

Well, she and Jennifer Ann were getting along marvelously. They enjoyed the same types of music, the same TV shows. And Lenore had gotten a surgery date and when she was home recuperating, she'd feel more secure if someone was there to give her a helping hand, if she needed it.

"Okay," Lenore chirped. "But if I meet a guy, and we become serious, you'll have to make other living arrangements."

"Fair enough," Jennifer Ann said. "And I have to buy myself a bed. I love you, girl. But I don't like sleeping with women." She chuckled.

A few days later, a four-poster bed, a chest of drawers, and a nightstand was delivered to the apartment and set up in the spare bedroom, which was now Jennifer Ann's room. From Circuit City, she picked out a big screen TV, which was just too big for her bedroom. So, she had the delivery men set it up in the living room. And she moved Lenore's 32 inch set into her bedroom.

She and Lenore spent many evenings on the sofa with a quilt over their legs watching movies on the new large screen set. They viewed *Gone With the Wind, Beaches, Stella Dallas, Patch of Blue, Valley of the Dolls,* to name a few. They adored the oldies, which were dramatic, overwrought and sentimental.

And Jennifer Ann respected the no-smoking house rule. Every time she had a hankering for tobacco, she went out on the balcony. "You should give up those damn things," Lenore suggested.

"Mind your own fuckin' business," Jennifer Ann jokingly replied.

CHAPTER 30

"Well, this is nice," Jennifer Ann exclaimed when she and Lenore were inside the suite that was going to be their *pied-a-terre* for two days.

The young bellhop placed their luggage on the floor. "Here you are," Lenore said, handing him a five-dollar tip.

"Merci, Madame," he said.

"Actually, I'm a mademoiselle," Lenore joked. If she remembered her French lessons accurately, a Madame was a married woman and a mademoiselle was single.

The guy smiled and exited the room, shutting the door.

It was late morning, and they were in Montreal. The following day, Lenore had an appointment to see Dr. Yves de Maupassant, the surgeon who was going to transform her penis into a vagina.

Jennifer Ann had agreed to accompany her. They got some brochures from the hotel's lobby and were going to do some sightseeing.

That afternoon, they went on a boat tour, cruising the St. Lawrence River. They visited the biodome, and Insectarium. They dined at a charming French bistro and ate quiche and fish with a three citron sauce. Jennifer Ann bought Annabelle an expensive box of chocolates, and Lenore purchased her a bottle of duty-free perfume. And Annabelle had phoned and asked if they had arrived safely.

Later that night, they got dolled up in tight, sexy clothes that showed off their cleavages, and went to a GLBT nightclub, which they had found in the Montreal edition of Frommer's.

They danced with each other and with sensational looking French-Canadian guys, who told them they were pretty and bought them glasses of wine.

Lenore got into a heavy make out session with Jean-Luc. Before she let him kiss her, she told him, "You do know, don't you?" The atmosphere was mixed with real women, drag queens and t-girls.

"You're a transsexual," he said.

"Yes," she replied.

"I like transsexuals. You are very beautiful." So was he. He was tall, with jet-black hair and emerald eyes. Drooling at her, he asked, "Have you had an operation?"

"Not yet," she said.

"Good. When transsexual has operation, she's no different from real bitch. And I like those," he said, nodding to her breasts. "And dick. I want us to make love," Jean-Luc said seductively.

Forget it, Lenore thought. For starters, she was in no mood to take it up her butt, and besides there was HIV. She figured if she mentioned that, he'd say that he had condoms. And who cared? She did not wish to go off with a stranger. It was dangerous. He could give her a disease. He could become violent.

To rid herself of Jean-Luc, she sweetly told him that tonight wasn't a good night for her, but she'd be there the following night, which she had no intentions of doing. He accepted what she said. "I can't wait to get your cock in me," he said.

Get HER cock in him! Ugh!

Suddenly, Jean-Luc was the ugliest thing Lenore had ever seen.

Lenore Cavanaugh was a *woman.* She did not fuck men and she had absolutely no interest in men who wanted to get fucked.

And yes, there were men who enjoyed getting their butts penetrated, and there were transsexuals of the he-she variety, who were willing to fuck them.

Well, Lenore wasn't one of them. She was totally steeped in the female role, so she found screwing a man repugnant.

Back in their hotel room, Lenore and Jennifer Ann lay in their beds, in the dark. Jennifer Ann was weeping.

Frowning, Lenore whispered, "Ann."

Jennifer Ann sniffed. "Oh, Miss Thang, I'm sorry. I didn't mean to disturb you."

"You didn't." She explained that she was too keyed-up to sleep. The following afternoon was her appointment with Dr. de Maupassant and she was excited about it. "Why are you crying?" she asked Jennifer Ann.

Jennifer Ann sighed. "I was thinking about what I was doing tonight. We were in a bar, drinkin' and dancin', and it wasn't that long ago, Wayne died. I feel like Scarlett O'Hara from *Gone With The Wind.* I'm a widow and I'm out tapping my toes. But at least, Scarlett wore a black dress. I had on a mini skirt."

Lenore chuckled. "Ann, Wayne would've wanted you to enjoy your life. You didn't do anything wrong. You didn't disrespect Wayne."

She sniveled. "I miss that boy, Miss Thang."

"I know, honey."

"I miss us talkin', jokin' around. Havin' dinner together. You know, he taught me how to fish. We used to go on bike rides in the park." She took a deep breath. "If it wasn't for you and Annabelle, I woulda cracked up."

"You underestimate your strength, sweetie pie," Lenore said. "And speaking of people offering support, I'm glad that you're here for me. Now, let's try to get some sleep. I have a big day tomorrow."

The following afternoon, in the rented vehicle, they rode to the doctor's office.

When Lenore arrived in Montreal, she had driven to the physician's, so on the day of the appointment, she'd know precisely where to go, and wouldn't get delayed. She didn't want to risk not seeing the doctor.

She parked the car, and she and Jennifer Ann began the short walk to his office, an unassuming brick building.

They slowed when Lenore caught sight of a sign that said, Dr. Yves de Maupassant, M.D., F.R.C.S. *Chirurgie Plastique Et. Reconstructive.*

Who knew exactly what any of that meant? She only cared that Dr. de Maupassant was a qualified plastic surgeon, who could make her a pussy.

She entered his office and informed the soft-spoken receptionist of her presence.

She and Jennifer Ann sat in the waiting area. Lenore was visibly edgy. Impatiently, she flipped through a copy of *Canadian Living.*

"Girl, calm down," Jennifer Ann advised, sotto-voce.

Smiling nervously, Lenore exhaled. After a seemingly interminable wait the doctor came out for her and ushered her to his office.

His office was lavish. The sex change business was obviously booming. But Dr. de Maupassant did other cosmetic surgery procedures, so it wasn't just transsexuals that kept him in business.

"How tall are you?" he asked, from behind his desk. He spoke in a soft French accent.

His question bothered her. She had heard about doctors rejecting trans girls for surgery because of their height. It was a ridiculous prerequisite. Tall women were all over the place.

"Six feet," she answered. She was going to fib and say she was 5'11. That five part sounded better than six something. But why lie? The doctor had eyes.

"My son is about your height," he revealed, making Lenore feel instantaneous relief, though she didn't like being compared to his son.

"You look quite feminine," he praised. "Did you have facial surgery?"

"No," she answered truthfully.

He looked doubtful. Which was always the case when she said she hadn't had any facial feminization procedures. She was a beauty and some folks didn't believe it was natural. He rose from his desk. "Turn your face to the left," he demanded.

Watching him step a few feet from her, she did as she was told. "I'll be damned," he acquiesced. "You didn't have anything done."

She resisted the urge to say, 'Told you so.'

Returning to his seat, he said, "Many women would love to have your face." He sipped from a mug that was sitting on his desk. "How long have you been on hormones?"

"A little over a year," she said.

"Has your name been legally changed?"

"Yes."

"Can you provide a court order proving that?"

She nodded.

"We'll need a copy of it."

"When I get home, I'll be sure to mail it," she said.

He explained the surgical procedure—penile inversion, removing the testicles. "In addition to a vagina, I'll construct vaginal lips and a clitoris."

"Will this simply be for cosmetic purposes?" she asked.

He frowned. "I don't understand your question."

"Will this vagina function? Will I have sensation?" With her very own eyes, she had seen a transsexual in action. How could she forget that incident with Annabelle? But still, she wanted to hear what the doctor had to say.

"Oh, definitely," he said. "Many of my patients have reported being pleased with their surgical results. They experience erotic feelings and orgasm."

He switched the topic. "Are you aware of the costs? My fee as well as the anesthesiologist's?"

She remembered the fees that were quoted in the email attachment she had received. She repeated what she had read.

"Well, it went up three hundred dollars since then," he said, looking sheepish.

It wasn't that long ago that she had received the attachment. And in that short time, the fee had increased? She had emailed Erica, one of the doctor's satisfied customers, whose name she had gotten from the doctor's guest book on his web site. Lenore had asked Erica if she was pleased with her surgery.

Erica wrote back, saying that she wasn't good at expressing herself on paper. She gave Lenore her number. Lenore phoned her, and Erica said that for the most part, she was happy with the surgery, but that her vaginal lips weren't as full as she'd like. "But hey, you can't have it all," she chirped.

She mentioned that without warning, Dr. de Maupassant had hiked his asking price a few hundred dollars. She said other trannies had told her the same thing.

And now he was doing it to Lenore. Well, she wasn't going to quibble about three hundred dollars.

The girls needed Dr. de Maupassant's services. So, he had them by the balls. Pun intended.

Besides, on the list of services, there was a disclaimer saying that fees were subject to change without notice.

The sound of the doctor's voice brought Lenore back to the present. "When would you like to have your surgery?" he asked.

"As soon as possible."

He picked up the phone and buzzed his receptionist, telling her that Lenore Cavanaugh would be coming out for a surgery date. "Celine, my receptionist will also provide you with a list of things you have to take care of prior to surgery."

Lenore rose from her chair. "Thank you," she said sincerely and shook his hand.

From the receptionist, she learned that an opening was available in three weeks.

"Three weeks?" Lenore said, in disbelief.

"Is that too soon?" the receptionist queried. Looking at her computer screen, she said, "I can give you something two months from now, if you'd prefer."

"Oh, three weeks is fine," Lenore said quickly, virtually shrieking. She was anxious to get this surgery over and done with.

Actually, she had expected a much longer wait. But she was ecstatic with the date she had received.

The surgery would take place at nine a.m. on a Monday morning, which was great. The doctor would have been off for the weekend, and he'd be alert and fresh and rested. The receptionist told her that they needed a fifteen hundred-dollar non-refundable deposit to reserve her surgery date. "If you cancel, you will lose your deposit," she explained. "If you reschedule, you'll have to pay another fifteen hundred dollar fee."

"I understand," Lenore said. No way would she miss the surgery date. In fact, she decided right there on the spot, that she'd come to Montreal two days before her surgery. She gave the receptionist a cashier's check for the amount requested.

She knew that she would have to pay money to reserve her surgery date, and that personal checks were not accepted. So, earlier that day, she had gotten a cashier's check from the Royal Bank.

With tears of joy dripping down her cheeks, she told Jennifer Ann the good news. "You are looking at a person who is going to have surgery in three weeks. Twenty-one days. Yippee!" She took a deep breath. "I'm so happy."

Jennifer Ann wrapped her arms around Lenore.

The next morning, shortly before noon, they checked out of the hotel, returned the rental car to the Hertz counter in the airport and learned that their flight had been delayed.

But Lenore didn't care. She was going to have her surgery.

CHAPTER 31

The next day, Lenore was alone in the apartment. Jennifer Ann had gone grocery shopping. They split the food bill.

Lenore was in her bedroom, naked, standing in front of the full-length mirror behind the door, gazing at her he-she status, her breasts and penis.

She took her penis, stretched it out a bit, and pushed it between her thighs, which she crisscrossed, creating the illusion of a vagina.

Looking at her breasts and her make-believe vagina, joy radiated from her brown eyes. She had engaged in this little game many times before.

She truly loved the look. This was how she was supposed to be.

Or maybe that was how she wanted it to be.

If it should have been that way, God would have made her female.

And many people felt that God didn't make goofs. Then, why was she born a male, but facially, looked female? Why did she sound female? Why were their no muscles on her body?

She was sure that some of her critics would argue that God had made her a pretty male, who sounded female and was muscle free. In fact, some of her opponents had uttered those very statements.

Okay, then, she didn't think like a man. And maybe she didn't think like a woman either. She could only say that her way of thinking was the antithesis to how most men thought.

It was all so very confusing. She only knew that she wasn't the way she wanted to be and God had given man the ability to make her into a woman.

And yes, she would be a man-made woman, synthetic, if you will. Synthetic in the sense that she wasn't born female. But hormones gave her, her ample breasts and curves. And her vagina would simply be her penis, recreated. So, she was as real as they come, in that sense.

Again, she looked at her fabricated vagina, and in a few weeks, this was how it would actually be. For several more seconds, she admired her totally female appearance.

When keeping her private parts in such an unnatural position became uncomfortable, she released her penis.

Her penis. How weird did that sound?

She dressed in panties and a floor-length silk robe and lay across the bed, gazing at the wall in front of her, her thoughts drifted to her impending surgery.

In less than a month, she'd have a vagina, a pussy, a snatch, a poontang, a secret place, a love box, a honey pot, new and improved private parts.

And after recovering, she'd seek employment, return to school and acquire a degree. She had attended college for two and a half years. So, after surgery, she'd juggle a job and school.

For months now, her life had been in limbo. But after the surgery, she'd have a full, purposeful life, and in time, she hoped to meet a man and fall in love.

She hoped to marry and maybe even become a mom. And of course, there were those who thought she shouldn't be a mom because she was a transsexual. Which had nothing to do with her ability to effectively parent a child.

So, screw her critics.

Lenore took a deep breath when she thought about the surgery. And going under the knife. Scary. But unavoidable.

Later that night, she and Jennifer Ann were curled up on the sofa, in silk pajamas, having a goblet of white wine and listening to George Benson's, *The Greatest Hits of All.* Trey was a huge George Benson fan and he had introduced Lenore to the talents of the magnificent crooner.

Lenore shared her fears about the surgery and recovering.

"Well, Miss Thang, I'm gonna be here," Jennifer Ann said and took a sip of wine. "If you need me to get you a pill or something, I can do it. I'll even help you bathe, if necessary."

Lenore's eyes got big. "God, I hope it doesn't come to that." She took a swallow of her Chardonnay. "I have to visit my family. Since I'm going to surgery, I should make them aware of it."

Jennifer Ann nodded.

Lenore sighed. "I don't look forward to dealing with them."

Later that night, around eight-thirty, Lenore was sitting on her bed, staring at the phone on the nightstand, cringing at the thought of calling her mother. *I'll do it tomorrow*, she thought. *No. Just get it over with,* said her inner voice. She knew her mother's routine, so by now, she'd have bathed and put on her cotton pajamas. She'd be sitting up in bed, gazing, undoubtedly thinking about unpleasantness that took place in her past. Lenore suspected that her mother had been emotionally abused as a child, which explained why she wasn't a good mother to Lenore.

She wasn't a good mother, period, but she treated her other children better than she treated Lenore.

But despite her failings and God knows they were bountiful, Mama's other children wouldn't speak a word against her.

She dialed the number. The phone rang three times before her mother answered.

"Uh, hi," Lenore said. She was going to say, 'Hi Mama," but the word Mama just wouldn't come trippingly off her lips.

"Travis," her mother said flatly, still refusing to call her Lenore. She made no attempt to respect Lenore. What else was new? She had never shown Lenore a drop of respect.

Lenore rolled her eyes. "How are you?"

"Fine."

"And how's everyone else?" Lenore asked, being polite. She really didn't care. She didn't hate her family, but she didn't care about their well being. They certainly didn't give a shit about hers. But deep down, she wished that she was closer to them. But she didn't see that happening.

"Good."

"Will you be busy this weekend?" Lenore questioned.

"I'm gonna clean the house. Why?"

"I'd like to drop by and see you. I'm going into surgery in a few weeks."

"What kind of surgery?" Mama asked, not sounding remotely concerned.

"My sex change operation."

"So you're still going to go through with that?" Mama stated.

"I most certainly am," Lenore replied graciously.

"I can't believe that you're gonna do some mess like that."

"It'll make me happy," Lenore said.

"If the Lord wanted you to be ..."

A woman, he would have made you one, Lenore said inwardly.

After uttering that cliché, her mother said, "And I bet you gone give that doctor a big piece of money to change you."

Lenore pretended not to care that this woman was annoying her. "I worked for the money. I'll spend it as I please," she said calmly.

"Well, my phone bill is two months behind, and I need a new wash machine. And you gonna spend money on some stuff like that. I don't know how you ended up like you did."

Trust me, sistah, Lenore thought. *I'd rather be just like I am than to be anything like you.*

"Look," Lenore said, keeping it courteous. "I wanted to let you know that I'm going to the hospital. I'm going to hang up now. Goodbye and take care." She politely put down the phone.

She was going to give her mother the name of the hospital and her room number when she saw her this coming weekend. But she had a change of heart. She wasn't going to visit her family. That little phone chat was a prelude to how the visit would have been. Unpleasant. So forget it.

There would not have been hugs and kisses. No one would have told her that they were glad to see her. There would not have been a ham decorated with pineapple rings. Or a bowl of punch and a coconut cake.

But there would have been insults, put-downs and snide remarks. Who needed the shit?

Her family, mostly her mother brought Lenore's spirits downs. And sometimes the depression lingered for days. Soon, Lenore would be going into surgery, and she needed to keep a positive frame of mind.

Lenore's mother hated her and she knew why. One night, when she was 18, during the wee hours, Travis/Lenore was jolted from a sound sleep by irate voices. "Whore," her father snapped in a sharp whisper.

They were in their bedroom, behind closed doors, but the walls were paperthin. "Look, Melvin, I don't appreciate you callin' me out my name like that," Mama said.

"That's what you are."

"Well, maybe I wouldn't have to go to other men if you knew how to please me."

No man liked being told that he was dull in bed. "How would you like it if I told Travis that I ain't his daddy?" he barked. "He's grown now. He can handle the truth. How would you like it if I told him that you left three young children and ran off with some man and that that man pimped you?"

"Shut up, Melvin," Mama shrieked. "I don't want to talk about that oh mess."

"And when you got pregnant by one of your customers, your pimp dropped you. How would you like it if I told Travis that we don't know who his daddy is cuz you used to be a prostitute and that he a whore baby?"

Lenore came out of her reverie.

Her mother had treated her like shit because another man was oh my pa-pa. Learning that her mother had been a tramp had not been particularly shocking. Lenore knew that her mother slept around, that she screwed various men in the neighborhood. "Your mother's a whore," brats told her.

One man told her—"I fucked your mama. She sucked my dick."

So, mama was a tramp, but that was no excuse for her to treat her child as she had treated Lenore. She constantly criticized Travis/Lenore. She'd prepare meals and sit in Lenore's face and eat and not give her anything. She would take Travis/Lenore and her siblings to the market and buy everybody candy bars or gum and when Travis/Lenore picked up something, she'd say, "You put that back." When the ice cream truck came to their neighborhood, she'd buy Lenore's siblings a popsicle or an ice cream treat. But Lenore would get nothing. The woman was abnormal, unnatural, an oddball.

A few months after learning the truth about her paternity, Lenore got the hell away from the beast, moving into her own apartment. On Christmas, her mother's birthday or Mother's Day, Lenore always gave her mother a gift or a card filled with lovely sentiments.

It was just a gesture.

She truly despised the woman, and sometimes she hated herself for feeling that way. The woman was her mother, after all. But Lenore's opinions and feelings had been shaped by her mother's deplorable treatment of her.

CHAPTER 32

Lenore and Jennifer Ann were sitting on the sofa, watching *The Young and The Restless.* Tumblers of Pepsi were on the coffee table in front of them.

There was a knock on the door. Jennifer Ann answered it.

It was UPS with a package for Lenore.

"Hey, Miss Lady," the black driver effervescently greeted Lenore. He knew her, sort of. From catalog companies, she frequently purchased clothes, shoes, books, CD's, DVD's, fruit and he delivered the packages.

Sometime ago, wearing a sheepish expression, Mr. UPS asked her out, but she told him a little white lie about having a boyfriend. "Ah, lucky dude," he had said. If she were a real woman, she would have gone out with him. He was about 6'5, quite handsome, with flesh the color of a Snicker's bar and the body of a personal trainer. She was tall, so they would have looked good together.

"Have a good one," he said, winked at her and handed her, her parcel. She wondered what his attitude towards her would be if he knew she was a t-girl.

Hmm. She opened her parcel, which were a couple of new nightgowns for her hospital stay. She had ordered them from a company that sold clothes for tall women.

In a little over a week, she'd be boarding the plane, going on her final journey to complete womanhood. Well, almost complete. She didn't have a reproductive system, after all.

In preparation for the surgery, per the doctor's orders, she had ceased taking hormones. The doctor had sent her a list of dos and don'ts. She had to abstain from the hormones for several days prior to surgery. Three days before the operation, she had to lay off alcohol.

Usually, she didn't imbibe hard liquor. Occasionally, she'd have a daiquiri. But wine was her adult beverage of choice. And although she had been told not to have it seventy-two hours before surgery, she was going to stop even sooner, just to play it safe.

She had had X-rays and an AIDS test done, and the results had been forwarded to the surgeon. On the day of the operation, she had to shave her entire pubic region. And take an enema.

She had bought a book on nutrition and read about what vitamin and mineral supplements to take before and after surgery, what nutrients accelerated healing.

Later that night, Lenore was sitting up in bed, and the phone on the nightstand jangled. She glanced at the caller I.D. and frowned. She didn't recognize the number.

She shrugged. "Hello."

"Hey," a male voice said.

She couldn't place the voice.

"How you doing?" he asked.

Perhaps, he had dialed the wrong number. "I think maybe you misdialed."

"Your name is Lenore Cavanaugh, isn't it?" he said, and his voice was beginning to sound familiar to her.

But still, she wasn't revealing her name to some unknown person.

"This is your brother, Jimmy," he disclosed.

"Oh, hey," she said, surprised to be hearing from him. Quite sometime ago, he had sent her an email, and she had never replied. "Sorry for not recognizing your voice, but—"

"It's been a while, I know," he said. "So I asked how you're doing?"

"I'm okay. Yourself?" She was quite intrigued by this unexpected phone call.

"Cool. We built a new deck onto the house."

Hmm. Maybe, the new deck had caused him some financial struggles.

So, he wanted to hit his long-lost sibling up for a loan. Well, he wasn't getting it.

"I had written you an email sometime ago," he said. "But you never wrote back. I figured you were still angry because of how I acted when you showed up at mama's house that Christmas looking like Miss America." His tone was jocular.

"Jimmy, it's my choice," Lenore stated wearily, but she would argue if necessary.

"I know, and uh … Hey look, I'm sorry for acting like a fuckin' fool. I talked to Ma the other day."

Lenore rolled her eyes. "Oh?"

"She told me that you're gonna have *the* operation."

"That's right," Lenore stated.

"Hey, if it makes you happy."

"I'm confident that it will," Lenore said.

"Somebody like you … a woman … A transsexual is at my job," he said. "Her name is Bridget. Well, she started to work there a few months ago, and some people have been pretty shitty to her."

"I can imagine," Lenore said.

"Behind her back, they call her names. Some of the bitches that work there complained about her using the women's bathroom." He paused. "I'm nice to her, so are a few of the ladies who work there …" He sighed. "And some of the people rag on us for even being polite to her. It's like they want to punish her for being different." He paused. "They don't want her there. And you know, I think they believe if they freeze her out or treat her like she doesn't exist, she'll up and quit. I told her to hang tough."

"Good for you, Jimmy," Lenore said. It seemed as though her brother had become enlightened.

He sighed. "You know, I got to thinking, who would put themselves through some shit like that unless it was very important that they change their sex? I ain't gonna lie, when you said that you were gonna have a sex change, I thought you were just out to have sex with as many men as possible."

"A lot of people think that of transsexuals," Lenore said. "But if all I wanted was to fuck guys, it wouldn't have been necessary for me to ever swallow a hormone. I could have simply been a gay man."

"You've been talkin' to Bridget, huh?" Jimmy said.

"She said that to you?" Lenore questioned.

"Yeah, we've talked about some of everything." After a pause, he added, "Look, when you have that operation, I'd like to be there."

Lenore's eyes filled with tears and she could feel a gasp, rendered by emotion, coming on. She covered her mouth to mask it. She couldn't believe it. A member of her family was offering support.

Jimmy said, "You're going through something heavy-duty, and you need your family in your corner. I wanna be there for you. You're my sister and I want to get to know you."

"Jimmy, you don't know how much this means to me," Lenore said truthfully. "I'd like for us to become closer."

"You should come down and spend some time with me and Tamika," he said. Tamika was his wife. "We can talk. Go to dinner. Just chill."

"I'd like that," Lenore said, meaning it. "And I'd like for the two of you to visit here."

She thanked Jimmy for the phone call. He offered his number. She said that it was on her caller I.D., and that she'd put it in her personal phone book. She told him her surgery date, and he said that he'd take the flight with her.

She explained that she was going to Montreal a few days before her actual surgery date. She chuckled. "I want to make sure that I'm there. I don't want any delays or cancelled flights to mess up my plans."

"Well, I'll still fly with you," he said. He explained that he had vacation time that he could use.

Lenore asked Jimmy if he would give Bridget her phone number and email address. If she wanted to make a connection, she could.

And a few days later, Bridget sent her an email. She and Lenore talked on the phone, and via their computers, exchanged pictures. Bridget was black, in her early thirties, pretty and quite passable. Like Lenore, she had been on the gay scene. And Lenore would wager that the women on her job were giving her a hard time because they were JEALOUS of Bridget's looks.

No natural woman wanted to be a transsexual, but many of them wished they looked as good as a beautiful t-girl or could carry themselves with the grace of a sophisticated t-girl.

🍁 🍁 🍁

It was a Saturday evening and Lenore, Annabelle and Jennifer Ann were at Lenore's dining room table, enjoying their weekly dinner. Jennifer Ann made a pan of lip-smacking lasagna and Annabelle brought over a salad, a bottle of red wine and homemade éclairs. "My mother used to love to bake, and these are from her recipe," she told them.

And they had teased Lenore about not being able to have wine. "Aren't you jealous?" Annabelle joked, holding up her glass. "We can get buzzed and you can't."

Lenore chuckled. "Go to hell, bitch! After I have my surgery, I'll celebrate with all the wine I want."

Jennifer Ann said, "Lenore got a phone call from her brother."

Annabelle's expression looked alarmed. "Was it ugly?"

"On the contrary," Lenore said, smiling. "It was quite pleasant. He wants to be at the hospital when I have surgery. He said that he wants me to be his sister."

"Oh, that's terrific," Annabelle said and tapped Lenore's arm.

"You've got plenty of support," Jennifer Ann said to Lenore. "I'm going to be at the hospital; so will your brother."

"And me too," Annabelle said.

"You?" Lenore said, surprised.

"You betcha," Annabelle said.

"But your job," Lenore stated.

"I'm going to take vacation," Annabelle explained. "Lenore, when I met you, I had no life. All I did was go to work, watch rented movies." She paused. "You came along, with your great idea for these weekly dinners … You and Ann introduced me to a bar where I could go dancing and not worry about risking my life." She eyed them both. "We're family. So, when you're wheeled into that operating room, I wouldn't be anywhere else. You're my sister, girl."

Lenore's eyes filled with tears. "You girls are the best."

After Lenore composed herself, Annabelle asked what made Jimmy change his mind. "At his job, there's a tranny, Bridget and everybody is cold to her. And he didn't think it was right, so he reached out to me."

"He's a good guy," Annabelle said.

"I've spoken to Bridget, and she sent me an email and a picture," Lenore explained.

"What does she look like?" Annabelle asked.

"Oh, she's a pretty bitch," Jennifer Ann said. "A black child." Lenore had shown Jennifer Ann the picture.

"I want her to drive down and meet us personally, or we could go to her," Lenore said.

Jennifer Ann and Annabelle were receptive to meeting her. Lenore said, "It's because of her, I have a brother." She bit off an éclair. "Jimmy said that Bridget was dealing with workplace discrimination. Stuff you're going through, Annabelle. Stuff I'm going to go through when I re-enter the work force."

"Me too," Jennifer Ann said. "I'm going to have to look for work. That money won't last forever."

"You know," Lenore said. "An excellent way for some trannies to avoid prejudice is to become self-employed." She shrugged. "Why not learn to do hair? Or electrolysis."

"If a t-girl became an electrologist," Jennifer Ann said. "Transsexuals would be guaranteed customers."

Lenore nodded. "And that tranny customer would probably be more comfortable with a transsexual electrologist. Also, there's catering. And a lot of women like us are excellent seamstresses. Some design gowns for girls appearing in those drag pageants. And some know how to do alterations. So a transsexual seamstress could make a living sewing." She sighed. "Everyone has a talent. I think to avoid disrespect and unfair treatment, a transsexual should take her gift and turn it into an income."

CHAPTER 33

It was 2:17 in the afternoon and Lenore and Trey were in his apartment, in bed, making love. She was moaning appreciatively as he alternately kissed her lips, cupped her breasts and sucked her nipples. He kissed and licked her entire breasts. Kissed her flat belly. His mouth traveled to her penis and he suctioned it into his mouth and enthusiastically gave it attention.

Ooh, feels so good. Feels so good, she thought, putting her fingertips in Trey's eager mouth. He stopped what he was doing and sucked her fingers. After making them nice 'n juicy, he resumed sucking her, and while he did so, she rubbed and pulled on her nipples with her wet fingertips, enhancing the magnificent feelings.

Trey went from sucking her to making love to her breasts and back again.

And after she came, she straddled him, kissing his lips, neck, chest, putting his roc-hard dick in her mouth, licking and sucking it. Tasting his balls. And doing so with zeal, acting like it was the most yummy thing she ever had in her mouth.

When she sensed he was about to come, she removed her mouth. "Don't come just yet," she whispered.

From the pillow, he looked at her, panting and bewildered. "Why you torturing me?" he joked.

She got on her knees. Twisted her head to eye him. Smiling lewdly and tapping a butt cheek, she said, "You want some of this, don't cha?"

He grinned. "You know I do."

"Well, fuck it and fuck it good." She wasn't that wild about anal sex, but she felt sexy and frisky, maybe because she'd be having surgery soon. And Trey liked anal. So, she'd show him a good time.

He stretched to the nightstand and got a condom and the lubricant. He squeezed some lube on his fingers and rubbed it on her asshole. He slid one finger into her ass and like a contortionist, twisted his head to her nipples and sucked them while finger fucking her, starting with one finger and eventually putting in three. He slid the condom on his cock, greased it and gingerly entered her. After seesawing for a few minutes, she began to moan. As Trey banged her, she played with her nipples and pulled on her penis.

"Ooh, ooh," she sighed happily.

"You love it, don't you?" he asked, pounding away.

"Oh, yes," she moaned. "Fuck me. Fuck me."

They came simultaneously. After it was over, Trey rolled off her and plopped down on his back. His head landed on two pillows. Taking a deep breath, he looked over at Lenore who lay next to him. "You're fantastic." He gave her a sexy kiss. Went to the bathroom and disposed of the condom. When he returned, she went to the bathroom and cleaned up. When she finished up, she saw Trey back in bed.

She reached for her dress, which was on the floor.

"Do you have to go?" he asked. "Why don't we spend some time together? Have some wine?"

"Wine's out," she said.

"Oh, yeah," he said, remembering. "In a few days, you're going to surgery."

"And I can't wait."

"I'll bet you can't. But hang out here with me for a while." His tone was earnest.

Smiling warmly, she rejoined him in bed, put her head on his chest, thinking how amazing it was that they were together.

Earlier that afternoon, she was at the mall, shopping for a new suitcase for her trip to Canada. The luggage she had used for her first excursion was battered and ugly and she wanted something new. So, she was in the luggage store, studying the suitcases and overnight bags. From behind her, she heard, "Hey, you."

She turned and saw Trey, smiling at her, showing off his gleaming white teeth. His smile always reminded her of those gorgeous male models in *Essence.*

Trey, who had cooked her Chinese food and who, did not want to be seen in public with her because she was a transsexual, was standing before her. In fact, she had tearfully said goodbye to him in this very mall.

"It's good to see you," he said, awkwardly.

"Good to see you too," she replied graciously. "How you doing?"

"Great," he said. "You?"

"Wonderful."

Looking around the store, he said, "Planning a trip?"

She nodded. "In a few days, I'm going to Canada."

"Canada? What's happening there?"

"THE surgery."

"I'll bet you're excited about that," he said. "Well, um, I don't have anything planned for the rest of the day. If you're free, why don't we have lunch?"

She smiled wryly. "Hmmm. What do you want to do, whip me up some Egg Foo Young? Your wok or mine?"

He made a face. "Sarcasm isn't necessary."

"No, it isn't," she said apologetically. "Sorry."

"I was thinking we'd go to a restaurant. You pick the place."

Lenore sighed. Made sure no one heard her. "Trey, look, I'm not interested in dealing with your hang-ups, okay? I don't want to go to some restaurant with you, and watch you feel self-conscious. Now, there's nothing about me that should embarrass you. I don't look like the bearded lady at the circus. Yeah, yeah, occasionally, some people question my gender, but for the most part, I'm accepted as a woman. And when you acted like you didn't want to be seen with me, it greatly affected my self-esteem."

He chuckled. "Yeah, but it didn't greatly affect that tongue of yours." He paused. "Listen, I've evolved since then." He shrugged. "I mean, I'm standing here in this store, filled with shoppers and I'm not shrinking away."

True, she thought.

"Let's have lunch," he said.

Girl, have lunch with the man. He's trying to make peace, said her inner voice. She smiled warmly and said, "Okay." She selected two pieces of luggage, which Trey took to the counter. Lenore handed the clerk her Visa card.

And after the clerk slapped a paid sticker on the items, Trey grabbed them and side by side, they walked through the shopping center, receiving glances from mall goers. And to Lenore, the looks suggested that people thought she and Trey were an attractive couple. Surreptitiously, she glimpsed at Trey and he didn't seem uneasy, tense or uncomfortable.

Outside, he put the suitcases in the trunk of her car.

They decided to eat at Mima's, a locally-owned trattoria that offered good service and tasty, plentiful food at a moderate price.

They got in their cars, and she followed him to the restaurant. They pulled into empty spaces. As she was dropping her keys into her purse, out of the corner of her eye, she saw him emerge from his vehicle. He opened her door.

And together, they strolled to the restaurant, and at the entrance, he opened the door for her. And at the table, he pulled out her chair.

And she loved the attention. The whole thing was impromptu, but it was her first date as a woman.

The waitress handed them menus. After they made their selections, they requested soft drinks.

Over her glass of soda, Lenore casually observed Trey as she had done in the mall. He didn't appear edgy. He wasn't shifting his eyes to see who was looking at them.

"I owe you an apology," he said.

"For?'

"How I acted in the mall that day," he said.

She didn't wish to quarrel. She shrugged. "It's in the past."

"Lenore, as I said, I had never dated a transsexual. And being out in public with you was difficult." He shrugged. "But it had nothing to do with you. It was *my* problem." He sighed. "I wanted to call and explain, but I figured, 'Hey, she doesn't want to be bothered. Forget it.' But this afternoon, I saw you and I thought why not clear the air."

"And you've done that," she said.

He smiled warmly. "And I have to tell you, I always knew you were a class act. And you really showed it by how you handled things at Ruby Tuesdays."

She frowned. "What are you talking about?"

"You saw me on a date and you didn't start any drama. Classy. A lot of women would've stirred up something."

Oh, okay, she thought. He was talking about the night that she and the girls were in Ruby's celebrating Annabelle's birthday and they saw Trey with that woman. And Jennifer Ann had wanted to stir up something.

After having some wonderful conversation and eating a delicious entrée and dessert, they went to his apartment and made love.

After which, they ate Chinese food delivered by a nearby take-out joint and watched two movies and listened to music.

And after making love yet again, Lenore slept in Trey's arms and when she kissed him goodbye, it was seven-thirty the next morning.

Lenore was standing in front of her apartment door, with her brand new luggage at her feet. She was poised to insert her key in the lock when suddenly the door flew open, astonishing her. "Well, it's about time you showed up," Jennifer Ann snapped.

Frowning, Lenore entered the apartment and sat her suitcases down while her roommate shut the door. "Where the hell have you been?" Jennifer Ann demanded.

Lenore chuckled. Her whereabouts were none of Jennifer Ann's business. "Out," she said.

"Out where? You've been gone since yesterday afternoon."

"I went shopping for luggage."

Jennifer Ann folded her arms. "You shopped for luggage all day? What happened, you get locked in the mall?"

"Not that it's any of your business," Lenore said, quite perturbed. Who the hell did Jennifer Ann think she was grilling her about her comings and goings. "But I bumped into Trey."

"And I assume you were off fucking," Jennifer Ann roared.

"Yes, ma'am," Lenore sang, lightheartedly. "And it was lovely with a capital L." She glided to the refrigerator and grabbed a bottle of water.

"I'm so glad that you find this amusing, Miss Thang," Jennifer Ann spat, watching Lenore toss ice cubes into a glass. "I was worried half to death. I didn't sleep a wink last night. The least you could've done was called."

"Ann, I don't have to check in with you," she said, pouring water over the ice. "I'm an adult. I can come and go as I please." She sipped the fluid.

"Yes, but we're roommates."

"So true. And why don't you act like my roommate instead of my mother?"

Jennifer Ann burst into tears. "Okay, fine," she shrieked. "Shoot me for caring."

Lenore frowned. "Ann, what's going on with you?" Her tone had softened.

Jennifer Ann sniveled. "Miss Thang, it wasn't all that long ago that Wayne died. And usually, he came home at a certain time, and the day of the accident, he didn't. And when you were gone so long, I started to worry. All those memories came a-floodin' back." She paused. "I didn't know what to think. I wondered if you had been in an accident." She paused. "Or if some lunatic clocked you and beat you up or knifed you or shot you. I didn't know if you were in an alley or the morgue. Lord, oh, Lord, I just didn't know what to think." Tears rolled down her cheeks.

Lenore sat her glass on the counter and hugged Jennifer Ann. "Ann, I'm sorry for causing you to worry. I should've called and told you what was going on."

If they were two natural-born women sharing an apartment, Jennifer Ann probably would not have cared that Lenore had pulled an all-nighter. But many transsexuals were insecure and felt things deeply. And Lenore was Jennifer Ann's friend, her loving, surrogate sister, so she was worried when Lenore was out all night.

"Miss Thang, I feared I was gonna have to deal with another loss." Wiping her eyes, she said, "So you said you were with Trey?

Lenore told her about the romantic, sexy afternoon they shared.

"Oh, that sounds nice," Jennifer Ann gushed. "Who knows, after your surgery, you and Trey may end up man and wife."

"I wouldn't have a problem with that."

CHAPTER 34

Lenore sat up in her hospital bed, clad in a brand new cotton gown. It was a Sunday night, and the room was dimly lit, which she supposed was conducive to putting patients in a tranquil frame of mind.

And her frame of mind was the antithesis of tranquil. She tried to distract herself from her woes by reading a novel by the overhead light. But she couldn't concentrate on the lives of fictional people. She had her own issues.

She took a deep breath. Tomorrow morning, she was going to be wheeled into the operating room to have her surgery. And that was something that she wanted, but she was nervous about being put under anesthesia, being cut.

She had people in her corner. Annabelle and Jennifer Ann were there, sharing a hotel room. And Jimmy, her brother was in a room next to theirs.

It was good to see Jimmy. He had put on a little weight since she had last seen him. And when he met her friends, he openly gawked at Jennifer Ann, looking for something that said, man. He didn't pay much attention to Annabelle, probably because it was clear what was what.

Earlier that day, they all went out to eat and did some sightseeing.

Jimmy and Lenore took pictures together while Annabelle played shutterbug. Lenore took a photo with Annabelle and one with Jennifer Ann and the girls took a group picture, which Jimmy snapped.

She was fairly upbeat when she was the happy, vacationing tourist.

But now she sat in this bed, unsure and scared. For the first time, she was scared. Terrified.

In several hours, she'd be wheeled into SURGERY.

And she was scared.

She never had a fear about taking hormones. For her, swallowing a pill wasn't a big deal.

When she had electrolysis, the technician told her that she'd never be able to grow facial hair and that pleased her. Who wanted the shit?

But this, going under the knife. She didn't care about losing a penis.

Women didn't have penises.

In preparation for the surgery, she had taken an enema and shaved her pubic area.

And later, the nurse appeared at her bedside, yanking her out of her thoughts and offering her pills.

"What are they for?" Lenore asked.

She held up a white tablet. "This will help you sleep. A lot of patients have trouble sleeping the night before surgery, so this will help."

Lenore could definitely use some sleep, so she swallowed the tablet with a few sips of water.

The R.N. extended another pill. "And this will constipate you."

Lenore frowned. "Constipate me? Why would I need a pill to do that?"

"After surgery, we don't want you to have a bowel movement for several days," the nurse said. "A bowel movement could cause the vaginal sutures to tear."

Oh, God, Lenore thought. *Sutures, and sleeping pills and tablets that caused constipation.*

But like a good little patient, she swallowed the pill. And tomorrow morning, the doctor would come at her with a scalpel.

Bright side, bright side, she told herself. *After the surgery is over, you'll be a woman.*

And then, her life could finally start.

CHAPTER 35

It was daylight, seven-thirty and Lenore was sitting up in bed. Despite the sleeping pill, she didn't sleep very well last night. And now she was hungry. But soon, she'd was going into surgery, so food or fluid was taboo.

So she waited. And a few minutes before nine, a nurse came to her bedside and told her that the doctor was ready for her. "Take the elevator up to the surgical suite," the nurse said.

Hmm. In the United States, an orderly would have come to her room, assisted her onto a stretcher and rolled her to the surgical suite.

But Lenore did as she was told and when she got off at her destination, she was greeted by a smiling man, who she learned was the anesthesiologist. He ushered her to a table, where she laid down. Bright lights were in her eyes, causing her to squint from the glare. "Light bothering you?" an R.N. quietly asked and twisted the light from Lenore's line of vision. Soon, Lenore felt a needle prick her arm.

Quickly, she began to feel drowsy. Her eyes became heavy, and two men lifted her from one table and transferred her to another. *God, please, watch over me.*

And hours later, she woke up, back in her hospital bed, still drowsy and feeling a burning sensation between her legs, an unfamiliar smell in her nostrils. *What is that smell?* she said in her head. She wanted to utter the question, but she couldn't bring the words to her lips. It was locked inside her brain.

A nurse was hovering around.

"What's that smell?" Lenore finally managed to get out. To her own ears, her voice sounded distant and whispery.

"Iron from the blood," the nurse explained.

Weakly, Lenore pulled back the sheet and her groin area was covered with blood soaked bandages, which the nurse changed.

Throughout the day, she bled and bled and various nurses changed her dressing. And at night, she sweated. And nurses rolled her on her side and changed the sheets.

The day following her surgery, all Lenore did was sleep. Waking up, she remembered, seeing Annabelle, Jennifer Ann and Jimmy, smiling down at her asking if she was okay.

And next to her on the nightstand were flowers, cards, a box of chocolates and a helium balloon. *So nice,* she thought, feeling incredibly weak and exhausted.

* * *

The next morning, the nurse sat a tray of scrambled eggs, toast and apple juice in front of her. Lenore wrinkled her nose. The food looked positively repugnant. "I don't want this," she told the nurse. "Take it away."

"You have to eat something," the nurse said.

Lenore found the smell offensive. *I can't eat this shit.*

But food would accelerate her recovery time. So with effort, she picked up her fork and it was like lifting a sandbag. She stabbed a few eggs, and briefly eyed them wriggling from the fork. She took a bite, followed by a nibble of toast, and regurgitated.

The nurse hurriedly fetched a plastic basin and placed it in front of her. Lenore threw up three times. The nurse brought in a green bottle of something. "Drink this," she said. "It'll settle your stomach."

It did. And for the rest of that day, she slept.

For the second day in a row, she was a prisoner in that bed and the railings that surrounded her were the bars. She couldn't even go to the bathroom. A catheter was attached to her urethra, so she was peeing in that. And when it became full, a nurse emptied it.

Days passed. Her appetite was returning. She could eat without throwing up. And the nurses continued to give her pills that constipated her.

She wanted to get the hell out of this place. She wanted to walk around. She wanted a goddamn Pepsi.

"I can get you a Pepsi," Jennifer Ann said. "There's a convenience store up at the corner."

"You'd better ask the nurse first," said Annabelle.

The nurse nixed the soda idea, saying that juice and water was better for her.

Still, Jennifer Ann smuggled in a Pepsi. *Nirvana,* Lenore thought, taking a few sips.

Lenore wanted to take a bath. And she'd pay a hundred bucks to take a shit.

Her stomach was cramping.

"This is horrible," she complained to the nurse. "I need to shit." She didn't care about manners, dignified behavior or ladylike language. She needed to take a dump.

"I'm sorry, but we can't allow you to do that," the nurse said.

"But I have to," Lenore said. "The cramps are unbearable."

Oh, they were terrible. Those near and dear to her were visiting, but she secretly wanted them to go away. She was in no mood for them. They were smiling and healthy and not confined to a bed and she resented them.

But they watched TV and played Scrabble and Cribbage with her.

She thanked them for the flowers, and in one of the arrangements was a card, which Lenore hadn't even looked at. Admiring the bouquet, Jennifer Ann asked, "Wonder who sent these?"

Lenore had assumed that all the flowers were from the gang that was with her. "Can I look at the card?" Jennifer Ann asked.

"Sure," Lenore answered.

Jennifer Ann plucked the card from the arrangement and read it. "Well, all right," she exclaimed. "They're from Trey, girl."

"How sweet," Lenore said. And later, she learned from the nurse that while she was sleeping, Trey Fuller had phoned, asking if she was okay, if the operation had been a success.

And that night, he called and they chatted for about twenty minutes. And she thanked him for the flowers. "I'll be checking in on you," he told her and made a kissing sound before saying goodbye.

Lenore lay in bed, thinking about the things people took for granted, defecating and showering.

Boy, she'd love to do both, sit on a commode and let it all come out, and then wipe herself.

And how wonderful would it be, to stand under a warm spray, and get her flesh soaked, and lather her body with her favorite soap and rinse it off with warm water, and rub a scented lotion into her damp flesh.

Oh and how she'd like to wet her hair, and wash it, filling her nostrils with the delightful fragrance of her favorite shampoo.

It would all be a gift.

She couldn't wait until she was healed and could go home.

Lenore had been hospitalized for a week. And on a Sunday afternoon, Dr. de Maupassant, dressed casually, came to her room, and told her that the vaginal area had been packed with a stent to keep it open. And in a few days, the packing would be removed.

That was good news, she thought.

Later that day, she had to defecate and those pills that were plugging her up weren't going to hold it back.

It was like a baby, ready to be born. It was coming.

She told the nurse that she could feel it. They gave her an enema. "The liquid will make it easier to pass, and that won't threaten the sutures," explained the nurse.

Lenore went to the bathroom, sat on the commode and after it was over, she felt like a new person.

That same day, she was allowed to take a shower, and afterwards, she was beginning to feel like her old self. Her first important dinner was roast beef *au jus,* buttered Brussels sprouts, mashed potatoes and for dessert, cherry cobbler.

And eventually, the catheter was removed, making it so that she could pee on her own. But when she sat down to do so, urine sprayed everywhere. *What in the world,* Lenore thought.

"I have to see the doctor," she told the nurse.

"What's the problem?"

She explained how she made a mess on the floor when she urinated.

When the doctor arrived to remove the packing, he said, "The urination problem will straighten itself out."

He gave her instructions on dilation. "What the hell is dilation?" Jimmy asked when she discussed it with Annabelle and Jennifer Ann, and Jimmy was in her hospital room, looking on.

"I'll have to use a dildo and penetrate myself with it a few times a day to keep the vagina open," Lenore explained.

Jennifer Ann said, "In other words, she has to fuck herself."

Annabelle chuckled. "Until she finds someone to do it for her."

Well, Trey should be able to help me out with that, Lenore thought.

CHAPTER 36

Dr. de Maupassant appeared by Lenore's bedside. "You will be released tomorrow," he said.

That was music to her ears. "Well, your staff has been just marvelous," she told him. "Thanks for everything."

* * *

And the next day she and her gang went to the airport to journey home. And it was crowded and she was weak. And she feared that their flight would be delayed or cancelled. Under the best of circumstances, who wanted to deal with that? But since, she just got out of the hospital, she definitely didn't want to be bothered.

She was so grateful when their flight was called, and even more so, when the plane was airborne. And the stopover was mercifully short, and she wanted to jump for joy when the cab containing her and Jimmy, and Jennifer Ann and Annabelle pulled up at her apartment building.

Jimmy and Annabelle's cars had been parked at her complex. "Now, if you need anything, don't hesitate to call me," Jimmy told her after visiting with her and her friends for about an hour. "And I'll be checking on you."

"Thanks, Jimmy," she said. He hugged her and gave her a kiss on the cheek. He playfully pointed a finger at Annabelle and Jennifer Ann, "Y'all take care of my sister."

Lenore liked how that sounded.

He also gave her friends a hug and a peck on the cheek, and when he was gone, Annabelle said, "He's a nice guy. You're lucky he's your brother."

Jennifer Ann complained of hunger, went to the kitchen, and returned a short time later, saying there was nothing worth eating in the house. Several days before the Canadian excursion, she and Lenore didn't do any food shopping. They didn't want stuff to sit in the fridge and spoil.

So Jennifer Ann grabbed her purse and headed out to the market, while Annabelle stayed with Lenore. "Get some wine," Annabelle said to Jennifer Ann when her hand was on the doorknob.

"Oh, I'm not ready for wine," Lenore said, from the couch, dressed in a robe, feeling better, but still weak. "Girl, I'm still fragile."

"It isn't for you," Annabelle joked. "It's for me and Ann."

So, while Jennifer Ann was at the store, Annabelle and Lenore chatted and watched a bit of TV, and about forty-five minutes later, Jennifer Ann returned, carrying two plastic sacks of groceries. "I got some deli meats," she explained, "And some Swiss cheese, lettuce, tomatoes and sub rolls. "How does a sub sound?" she asked them.

Annabelle and Lenore nodded.

So Jennifer Ann served them subs, and she and Annabelle sipped wine, while Lenore drank sparkling water.

Eventually, Annabelle hugged Jennifer Ann and Lenore and said goodbye.

Lenore slept peacefully that night. It was terrific being back in her own bed, which was a nice roomy queen-size. The next day, while brushing her teeth, she caught a glimpse of herself in the mirror. God, she was so pale, a shade lighter than she was before the operation. The veins in her face showed.

Maybe that would go away when she got her coloring back.

She stepped into the bathtub, and allowed the warm shower spray to saturate her skin. Absent-mindedly, she washed herself, soaping her armpits, her chest, under her breasts and her stomach. She reached for her penis. She was going to raise her scrotum and wash below. But nothing was in her hand. She no longer had a penis. In the hospital, she had bathed a few times, and she hadn't thought to reach for her former penis. But at home, in her usual habitat, with her defenses down, she had reached for it and it wasn't there.

She had had surgery.

Wow!

For so many years, her penis had been a part of her, and now it was gone. And who cared?

Good riddance.

* * *

The doctor had told her to douche a few times a day during the healing process, so she used a vinegar and water solution, greasing the nozzle and gingerly inserting it in her vagina. She squeezed the bottle and water spurted everywhere. The smell vaguely reminded her of salad dressing.

After douching, she felt clean, refreshed. But she had to find a more pleasant smelling douche.

Prior to surgery, when she bathed, she had simply used a deodorant soap, which she still used. But she washed her vagina with a floral fragrance feminine wash. And she adored the smell.

And she continued to dilate, a few times a day, greasing the dildo or the stent as it was called and pushing it in and out.

She was beginning to heal. Her vaginal lips were no longer raw looking.

But she still lacked energy, and Jennifer Ann was pushing the vacuum, squirting Windex and Pledge and sprinkling Comet. "I really appreciate everything you've done," Lenore said from the couch. "And I'm not malingering."

"Miss Thang, what the hell is malingering?" Jennifer Ann asked, folding laundry while *The Young and The Restless* played on the TV. "It sounds like a disease."

Lenore chuckled. "Malingering is pretending to be sick to avoid working."

"Oh, girl, I know you ain't like that. After Wayne died, you were there for me. You helped me through some tough times. So I don't mind helpin' you out. 'Sides, I do live here."

When Lenore felt up to a mall excursion, she'd ask Jennifer Ann to accompany her, and she'd treat her to an outfit from the tall store. Since she was so enervated, she shuddered to think what the apartment would look like if Jennifer Ann weren't there.

* * *

A few days after Lenore was home from the hospital, Trey dropped by for a visit, bearing Godiva chocolates. Of course, before actually seeing her, he had phoned a few times to chat, and when she was hospitalized, he had called. They were in her bedroom. To have privacy, she had shut the door.

She was sitting up in bed. "So, how you feeling?" he asked from the side of her bed.

"Weak, but slowly, my strength is returning," she answered.

"You look great."

He had phoned to ask if he could drop by, so she had shampooed and blow-dried her hair and put on makeup and fragrance.

She smiled warmly. "Thanks."

He chuckled.

"What?" she asked, frowning.

He shrugged. "There's something I want to ask you, but I don't know how to go about doing so."

She shrugged. "Just spit it out."

He did just that. "Can I see your vagina?"

She giggled incredulously.

"Hey, I'm curious," he said.

"And why is that?" she joked. "You want to have surgery?"

"Ah, my little stand up comedienne. I just wanna take a peek at your poo poo?" he kidded.

She didn't mind him seeing. After all, he had seen her naked many times previously. And eventually, he'd be making love to her.

She rose from the bed and pulled the fabric of her satin gown from her left shoulder, and watching her, Trey wiggled his eyebrows.

And then she did the same to the right shoulder, and allowed the garment to cascade to the floor, revealing her nakedness. Because of her poor appetite during her hospitalization, she had dropped a few pounds—not because she needed to—but the weight loss made her body look even more alluring.

Trey looked serious. Aroused. She was a little turned on herself.

But she knew she was in no condition to have sex. But by God, there had been all the waiting ... the visits to the shrinks ... the hospital stay ... the pain ... the cramping.

The least she could do was play the seductress, the femme fatale, use her womanhood to thrill and tantalize Trey. She had earned it, damn it. "You want to see," she said and returned to the bed. She lay her head on the pillows and spread her legs like an Oriental fan.

She had healed sufficiently. "Wow," he said, looking between her stretched thighs. With his fingers, he separated her vaginal lips, and said, "You have a clitoris and everything. Amazing."

"So it looks authentic?" she said.

He nodded. "I've seen my fair share of pussies, and yours looks real. You have a pretty little love box there, girl."

She chuckled. And she believed him. After surgery, she bought a magazine that featured naked women. And she compared the pictures to her vagina. And there was no distinction.

Trey kissed her, and made love to her breasts, sucking her nipples and covering each of her breasts with a thousand little kisses. Cooing with delight, she muttered that the time for them to have intercourse wasn't right. But she suggested he get naked, which he did. And she gave him head, licking and sucking his dick and his balls and loving every juicy minute of it.

Later, he got dressed, went and got a bunch of Chinese food from a takeout joint.

And they ate in the kitchen, sharing the food with Jennifer Ann. After dinner, Lenore and Trey returned to her room and snuggled in bed and giggled at a handful of old sitcoms on cable, *The Jeffersons, Sanford and Son, I Love Lucy, Roseanne.*

And in the middle of one, she fell asleep on his chest, and shortly after two a.m., she opened her eyes, and saw Trey getting undressed. He stripped down to his underwear and spread the blanket on her, and climbed into bed next to her. And spent the night.

CHAPTER 37

A few weeks had passed, and Lenore had been chatting with Trey on and off, and her vagina had healed, but still, she was deficient in energy. But everyday, she got dressed and assisted Jennifer Ann with the household chores. She had gone shopping a few times. She and Jennifer Ann were in the tall girl store. "I want to buy you an outfit," Lenore said.

"Oh, Miss Thang, you don't have to do that," Jennifer Ann objected.

"I know, but I want to. You've been so helpful to me during my convalescence."

"Look, you and I have been down this road before. You helped me out when I was in trouble, so I just returned the favor."

"Ann, look, you went to the store for me, cleaned out my bathtub. Girl, let me do something for you," Lenore said, refusing to take no for an answer.

"Well, an outfit is just too generous. We can go over to the Outback, and you can buy me a big, juicy T-bone."

Hey, if Jennifer Ann wanted to decline a free outfit, fine, Lenore thought.

Lenore still felt weak, but certainly not as much as she did after the operation. Also, women were called the weaker sex. That made her wonder if she'd always feel lethargic. "Well, you definitely won't have the physical strength you used to have," Annabelle said. "Your primary source of testosterone has been removed."

Actually, Lenore began to lose physical potency after she had been on estrogen for a while. Lifting heavy objects was harder to do. "But don't worry," Annabelle had assured her. "You'll get your energy back."

Annabelle should know. She had undergone the surgery as well.

❧ ❧ ❧

Lenore was on the phone with Trey. "I don't feel up to it," she said.

"Well, why don't I pick up something and bring it to you?" he suggested. He had invited her out for dinner and she declined.

"Oh, that's sweet of you," she said politely. "But I really don't want to see anyone."

"Okay," he said, sounding disappointed. "Then, I'll talk to you later."

❧ ❧ ❧

Another time, he called and said, "I know how much you like Usher."

"Yeah, he's my man," she said from her bed, where she had been relaxing.

"He's your number two man," Trey joked. "I'm number one. The main man. Your main squeeze. Your boo." He chuckled. "Anyway, I got us tickets to an Usher concert for this coming Saturday night, so that gives you a few days notice. You can get your hair done. Buy a new outfit."

Lenore made a face. "Oh, Trey, thanks, but I can't go."

For a moment, there was silence. He asked, "What's the problem?'

She pictured him frowning. "I don't—"

He cut her off. "You don't feel up to it, right?" He scarcely managed to keep the annoyance out of his tone.

"Well, yeah."

"You know, I'm beginning to get the impression that you're blowing me off," he said.

She didn't comment on that. If he got that impression, so be it.

"Well, I'm going to hang up," she said, sounding blasé.

"Don't you think we should talk?"

"About?"

"Your attitude. I mean, shit, lately, you've been as cold as a seven-pound bag of ice. I wanna know what's going on. Let's discuss it."

"There's nothing to discuss. Bye." She hung up the phone, left her bed, went to the kitchen, where Jennifer Ann was cutting up a honeydew melon and a cantaloupe and dropping the slices into a bowl. Lenore removed a fork from the cutlery drawer. "Do me a favor," she said, stabbing a cube of honeydew.

"Sure," Jennifer Ann said.

"If Trey calls, and you answer the phone, tell him that I'm not here." She popped the fruit in her mouth.

Jennifer Ann frowned. "What's wrong? You two have an argument about something?"

Lenore shook her head. "I just don't want to be bothered with Trey Fuller."

"And why is that?" Jennifer Ann inquired, scowling.

"I don't want to discuss it," Lenore said.

"But he's such a nice guy. And he's given you flowers and chocolates and not cheap shit, but Godiva's. He comes by to see you." She paused. "Miss Thang, he's a winner. So, why you actin' like this?"

"I don't want to talk about it," Lenore said in a tone that refused to brook any argument.

Jennifer Ann held up her hands in surrender. "Okay, fine."

Lenore returned to her bedroom and got cozy on the bed. Jennifer Ann was right. Trey was a nice guy. Terrific, actually. In the beginning, he had a problem going out in public with her, but he resolved that issue. He had taken her to dinner a few times.

One afternoon, they got some food and ate in the park.

They regularly visited the mall. They went walking hand-in-hand through the botanical gardens. They had gone to Starbucks and over cappuccinos sat and talked. He was now comfortable being out in public with her. He didn't cut his eyes to see how people were reacting to her, if they had ideas about her.

And here and there, there had been a few is she or isn't she looks. That would always be the case.

Recently, he shared his dreams with her, about how one day, he wanted to open his own store and years down the road, teach at a pharmacy school.

Yes, Trey Fuller was perfect. Wonderful.

But he couldn't be her guy.

Trey was a sensual man, who enjoyed lovemaking and Lenore had nothing to offer him.

Her surgery had proven to be a bust, a failure. The doctor told her to dilate a few times a day, and she conscientiously did so. Every day and night, she oiled up her plastic man—her pet name for that stent/dildo—and pushed it in and out of her new vagina, following the doctor's instructions to the letter.

One would think that a woman would derive great pleasure from pushing a penis-like device in and out of her pussy, but Lenore found dilation to be a chore. And quite boring, not something that she looked forward to, at all.

And after doing it for several minutes, it became uncomfortable, not really painful, but something that she could do without.

Maybe, that dildo was hitting her nerve endings and not in a pleasant way.

And the longer she fucked herself, the more difficult dilation became.

And when she urinated, she had to hold a wad of toilet paper in front of her, to keep from making a mess on the floor.

Dr. de Maupassant, the so-called sex change specialist had told her—"The urination problem will straighten itself out."

Well, it hasn't happened, Lenore thought.

Something was not right. She was avoiding Trey because she knew that he wanted to make love to her. For that matter, she wanted to make love to him.

But because her vagina didn't function properly, she couldn't.

She was embarrassed.

Ashamed.

She knew of a surgeon, nearby, who did sex change procedures. When she was in the market for someone to perform her operation, that particular doctor was not a consideration. She thought his fee was excessive.

But the other day, she made an appointment with him to ascertain if he could possibly repair the problem. She had some savings left, and credit cards with good size lines of credit. And if he could help her, she'd max them out.

The doctor's name was Gavin Wyndham. He was tall, white, soft-spoken, and his bailiwick was cosmetic surgery. Lenore had seen advertisements of his services on television, procedures like rhinoplasty, body sculpting, cheek implants and face-lifts.

For information about his sex change procedures, one had to visit the Internet.

Lenore entered his office and shook his extended hand. She could tell by his expression that he was impressed with her appearance. "You're very passable," he said after they were seated.

"Thank you," she replied.

"Now, what's the problem?"

"I had surgery a few months ago," she explained. "I've healed. The soreness is gone, and I've been dilating. But it's not exactly a pleasurable experience."

"Could you clarify, please?" he requested.

"When I dilate, there is some arousal. I am not overjoyed and ecstatic, but I am turned on. The clitoris enlarges."

"That tends to happen during stimulation," he said.

"But when I'm aroused, the vaginal opening constricts."

"Which makes dilation difficult," he said.

She figured that he had heard it all before. "Yes," Lenore said. "And when I urinate, urine sprays everywhere like a broken faucet."

"Well, I'll have to examine you," he said. He ushered her to the examination room, and told her to change into a gown and wait on the examination table.

"I'll be back shortly," he said and departed the room, quietly shutting the door.

She went to a changing cubicle, which had a curtain, similar to a dressing room in a department store.

There was a chair and on a counter, a box of paper gowns. She undressed and put on a robe. *I'm making a real fashion statement here,* she said inwardly, looking at herself in the mirror.

She exited the dressing room, and sat on the edge of the examining bed. On the adjacent table were glass jars of cotton balls, wooden tongue depressors, bandages and a bottle of alcohol.

Why did Lenore have to go through all this shit? She felt like crying, even though the doctor hadn't said anything to make her weep. Well, she had sufficient reason to shed tears. Barrels of them, in fact.

That damn surgery didn't work. She was not the complete woman that she wanted to be, that she longed to be. But who knew. Perhaps, Dr. Gavin Wyndham would report good news. She hoped.

Dr. Wyndham returned, with his nurse, Tovah, a pretty black woman in her late twenties. Tovah smiled warmly at Lenore, who smiled back, but secretly wished Tovah would vanish. But when a doctor examined a female patient, a nurse had to be present. That was the law.

"Please lie down," Dr. Wyndham told Lenore.

She did as he asked; placing her head on a pillow covered with a paper pillowcase, which rustled against her head. Out of the corner of her eye, she saw the doctor snatch rubber gloves from a box and put them on.

She could feel him spread apart her vaginal lips. "I'm impressed with Dr. de Maupassant's work," he said. "Your vagina looks quite natural."

So what! It doesn't function. And she saw Miss Tovah, standing there, acting nonchalant, but fighting the desire not to gawk.

And since Tovah was Dr. Wyndham's employee, seeing a transsexual's pussy wasn't a new experience for her. And Lenore would bet a month's rent that later today, Tovah would tell her family and friends that a transsexual had come to the office that afternoon. And of course, Lenore's appearance and vagina would be discussed. The scrutiny never ceased.

"I see the problem with the urethra," Dr. Wyndham announced. "It isn't major."

"What's wrong?" Lenore asked.

"It wasn't repositioned properly. That can be easily repaired. I'll forward you to a urologist. He will fix you right up."

Well, hearing that was some good news. She'd be able pee without having to hold crumpled toilet paper in front of her.

From a nearby table, the doctor got a tube of lubricant and squeezed a squiggle onto a gloved finger. "I'm going to insert a finger in you," he said.

And that was what he did. And she hated it. She became tense.

"Relax," he said in a soft, coaxing tone.

Lenore *tried* to loosen up, while the doctor poked his finger inside of her, going as far back as possible, moving his fingers back and forth, from side-to-side. *God! This is horrible,* she thought. "I know what the problem is," he said. "You can get dressed." He took off his gloves and tossed them in the wastebasket.

Tovah's eyes were on Lenore. "You can discard the dressing gown in the trash can when you're done," she said.

Dr. Wyndham told Lenore—"After you're dressed, please return to my office."

And he and Tovah left the examining room, and after Lenore got dressed, she checked herself in the mirror, smoothed her hair and returned to the doctor's office and found him behind his desk, smiling benignly. "Please have a seat," he said, pointing to the chair facing his desk.

She did as he suggested.

"Lenore, you have stenosis," Dr. Wyndham said without preamble.

Lenore scowled. "Stenosis?"

He cleared his throat. "The doctor did a first-rate job with your vagina. But a portion of it has closed. The skin has grown back together, which is why you are experiencing discomfort when you dilate. In addition to that, there is excess bone which constricts after a few minutes of penetration."

She took a deep breath. “Can this be remedied?”

“Possibly.”

“You can’t say for certain?” she stated.

He shook his head. “I can’t give you any guarantees.”

“Well, what can *possibly* be done?”

He rubbed his chin. “For starters, as I said, the urethra can be fixed. You’d have to be hospitalized for one night.”

She could deal with that.

“I can shave some of the bone; reopen your vagina, but it could close again.” He paused. “I have reopened vaginas that had stenoted and they did close a second time.”

Oh, God, Lenore thought. *This was so depressing.*

“There is another option,” Dr. Wyndham said.

“What?” Lenore asked, thinking this man was acting like she was some goddamn laboratory mouse, somebody to be experimented on. Cut her up. Reposition this. Move that around. That didn’t work. So, let’s try this. If that doesn’t work, how about that?

And of course, with every procedure, the doctor picked up a hefty paycheck.

Dr. Wyndham said, “We could create you a vagina by using a piece of your colon.”

“A piece of my colon?” she said, not quite believing her ears.

“Yes, the procedure is called colon re-sectioning.”

“Now, okay, you want to take a piece of my colon and use it as a vagina?” Her expression was twisted with confusion.

“It’s been done before.”

“Now, I didn’t go to medical school, but isn’t feces stored in the colon before it passes through to the large intestine.”

“That’s right,” he said.

“And you’re telling me that you want to use a portion of that as my vagina?” A horrified expression appeared on her face.

“Lenore, as I said, it’s been done before with transsexual patients and with natural-born women.”

“Why would a real woman need to do such a thing?”

“Some real women, as you put it, were born with Rokitansky syndrome and being devoid of a vagina is a symptom,” he said. “Doctors have successfully used a portion of the colon as an artificial vagina, which functions like a genuine one. You wouldn’t have to worry about it closing up. Or using a lubricant. It’s quite natural.”

"There is nothing natural about using a section of my body that shit passes through and turning it into a vagina," she spat and took a deep breath.

"Lenore, when a piece of the colon is re-sectioned, feces will no longer pass through it."

"That's good to hear," she snapped sarcastically.

"It could be a solution to your problem. Of course, what we discussed earlier, reopening the vagina is an option."

"But it could close up again?" she said.

"And with the colon re-sectioning, you wouldn't have to worry about that."

Was it her imagination or was he pushing this positively macabre colon re-sectioning operation? "Have you ever done this colon thing?" she asked.

He nodded. "On a few patients."

"Were they pleased with the results?"

"They said they were."

And if they were unhappy, of course, you wouldn't admit it. That wouldn't be good for business. She sighed. "This is just too much to take in."

"I understand."

You couldn't possibly understand what I'm going through. You don't have a clue. You are a man and you want to be a man. You can't began to comprehend what it was like being born a male and craving to be female and going through a sex change operation, only to have it not work. "I'll have to digest all you've told me," she said.

Graciously, she cracked a smile for the doctor, went to the outer office and wrote a check for the consultation. The office manager said that she would be billed for the other services that she received.

What other services, she thought, exiting the office and going to her car? He had shoved his finger up that pathetic excuse she had for a vagina. So, was that considered a gynecological exam?

She climbed in her car and began driving down the road and reflected on what the doctor had proposed. He wanted to take a piece of her colon and use it as her vagina.

That sounded repugnant.

How could she live with that, knowing that her vagina was actually a part of her colon?

She could feel herself disintegrating. Why did she have to go through all this? What in the name of God had she done to deserve it? Was she a wretched person in a previous life? Was she now paying for it?

Or maybe the answer was ridiculously simple. Perhaps, things weren't working because she was trying to become something that God didn't mean for her to be. *Oh, that's nonsense,* snapped her inner voice.

If having a sex change was opposing God's wishes, why had Annabelle's surgery worked? And surely, Annabelle Morrison wasn't the only transsexual who had had successful surgery.

While driving, she beat the steering wheel with her fist. Why? Why did she have to go through all this?

CHAPTER 38

Lenore entered the apartment and found Jennifer Ann sitting at the kitchen table, filling out an application. "I need three references," she announced to Lenore, who went to the fridge and grabbed a bottle of water, which she poured over a tumbler of ice cubes.

"For?"

"I'm applying for a job at Kroger, working in the deli/bakery. I saw a 'help wanted' sign on the door."

"You think you'd like doing that?" Lenore asked, taking a seat at the table.

"Oh, sure. I'd enjoy slicin' cold cuts and scoopin' out rice puddin'. Back home, as a boy, I worked at a Dairy Queen." She chuckled. "I would do something with the name queen in it, wouldn't I? But I loved it."

"As long as it makes you happy," Lenore said, lackadaisically.

"Now, I ain't gone make no career of it. I'm not sure yet, but I was thinkin' about what you said about how transsexuals should become self-employed. Maybe, I'll get a license and become a hair stylist." She paused. "I still have a chunk of the money Alice gave me. But it won't last forever, so I have to find work. I want to keep somethin' comin' in instead of burning every penny I have."

"That's smart, Ann," Lenore said.

"So can I put you down for a reference?"

"Sure. Why would you even ask?" Lenore said, her eyes filling with tears. It had been a most trying day.

"Well, I didn't want them possibly callin' you, and you not know that I even applied for work there," Jennifer Ann said. "If you're hungry, I made a pot of beef vegetable soup. It's in the fridge. You can heat yourself some."

"I don't want any, thanks. Oh, God," Lenore whimpered, with tears dripping down her cheeks.

Frowning, Jennifer Ann looked up from her task, with an ink pen between her fingers. "Lenore, what's wrong?"

Lenore sniffed. "Nothing."

"You just don't start boohooing for nothin'. Now, Miss Thang, what's going on?"

Sighing, Lenore shook her head. "I don't want to discuss it."

"Is it about Trey?"

"Ann, just leave it alone," Lenore said firmly.

"Well, I know you don't wanna talk to Trey. For weeks, you've been mopin' around here. And now you're sittin' there with tears in your eyes. But you say nothin's wrong. But I know better."

Wordlessly, Lenore vacated the kitchen. Trudged to the bathroom and after a leisurely bubble bath, she put on a long silk robe and poured herself a glass of white wine.

On her bed, she turned on the TV to her favorite soap opera. Sipping the spirit, she watched a beautiful girl clad in a camisole kissing a shirtless, muscular man. They were breathing heavily while sexy music played in the background. Rolling her eyes, Lenore turned off the TV.

I'll read. She stretched to the nightstand and grabbed a book she was reading.

Oh, God. On the cover were a gorgeous black man and woman. He was shirtless and she was dressed in a lacy bra and skimpy panties. He stood behind her, with his muscular arms wrapped around her tiny waist. And her head was twisted in the direction of his handsome face and their lips were almost grazing. Lenore rolled her eyes and threw the book across the room.

She didn't want to look at those *normal* people, loving each other, even if it was simulated.

Lenore had traveled down this road before, being envious of normal people. She didn't want to look like them. She was happy with her appearance. Thank you very much.

She didn't want to think like them. She liked her perception of things.

For the most part, Lenore liked who she was, but she wished she could express sexual love for a man. So, yes, she envied a natural-born woman's ability to do that.

And she thought it was something she'd be able to do after surgery.

But that wasn't the case and because of her botched operation, it never would be.

She wondered just how many transsexuals like her were running around the place, beautiful, articulate, but incapable of having sex with a man?

Lenore was essentially, a beautiful eunuch.

Describing herself that way made her cringe, but her "vagina" was nothing more than an intricate scar that resembled a pussy.

Prior to surgery, she had hope of a bright future, something to look forward to, to have faith in.

Now, she didn't even have that.

Because of bad surgery, her dream of getting married and having a great life with her husband would not be realized. She had to view this situation, realistically. Sex was a part of relationships and the sad fact was a man couldn't make love to her. So, what man would want to marry a woman that he couldn't fuck?

And this would be Lenore's secret. No one would know that her surgery had failed, that her vagina was useless.

And if some 'normal' people became aware of it, she was confident they'd be pleased to hear that her surgery had been unsuccessful.

They'd think she had played God and was being punished for it, that she had gotten what she deserved. They would think that she had tampered with nature and that it had backfired on her. They would feel no compassion for her. Their opinion would be that she had brought it all on herself.

She would not give them the satisfaction of saying that to her, or even thinking it to themselves. They wouldn't know about her bungled surgery. They'd think she could do it all, save menstruate and have babies.

She was not going to share this sad story with anybody, not even Annabelle and Jennifer Ann.

This would be Lenore's secret.

CHAPTER 39

Jennifer Ann had gotten the job at Kroger. Her uniform was a baby-blue smock and matching pants. She worked forty hours a week and she told Lenore that she enjoyed the job and having it to go to seemed to improve her disposition.

It was a Saturday night, and the girls were having their weekly food-a-rama. Jennifer Ann made pulled pork and homemade slaw. And it was yummy.

Lenore recalled her first meeting with Jennifer Ann, who had served Lenore barbecue that afternoon. Also, they had listened to music and lip-synched songs. It had been such a fun day.

That seemed so long ago, but actually, only four measly months had passed. And so much had happened since then.

Wayne had died and Lenore had undergone surgery, and Jennifer Ann and Lenore were roommates.

And Jennifer Ann had found employment, something Lenore needed to do. She was healed and her energy had returned and her nest egg was dwindling and she needed to replenish it.

After dinner, the trio sat on the sofa and sipped wine and talked.

With her eyes on Jennifer Ann, Annabelle asked, "How are things going at your new job? Have there been any problems?"

"Oh, a few people have looked at me funny. But for the most part, they think I'm one of the girls," she said cheerily. "Most of the clockin' comes from black people."

"I agree," Annabelle said.

"I'm not taking offense to your comments, because I'm black," Lenore said. "But people from all walks of life spook us. I've been read by blacks, whites, young people, old people."

Jennifer Ann said, "So have I, but it seems that most of the spookin' comes from blacks."

"I guess black people are just more suspicious," Lenore said.

"Next topic. Next topic," Annabelle said. "Getting clocked, spooked, whatever the hell you want to call it, is part of the transsexual experience. So what are we going to do this evening? Music? A movie?"

"Why don't we go to Lovers and Friends and shake our butts?" Jennifer Ann suggested.

Annabelle nodded.

Lenore sighed. "You two can go to Lovers and Friends. I'm in no mood for partying."

"Well, you're all better," Annabelle said. "You look better."

"And I feel it," Lenore said.

"Physically, you might be better," Jennifer Ann stated. "But emo—"

"My emotions are none of your business," Lenore snapped.

Jennifer Ann looked at Lenore as if to say, Excuse me.

"Lenore, we're here for each other," Annabelle said, with warmth. "If something's bothering you, you can talk to us."

Lenore rolled her eyes. "Who said anything was bothering me?" And then it hit her. Looking at Jennifer Ann, she said, "I guess I know who said it."

Jennifer Ann said, "Well, you're upset about somethin' and you know it."

"That's what you think," Lenore hurled and stretched to the coffee table, got her glass of wine and sipped. Ugh. It was warm. She went to the refrigerator and poured a fresh glass.

Looking at Lenore who had resumed her position on the couch, Jennifer Ann said, "After some women have babies, they go through post-partum depression. I wonder if after surgery, some transsexuals go through something similar." With her eyes on Annabelle, she said, "She's been walkin' around here lookin' all sad. But she says nothin's wrong."

"Um, Ann, I'm in the room," Lenore yelled.

"Look, we want to help you, but if you won't tell us what the damn problem is, what can we do?" Jennifer Ann said.

Help me, Lenore thought. What the hell could they do? They didn't have magical powers that would make her vagina function. Lenore wanted this conversation over. "You are such a dumb ass," she spat to Jennifer Ann. "A rude, overbearing dumb ass."

Chuckling, Jennifer Ann's eyes dilated. "Pardon me."

"What, you need a Q-Tip?" Lenore flung. "You want me to repeat it?"

"Look, Miss Thang, I don't appreciate you talking to me like that," Jennifer Ann rejoined, her voice rising and becoming jittery with anger.

"Girls, calm down," Annabelle said patiently, sounding like a mother admonishing her sparring daughters. "Now, you're great friends. Don't do anything to ruin it."

"Well, Ann should learn to back off when people tell her that they don't want to be bothered," Lenore snarled.

"Well, just fuck it!" Jennifer Ann snapped.

There was a knock at the door.

"Saved by the bell," Annabelle said, sounding relieved.

Jennifer Ann practically skipped to the door. She was acting unfazed by the heated exchange she and Lenore had had, but Lenore knew she was pissed. Jennifer Ann glanced through the peephole. "Oh, it's Trey," she caroled and put her hand on the knob.

Lenore parted her lips to tell Jennifer Ann to ignore the door, but Miss Fast Ass opened it.

"Hi, Trey," Jennifer Ann sang.

"Hey," he said.

"Well, I know why you're here. Come on in." She stepped aside so he could enter. While she closed the door, Trey said hello to Annabelle.

Lenore remembered when Trey had told her that she shouldn't hang out with Annabelle because of Annabelle's appearance. 'You could be asking for trouble,' he had warned, explaining that when Lenore was in public with Annabelle, someone could read Annabelle and respond violently and Lenore could get caught up in an ugly situation.

Lenore scoffed. Annabelle was a nice person and had proven herself to be an invaluable friend.

Friends like Annabelle Morrison should be treasured, not cast aside because she didn't look like a middle-aged model and she told Trey so.

"Hi," Trey said to Lenore, smiling warmly.

"Hi," she said, being Miss Apathetic.

"How've you been?" he inquired.

She shrugged. "Okay."

"Well, Trey, why don't you sit down?" Jennifer Ann suggested. "We're having wine. You want a glass?"

"Yeah that would be ni—" Trey said.

"Trey won't be staying," Lenore said rudely. "So, don't bother getting him any wine."

"Lenore!" Annabelle shrieked.

Trey took a deep breath and said to Lenore—"What's going on here?"

Observing Jennifer Ann, Annabelle said, "Maybe we should go to another room."

Jennifer Ann and Annabelle made a motion to rise from the couch.

"That won't be necessary," Lenore said, stopping them. "You two can hear what I have to say."

Trey sighed. "I'd like to hear what you have to say … I mean, you don't take my phone calls. I'm not stupid. I know that you've been ignoring me."

"Well, you're very quick," Lenore said brusquely.

He frowned. "What the hell have I done to make you act this way towards me?"

"Trey, I've had my operation," Lenore said casually. "I'm now a woman, and I don't want to be involved with somebody like you."

His expression looked as though something foul smelling filled his nostrils. "Somebody like me? What the fuck does that mean?" he snapped.

"Well, you're bisexual, and I've decided that I don't want to deal with that." She sighed theatrically. "I mean, who knows? You could get a yen to fuck some guy in the ass. And bring me HIV."

"Oh, Miss Thang," Jennifer Ann gushed, in disbelief. "This ain't right. Stop."

Trey's face was creased with hurt and confusion. "I can't believe you said this shit to me … I guess you think because you've had that operation that you're hot shit or something. Well, let me tell you something, sweetheart, operation or not, some guys would have a problem with you."

Lenore said, "Well, that remains to be seen."

"I guess you never really liked me, anyway, huh? Just biding your time until something better came along."

"Possibly," she said, apathetically.

"Well, like I said, you're wrong if you think it's going to be easy because you now have a vagina. Some guys wouldn't want to date you. They'd be willing to try you out. But they won't care anything about you. And I really like you, and you just threw away something solid."

"I don't think it's all that solid," she said.

He shook his head in disbelief. "I can't believe you disrespected me like this in front of people." He took a deep breath. "But hey, it's okay. To hell with you." He exited the apartment, politely closing the door.

"Oh, Miss Thang," Jennifer Ann moaned. "I can't believe that you did that boy like that in front of us."

"It was cruel," Annabelle scolded. "I never knew you were capable of such nastiness."

"It had to be done," Lenore snapped with tears in her eyes. "I tried breaking off with him by ignoring him, but he was too dense to take the hint."

"You could have let us leave the room," Annabelle said. "And told him how you felt in private. It was like you wanted to debase him. Being a transsexual who has been humiliated, I can't believe that you'd demean someone like that."

"He looked so hurt," Jennifer Ann said sorrowfully. "My heart goes out to the boy."

"I think you're nuts to let him go," Annabelle said. "Many of us are alone and we'd like to find someone like Trey. And you just tossed him away."

"Look, I don't need a lecture," Lenore yelled in a piercing, high-pitched tone. Because of her goddamn defective vagina, she and Trey had no future. She had to make him despise her. She hated disrespecting him that way, but the phone calls and the visits had to stop.

Jennifer Ann said, "I wonda if he likes white girls. If you don't want him, I'll happily take him off your hands."

Eyeing Lenore, Annabelle said, "Oh, he was wonderful to you. He gave you flowers. Visited you. Took you out." She shook her head. "Finding a replacement won't be a cinch."

Lenore released a frustrated breath. "I don't want a replacement. I'll spend my life alone. I'll be an old maid."

"Well, that doesn't make any sense," Annabelle said. "You had talked about getting married one day, and finding a genetic woman to have children for you and your husband."

Lenore sipped her wine. "Well, I don't care about that anymore," she said, pretending not to give a shit. "I'll just be a spinster … just one of many transsexual spinsters. The world is overflowing with us, you know. Maybe, I'll start a quilting bee for trannies."

Annabelle and Jennifer Ann exchanged glances. "Lenore," Annabelle said, solemnly. "Have there been complications with your surgery?"

"No," Lenore said, too quickly.

"You sure about that?" Annabelle stated.

"Annabelle, I know better than you what is what with my surgery."

"True. But you talked about wanting a future with Trey, but you blew him off."

"And you've been moping around here like something's bothering you," Jennifer Ann added.

Lenore rolled her eyes.

Annabelle said, "Something's not right. And I wonder if it could be related to your surgery."

Jennifer Ann said, "I never considered that there could've been problems with the surgery."

Lenore had sworn to herself that she wouldn't tell anyone that her surgery had failed.

Annabelle took Lenore's hand and in a caring, soothing tone, said, "You can talk to us."

Oh, God, Lenore thought. The benevolent gesture increased the tears in her eyes.

"Yeah, Miss Thang, you can tell us," Jennifer Ann whispered.

Annabelle said, "You've always said that we're family. Well, families support each other during trying times."

Sighing, Lenore gradually shut her tear-filled eyes. Water dripped down her cheeks. She covered her face with trembling hands and howled into them. She felt caring hands patting her on the back. "Shush," Annabelle murmured.

"It'll be okay, Miss Thang," Jennifer Ann said softly.

For a while, Lenore sobbed against Annabelle's chest. Annabelle's delightful smelling perfume filled her nostrils. When she was a little composed, she removed her head from Annabelle's small bosom and saw Annabelle and Jennifer Ann's compassionate expressions.

"You okay, girl?" Jennifer Ann asked. Lenore simply looked at them. They would be able to comprehend her disappointment. They would have empathy. She had wished that she had confided in them earlier instead of suffering in silence.

Lenore nodded.

"You broke off with Trey because the surgery didn't work?" Annabelle said, knowingly.

Lenore shrugged. "What other choice did I have? Sex is a major part of a relationship. And since I can't function ... what could I do?"

Annabelle said, "Lenore ... Trey admires you. Maybe, he can deal with this problem."

Lenore sighed. "Annabelle, I've known Trey for only a few months. And yeah he cares about me ... But he doesn't have an emotional investment in me." She paused. "He wants sex. That's part of the attraction."

"Miss Thang, exactly what went wrong with the surgery?" Jennifer Ann asked.

Lenore sighed. "After surgery, I had six or seven inches of vaginal depth. And now it's down to a little under three inches." Using a tape measure, she had checked the artificial phallus she used to dilate her vagina.

Jennifer Ann frowned. "What happened to the other inches?"

"I've seen a doctor. He said there was some partial closing. He also said I could go back into surgery and have it reopened."

Annabelle's expression went from overcast to sunny. "Well, that sounds hopeful."

"Yeah, Miss Thang," Jennifer Ann added brightly.

Lenore sighed. "But he said that it could close a second time."

Jennifer Ann said, "But maybe it won't."

Annabelle said, "Some people have had cosmetic surgery and they weren't pleased with the results, so they returned to have it redone."

Lenore sighed. "And in some instances, additional surgery made matters worse." She had seen unhappy people on talk shows bemoaning their botched plastic surgery.

And with the exception of herself, Lenore didn't know of any transsexuals who had had lousy surgery. But she was confident that there were plenty of nightmarish stories to be told on the subject.

She said as much to her friends. "Lenore, you have to think positively," Annabelle said.

Lenore sighed. "I also have to be realistic. You know, right from the start, I always found dilating uncomfortable. My genital area is so screwed up." She sighed. "Having sex isn't possible."

Annabelle said, "Perhaps, it can be corrected."

"Miss Thang, I doubt if you're the only girl who's had this problem," Jennifer Ann said. "Maybe you could talk to other t-girls who had surgery and had to go back."

"Where would I find them?" Lenore said wearily. "A doctor isn't going to refer me to an unhappy patient."

"Check the Internet," Jennifer Ann suggested.

Lenore could do that. "The doctor also suggested another type of surgery," Lenore rolled her eyes. "He would take a section of my colon and turn it into a vagina."

Jennifer Ann looked horrified. "That sounds major."

"It is. He said that I wouldn't have to worry about dilating or it closing up or lubrication because it's a natural cavity."

"Well, that's hopeful," Annabelle said.

Lenore curled her upper lip. "I think it's disgusting." She paused. "With penile inversion, it was a penis in exchange for a vagina." She shrugged. "And to me that didn't sound crazy or unnatural … It made sense. But this colon thing."

"Well, I've heard of people transferring one part of their body to make another part function," Jennifer Ann said. "I know this woman who lost one breast to breast cancer. So, the doctor used fat from her stomach to build a new breast and a tattoo artist created a nipple."

"Oh, my God!" Lenore's expression looked as if she had put her finger down a drain and felt that slime that collects on the pipes.

"Lenore," Annabelle said, "if you want to have a vagina that functions, you're going to have to take a chance by either having your vagina reopened or maybe doing the other procedure."

CHAPTER 40

A few days later, Lenore had an appointment to see Dr. Eleanor Castle. Of all the shrinks she had spoken to, she thought Dr. Castle was the most effective. She had asked Lenore probing questions, making her contemplate what was going on in her life and why she made certain choices.

So, maybe Dr. Castle could help put it all in perspective.

A few hours before the appointment, Lenore bathed, massaged some perfumed body lotion into her skin. Applied a perfect makeup and added a little gloss to her mango-colored lipstick. She hot-rolled her thick shoulder-length hair and brushed it back, letting it hang loosely.

She donned off-black hose, a hunter Green two piece ensemble, and suede pumps of the same hue. She knew it was a bit overdone, just to see a psychiatrist. But getting dolled up always lifted her spirits. So, hey, why not look pretty while being psychoanalyzed.

And she knew that her appearance would bring favorable attention from men. She enjoyed handsome guys checking her out. She loved how that made her feel. It turned her on. And she could use a pick me up.

Lenore was sitting on the sofa facing the psychiatrist's desk. She was offered a beverage, which she declined.

"What brings you here?" Dr. Castle asked.

"I had the surgery and my vagina doesn't function."

"I'm sorry to hear that," Dr. Castle said.

But she didn't sound particularly shocked by Lenore's disclosure. "I'm sure you are, but it isn't exactly a news flash to you." She barely concealed the annoyance in her tone.

"What are you getting at?" Dr. Castle inquired, almost squirming in her seat.

"Surely, other transsexuals have told you that they weren't happy with their surgical results."

"Yes, I've heard it before."

"Well, if you knew that the surgery could have failed, why didn't you say anything?" Lenore took a deep breath. For that matter, Dr. de Maupassant didn't warn her of the risk she was taking.

"Lenore, no one knows what the outcome of any surgery will be," Dr. Castle said. "Each body is distinct and each body responds differently to surgery." Her tone was not hostile. "And as a consumer, it is the patient's responsibility to make sure that the surgeon is qualified … that there have been no complaints or malpractice suits against the doctor … Also, the patient should speak with people who have had work done by the doctor the patient is considering using."

"I did all that," Lenore said shortly. "That damn doctor should've told me that something could have gone wrong."

"Well, as I said, no two bodies responds to surgery in the same manner, so he had to wait and see. He probably figured that you were under a tremendous emotional burden, and he didn't want to add to it by speculating about problems that may or may not arise."

Lenore rolled her eyes. "That bastard could care less about my emotional burdens. All he gave a damn about was getting paid."

"You sound angry."

"No shit," Lenore spat.

"Let's discuss your anger."

Lenore sighed. "My dreams didn't pan out."

"Your dreams?"

"To have successful surgery, to find Mr. Right."

"Couldn't you go back into surgery and have repairs made?" the doctor stated.

This woman knew damn well that Lenore could return to surgery and that the vagina could close a second time. And Lenore wasn't even going to talk about that colon re-sectioning insanity. It was aberrant and too bizarre for words.

Lenore pulled on a tendril of hair and sighed. "I'm not too sure that I want to be bothered with that."

"You're not too sure? So, you've considered going back?"

Lenore nodded. She had done some research on the Internet and found some postings from people, who said that their initial surgery had failed, so they had it redone. One person said it didn't do any good. Another said that she had developed other medical problems.

Lenore said, "But I don't know if I want to gamble with more surgery." She sighed. "But there's my dream of becoming a wife and maybe even a mother." She shrugged. "I guess it's shot to hell."

"You do realize that you could still have a decent life, despite your unhappiness with your surgery."

Lenore rolled her eyes. "Oh, really?"

"There are friendships. You could travel. Socialize with good friends. There are books to read and enjoy. Music. Movies. You could get some hobbies, if you already don't have any. Hobbies can bring you joy. You could find pleasure from other sources besides sex. Your life doesn't have to be joyless." She paused. "And who knows, you could still meet someone and fall in love?"

"In this physical state?" She rolled her eyes heavenwards.

"You are still lovable." Dr Castle said. "Since you're unhappy with the results, do you regret having had the surgery?"

Lenore shook her head. "Knowing what I know, I'd have the surgery again ... Hey, look at the alternative. I could have facial hair ... a deep voice and a dick. But I am a fairly striking chick."

Dr. Castle smiled. "You are indeed."

"I prefer this ... So, no, I don't regret having surgery. I'm just enormously disappointed with the results. And I'm going to make my peace with it."

But where did she start?

CHAPTER 41

After her appointment, Lenore climbed into her car and hit the highway. She definitely didn't want to go home, where she'd do nothing, but obsess about her issues.

At a stoplight, her thoughts drifted to her faulty urethra. She had the name of a urologist, so soon, she'd have that problem corrected, which would enable her to pee without holding a wad of tissue in front of her.

And as she had told Dr. Castle, she had no regrets about having had surgery. But still, she felt those goddamn doctors were duty-bound to warn patients that something may go wrong.

A sex change operation is irreversible. And anybody considering one has a right to know the pitfalls involved.

And those money-grubbing quacks made sex reassignment surgery sound as simple as untwisting the cap off a bottle of Dr. Pepper.

She saw the sign for Mima's, an Italian bistro. She and Trey had eaten there a few times and the food was marvelous.

They offered lunch from 11:00 till 3:00. According to the dashboard clock, it was a few minutes after two, so lunch was still being served. And she hadn't had a crumb since that bagel with pineapple cream cheese she had consumed that morning, so she decided to grab some lunch.

She entered the eatery. Business was moderate. A few businessmen, old ladies and soccer mom types with fidgety kids were scattered here and there, eating Italian cuisine.

The hostess ushered Lenore to a table. A smiling waiter appeared, carrying a menu. She knew what she wanted without viewing it. She requested Linguini

Bolognese and while waiting for it, she sipped white wine. Sure, red wine accompanied what she ordered, but she was in no mood for the crimson stuff.

With her lips on the wineglass, she heard a deep voice say, "Hello."

She looked up and saw a handsome man, with luminous skin the color of Pepsi, smiling down at her. "Hi," she said, sensing that a come-on was on the horizon, and she truly didn't want to be bothered.

"I saw you walk in," he said, offering her a warm smile. "And I had to meet you. I hope you don't mind me coming over and introducing myself. My name's Randy."

"Hi, Randy," Lenore said, knowing what she'd say to get rid of him. When guys approached her, she always graciously told them that she was flattered by their attention, but she was happily married. That didn't always deter them. Some of them wanted to turn her into an adulterer.

"I'd like to buy you lunch," he offered.

Wonder if you'd still want to do that if you knew that I'm a transsexual with a pussy that didn't function properly, she thought, ready to tell him that she had a hubby. Smiling sweetly, she said, "Well, I'm—"

"She's meeting me," Trey said, popping up out of no where like a warlock from *Bewitched.*

Randy looked mildly embarrassed. "Sorry, man. I didn't know."

"No problem," Trey said, watching Randy strut off.

Looking down at Lenore, Trey said, "Hey."

"Hey yourself," she said pleasantly, recalling how she had behaved the last time they had seen each other. And she felt just horrible about it, but it was in Trey's best interest. "Thanks for rescuing me."

He shrugged. "Mind if I sit down?" His hand was on the top of the chair facing her.

"Sure." Watching him sit, it occurred to her that he would probably broach the subject of their previous conversation and she had no desire to deal with it. Looking at him, she thought, he was so good looking, so strong looking, so virile looking and he wanted her. Or whom he thought she was.

For a moment, there was awkward silence between them. "Um, are you here for lunch?" she asked, making conversation.

"I'm here to pick up an order I phoned in. When I walked in, I saw you sitting here." For a while, he studied her. "You know, I could be asking for trouble, but are you going to have your surgery redone or not?"

Lenore scowled. "How'd you find out?"

"The other day, I was in Kroger. I saw Ann behind the deli."

"And she told you?" Lenore snapped.

"Hey, don't go getting pissed with her. I told her that I didn't understand your change of attitude towards me, and she explained what was going on."

"She was out of line." She sipped her wine.

"She cares about you. She wants you to be happy, and so do I." His expression became serious. "Look, I'm sorry that your surgery didn't work out."

"I'll be okay," she said.

"Why didn't you tell me what was going on?"

"Trey, look, I have nothing to offer you ... I'm defective."

"Don't talk about yourself like that," he said.

"It's the truth."

He took one of her hands and while massaging it with his thumb, he said, "Lenore, look, I admire you. Your beautiful face. The way you speak. The way you dress. Your taste, your style, so my interest in you is not just about sex."

She rolled her eyes. "Oh, come on. Sure you care about sex." She remembered his rock-hard erections and all that huffing and puffing he did when they were together.

"Well, sure, I do." He chuckled. "I enjoy the stuff. But I also enjoy spending time with you. Doing things with you socially. Just because your surgery didn't work out doesn't mean we can't see each other."

She frowned. "Despite the surgery problem, you're willing to date me?" she questioned in disbelief.

He shrugged. "Sure, why not?"

"Trey, making love is a part of a relationship."

He nodded. "And there's no reason why we can't be intimate."

"My vagina doesn't function."

The waiter appeared at the table and placed steaming Linguini Bolognese, a small salad in a wooden bowl and a cruet of house dressing in front of Lenore. The sight of the food thrilled her taste buds.

"I wonder if my order's ready," Trey said. "If so, wanna have lunch together?"

Smiling warmly, Lenore nodded.

He left the table, and while twirling pasta on her fork, she saw him pay for his order with a credit card.

He returned with a brown paper bag, which he tore open, squashed and set aside. An efficient waitress got rid of it. "Thanks," he told her, removing the plastic lid off his food. And put a forkful of pasta in his mouth.

Lenore thought his meal looked enticing. "What's that?" she asked.

"Fettuccini Alfredo."

"Mind if I try some?" she said.

"Help yourself."

She twined some of the fettuccini around her fork, stabbed a broccoli spear and a chunk of chicken and popped it in her mouth. "Mm-m. Divine," she said. "I'll have to order it next time."

"You can make love without a vagina," he stated, resuming the topic. "We were intimate before you went to surgery, remember?" He lowered his voice. "We did it anally." He sprinkled sea salt on his salad.

Don't remind me, she thought, simply smiling at Trey. She wasn't that wild about anal sex. But Trey liked it, and she didn't have a vagina, so she did it.

"So we could do anal. And oral," he whispered. With his eyes on her prominent breasts, he said, "We could have fun with those."

"It's all about sex," she said, shaking her head.

Trey gently shook his head. "That's not true. Initially, my interest in you was purely physical … but I've gotten to know you … the person. And I'm very fond of *the person.*" He shrugged. "And I'm not going to lie. I like making love to you." He paused. "You can have your surgery redone, but if you choose not to, we can still have a satisfying sex life. We did it before surgery."

He had a point, she thought. But she had wanted to have traditional man/woman sex. But her messed up surgery prevented that.

Trey said, "You often said that despite being a transsexual, you were going to make the best of your situation. That you were going to enjoy your life, and not allow who you were or how people felt about you to be an obstacle to you having a good life."

"I recall saying that," she replied and sipped her wine.

"I liked how that sounded. It showed that you had spunk. But where this bad surgery is concerned, it's like you've thrown your hands up in surrender, and decided that you couldn't have a man because your vagina doesn't work." He sighed. "That sounds like the thinking of a defeatist, not the Lenore I've grown very fond of … That Lenore would have said, 'Okay, the surgery didn't work. But let's see how I can turn this negative into a positive.'" He paused. "I'm not saying that I'm all that, but I accept you as you are. If you want to go back to surgery, okay, that's up to you. But if you want to make your peace with what's what, we can deal with it."

We can deal with it. Tears sprang to her eyes.

"You don't have to be alone," he said.

Tears dripped down her cheeks.

He chuckled. "Ah, don't be up in here crying." He stretched his hand across the table and with his fingertips wiped away her tears.

She sniveled and with all sincerity, said, "I'm sorry for the way I spoke to you when you were at my apartment."

"Don't sweat it. It's in the past."

"Trey, you're a very special man."

He took her hand and kissed it. "And baby, you're a very special lady."

CHAPTER 42

One day, perhaps, Lenore would return to surgery. But right now, she wasn't interested in going under the knife. She had no faith in the operation. And she was not going to risk getting disappointed a second time or possibly creating new problems for herself.

For some reason, it hadn't been possible for her to become a complete woman. For some people, it worked. But that had not been the case for her.

And her life was not a total loss. She had plenty to be thankful for. She was attractive. Intelligent. So what if her vagina didn't work.

She could still be intimate with Trey. Like he said, they could do oral and anal.

* * *

One night, she and Trey were dining at a seafood restaurant. Earlier, they had gone to the mall and he treated her to a pair of beautiful diamond studs and four gift sets of perfume, *Very Irresistible* and *Organza* by Givenchy as well as some scents by Donna Karan and Vera Wang. Lenore loved fragrances and Trey loved to smell them on her. He helped her select the scents.

"Why don't you move in with me for about a month?" he said at the restaurant. "I'd like for us to see if we can live together."

* * *

"Oh, go for it, Miss Thang," Jennifer Ann exclaimed after Lenore told her about Trey's suggestion. "See what it leads to."

Lenore did not need Jennifer Ann's advice. She was simply sharing her happy news with one of her best friends. She had already decided to give the trial living arrangement a whirl. "But I'm not giving up my apartment," she told Jennifer Ann. "If this doesn't work out, I'll have a place to come to."

So, she moved into Trey's apartment, bringing along clothes, cosmetics, jewelry and the pillows that she slept on. She had no desire to try and get used to someone else's pillows. Becoming acclimated to Trey's firm queen-size mattress wouldn't be difficult for her.

Prior to Lenore moving in with Trey, she and Jennifer Ann had gone shopping, and Lenore purchased some silk kimonos in various hues, peach, beige and lavender.

They were short with a sash at the waist, and would put her firm slender legs on display and accentuate her 27 inch waist, which was a fairly small waist for a woman 6'0. She couldn't wait to prance around in front of Trey dressed in these delightful little get-ups. She was confident that he'd appreciate them as much as she did.

Oh, it was so wonderful waking up with Trey in the morning, and retiring with him at night.

While he worked, Lenore tidied the apartment, and cooked mouth-watering meals for them. He adored her lasagna and fried chicken. "This sure beats the Colonel," he complimented, eating a moist crispy, chicken breast.

And of course, he prepared delicious Chinese food for them.

After dinner, they lounged around and listened to music and watched TV or movies.

Once a week, they dined out, enjoying German, Russian, French, Japanese food.

They went to see movies, concerts, and a few times on their outings, he bumped into friends and people with whom he worked. "Trey, my man," one man greeted him in a winery. He and Lenore were there to pick out some spirits.

"Hey, man, how's it going?" Trey said, shaking the man's hand.

"I'm cool, dude. And who's this lovely lady you have here?" the man asked, openly admiring Lenore, making her feel uneasy. She knew she was a beautiful woman, but she wasn't naïve. Not everyone accepted her unequivocally as female. Some folks had ideas about her. And if one of Trey's friends read her, it could embarrass Trey. Make him uneasy and possibly put their blooming romance in peril. If people realized she was a transsexual, he could want to back off from a relationship with her. "This is Lenore," Trey stated proudly. "She's my lady."

"And she's a very lovely lady," the man said. "My name's Patrick," he revealed. Lenore learned that he owned a sporting goods store in the same shopping center where the pharmacy where Trey worked was located. "It's a pleasure to meet you, Lenore."

She smiled. "Nice to meet you too, Patrick." He hugged her.

When the man walked off, Lenore said, "You acknowledged me."

"Sure, I acknowledged you," Trey said. "We're going to have an open and honest relationship."

She was happy to hear that. And had he not acknowledged her, she would have packed up her stuff and returned to her former residence.

But she had to be honest with him. "From time-to-time, people are going to think things about me," she said. "They're going to whisper things about your girlfriend."

"Let 'em." He shrugged. "I'm living for myself." He kissed her cheek.

Although Lenore's vagina wasn't working the way she wanted it to, she still felt sexy and sensuous. Perhaps, having a gorgeous man who treasured her contributed to that.

And when they were intimate, oral sex was a part of their lovemaking. And she made a production of giving him head.

She got on her knees and kissed his lips and neck, while he played with her breasts, jiggling them around. She covered his chest with kisses and swished her tongue in his navel.

And then she'd put his penis in her mouth, and lick it like it was a double scoop of her favorite ice cream or suck it like it was a yummy piece of hard candy.

She'd alternately suck his cock and lick his balls and gently nibble his firm thighs. And sometimes, she'd make a mug of hot tea and alternate sipping it and sucking his dick. "Ooh, baby, this is nice," he'd moan, appreciating the feeling of her hot, wet mouth stimulating his penis.

She had read in a sex manual that the perineum was an erogenous zone, so when she sucked his cock, she made sure that she licked his perineum and his moans suggested that he thoroughly enjoyed it.

She straddled him and fed him her ample breasts and he'd greedily suck her nipples, acting as if they were the most delectable things he had ever had on his tongue.

At his request, she pushed her breasts together and he'd fuck her between them.

And he'd stroke, lick and suck her vaginal lips, and tantalized her clitoris, making it hard and turning her on.

She found oral sex pleasurable, but she LOVED it when he squeezed lubricant onto his fingers, and inserted his greasy fingers in her vagina and finger-fucked her. She could not be penetrated with his penis. But his thick fingers provided delightful thrills.

He'd stroke her vaginal lips and play with her clitoris, using a circular motion, giving her glorious feelings that were just indescribable, certainly more delightful than dilating with that dreadful plastic penis.

She had not as yet experienced an orgasm, but she had damn sure enjoyed some wonderful sensations, and the intimacy made her feel connected to Trey. She loved when they kissed. Loved when he sucked her breasts and finger fucked her. She loved sucking his cock and making him moan with delight.

She loved giving him hand jobs.

Being with Trey gave her a sense of incomparable bliss.

Three months later, Lenore and Trey were still living together, growing closer every day. They decided to move into her apartment, which was more homey and feminine. Jennifer Ann rented an apartment not far from Lenore's residence.

Trey paid Lenore's rent. Initially, she had balked at the idea. "Trey, we can go half," she said with a whine in her voice.

He shook his head. "If I want a roommate, I'll advertise for one on the bulletin board at the Laundromat. I can swing the rent and utilities. It's no hardship. Hey, you cook for me, wash my clothes."

"And I love doing it," she said truthfully.

He shrugged. "So, let me take care of you." He wrapped his arms around her. "I like doing it."

She truly appreciated Trey watching out for her, but she didn't want to become dependent on him. She wouldn't be comfortable with that. She would earn her own dollar bills. Right now, their relationship was in the honeymoon stage. But she had to be realistic. At some point, he could grow weary of her. And say adios. Considering that, it would be practical for her to earn a paycheck. So, soon, she'd seek employment.

Lenore had the problem with her urethra corrected, and the doctor was right, the procedure was simple. She stayed in the hospital one night, and now she could urinate without holding bathroom tissue in front of her.

Sometimes, she felt depressed about not being able to use her vagina during sex, and she thought about going back into surgery and emerging with a pussy that functioned the way most women's vaginas did. And then she'd think about the risks, the possible disappointment and the mental drama of going through surgery.

Who needed it?

But on the other hand, if she took a chance and tried surgery again, she may end up a complete woman.

But Trey's okay with me, just as I am, she thought. He loved her pretty face and beautiful breasts. He frequently paid her compliments.

But so what if Trey's okay with you, countered that devil on her shoulder. *You aren't okay with yourself.*

"And Trey can make love to me," Lenore mumbled to herself.

Yeah, in the ass, said that devil.

She and Trey did it anally a few times a week and he enjoyed it. But she could definitely live without it.

She had never been that wild about butt sex, but when she had a penis and testicles, she was producing large amounts of testosterone, the hormone that made people feel sexy. So during sex, she was aroused, which made anal sex bearable.

Now that she no longer produced male hormones—at least not in huge quantities, she wasn't as stimulated, making anal sex even harder to deal with.

She sighed. She wanted to be a woman, completely. She wanted a vagina that operated properly. Should she go back into surgery?

♣ ♣ ♣

One early evening, Lenore and Trey were at home, dining by candlelight. He told her, "You know, Lenore Cavanaugh is a nice name, but Lenore Fuller sounds nicer." He left it at that.

Hmmm. Trey's last name was Fuller. Was he trying to see how she felt about them getting married? She simply said, "Yes, Lenore Fuller does sound nice." But she wasn't going to push it. But if he popped the question, her answer would be yes. Let's go find a reverend, a church, cleave with me, baby.

CHAPTER 43

Jennifer Ann and Lenore went into business together, becoming the happy proprietors of Long-Legged Beauty, a clothing store that specialized in attire for tall women. They sold casual clothes, office and formal wear; teddies, pajamas and robes.

The store was open from 10 a.m. till 6 p.m., six days a week, closed Sundays.

Lenore had several credit cards. Over the years, various companies had sent them to her, and because she paid her bills promptly, her credit limit was frequently increased. So she got some cash advances to start the business.

Jennifer Ann had used some of the money from Wayne's insurance.

Jennifer Ann and Lenore always went to work, looking stylish, with flawless hair and makeup and tasteful jewelry. Genetic women came in and made purchases. And of course, some of their customers were transsexuals and cross-dressers.

Jennifer Ann had placed an ad in a few transsexual magazines and t-girls dropped by to shop.

Jennifer Ann had resigned from Kroger. She was unhappy with the pay.

Lenore suggested that she go into business with her and Jennifer Ann jumped at the chance.

Also, Jennifer Ann was dating Deshawn, who drove a Pepsi truck. They had met at Kroger, one of the deliveries on his route.

Jennifer Ann had introduced him to Lenore. And he was a good-looking black dude. He took Jennifer Ann to dinner. He was a basketball aficionado, so they went to games. And Jennifer Ann was learning everything she could about the sport. "I feel kind of guilty, running around with him," she told Lenore.

"Why?" Lenore asked. They were in the store, putting away a new shipment of fall sweaters that had arrived that afternoon.

"Miss Thang, it wasn't that long ago that Wayne died, and I think a widow woman should go through a respectable period of mourning." She paused. "But girl, I'ma tranny, and finding boys that will totally accept me ain't as easy as finding Double mint gum in a vending machine ... So, I'm gonna date him and ignore my guilt."

"Wayne would want you to have a life," Lenore said, sagely. "And besides, you're a transsexual. When have we ever paid attention to protocol?"

* * *

Dr. Kenneth Arrington was a doctor in Los Angeles who did corrective work on transsexuals who had had shoddy surgery. Lenore had gotten his name from a t-girl in an online transsexual support group. Lenore phoned Arrington, explaining the problem with her vagina. "Well, I'll have to examine you before I can definitively say what the problem is and what, if anything, can be done to rectify it," he said.

So, she made an appointment to see him. "I'll go with you," Trey said when she told him about speaking to the doctor. It was night. They were sitting up in bed. Trey had been reading a novel. "Lenore, you're fine the way you are," he said earnestly.

"To you," she said. "But I want a vagina that works. I feel like half a woman."

"Well, you're *all* woman to me."

Maybe the doctor in Los Angeles could make that be the case.

* * *

Lenore and Trey took a flight to see Dr. Arrington. Trey was in the waiting room while Lenore talked to the doctor, who was an affable, distinguished looking white man in his early fifties. After examining her, in a soft spoken voice, he explained what was wrong with her vagina. "It can be repaired," he said.

Her eyes got big. "You mean that?" she gushed. The previous night, she had tossed and turned, fearing that he would tell her that there was nothing that could be done to fix her problem.

"Absolutely," he said.

He told her that she had stenosis, which was the same thing the other doctor had said. She remembered what the other doctor said about reopening the vagina and the stenosis returning. "But after surgery, I could get stenosis a second time."

"Your stenosis is quite minimal. You have excellent vaginal depth. But excess bone is obstructing part of the depth, making penetration impossible. I can shave the bone. And that should take care of the problem."

Hmm. That other doctor made it sound like her only hope of having a vagina that functioned was to use a piece of her colon. And she damn sure wasn't interested in doing that.

And she trusted Dr. Arrington. He seemed sincere, straightforward. And she believed that he could help her.

He referred her to two other patients he had done corrective work on and Lenore phoned them. Initially, they were displeased with their surgery, which had been performed by other doctors. And Dr. Arrington fixed the problem. They were quite happy with the results.

Lenore made an appointment to have surgery two weeks after meeting with the doctor. She had to stop her hormones for a week. Have some lab work done. Avoid alcoholic beverages three days before the surgery. She knew the drill. Been there. Done that.

Dr. Arrington's fee was twelve thousand dollars and if he gave her a vagina that functioned, it would be twelve g's well spent.

At eleven a.m. on a Wednesday morning, Lenore was wheeled into surgery while Trey sat in the waiting room drinking Pepsi from a can and reading a Dean Koontz paperback.

Jennifer Ann was back home watching the store. Annabelle said she'd call later that evening to see how Lenore was doing.

After the surgery was over, a nurse came out and told Trey that Lenore had been taken back to her room. "How is she?" he asked, full of concern.

"Fine," the nurse answered. "The surgery went without complications."

CHAPTER 44

Four months later …

Jennifer Ann, Lenore and Annabelle were still convening for their Saturday night dinners, and on one such occasion, Annabelle tearfully said, "I have some good news … I think."

"What?" Lenore asked while Jennifer Ann looked on.

Annabelle took a deep breath. "Well, I visit a number of transsexual groups online."

Lenore nodded. She was a member of one group and occasionally, she read the letters and posted a response.

Annabelle said, "Someone told me about facial feminization surgery for transsexuals. I went to a site that had before and after pictures of transsexuals who underwent the procedure. It's amazing what the surgery can do for a t-girl. Before surgery, their faces were very masculine looking. They had square jaw lines, a block forehead, a manly looking nose. And the doctors feminized them."

"So you're going to have it done?" Lenore asked.

Annabelle nodded. "I've already talked to a doctor and he showed me a computer image of what I'd look like after the surgery. It was astonishing. Now I'm not going to look like a supermodel afterwards, but the surgery will make a difference. It would cut down on some of the staring I get from people in public." Looking at Lenore and Jennifer Ann, Annabelle said, "You girls look like women and people treat you differently from how they treat me." She took a deep breath. "I'm hoping that the surgery will change how people react to me. I'm hoping that it'll change my life for the better."

Lenore had certainly heard of facial feminization surgery and she thought Annabelle was a definite candidate for it. But she just didn't know how to bring it up. She thought facial feminization surgery would benefit Annabelle's life. "Whatever you chose to do," Lenore said. "You know you have our support."

Jennifer Ann nodded.

"Also, I received an encouraging letter from my daughter," Annabelle said.

"Girl, you have all kinds of good news tonight," Jennifer Ann said.

Annabelle smiled. "My daughter's pregnant. And she and her brothers had a talk, and they want me to meet them for coffee and conversation." She moaned happily. "Maybe they want to work it out."

"Oh, I hope so," Lenore said.

"Yeah, you can get your family back," Jennifer Ann added.

"I'd like to reunite with my kids. But you girls are my family," Annabelle said. "And if I do patch things up with my children, I'm not giving up on you two."

"And we aren't giving up on you," Lenore said and they all took turns hugging each other.

CHAPTER 45

The room was dimly lit by scented candles that surrounded the bed. "Yes, yes," Lenore screamed, as Trey was behind her pounding away in her VAGINA. She was on her knees; they were doing it from the back. She hated the expression, doggie-style. She didn't like her favorite sexual position being compared to an animal. "Give it to me," she yelled, egging Trey on; his dick becoming even harder inside her.

Four months had passed since she had had corrective surgery done to her vagina and after eight weeks, the doctor suggested that she start having intercourse. "To keep your vagina open, you'll always have to dilate," he had told her. *Yeah, Yeah, I know,* Lenore thought, loathing the very thought of screwing herself with a dildo. But a transsexual had to do that to keep her vagina from closing.

Dr. Arrington said that it wouldn't be necessary for her to dilate if she had sex regularly.

And Lenore did just that. She and Trey made love five times a week, so Trey's penis dilated her. He was her human dildo.

Trey began huffing and puffing loudly, pounding away faster. As he did his thing, Lenore played with her boobs. "Ooh, yeah, baby," he said, in a guttural tone. And then she felt his warm sticky explosion spurting inside her and he slowed his pumping and rolled off her, landing flat on his back, panting loudly.

Lenore clutched his penis, which had lost some of its firmness. She moved it up and down, squeezing the last droplets of cum from it. Trey chuckled. "Woman, what the hell are you tryna do to me?"

"Oh, be quiet," she teased. "I love your dick."

"Do you now?"

"I love playing with it. Sucking it. Getting screwed with it. It's the best dick in the whole wide world." She always loved performing fellatio on him and giving him hand jobs. But after her vaginal problems were resolved, she really discovered what a source of ecstasy Trey's penis could be. But of course, his penis was only a part of him. She loved everything about him. The way he looked. How he treated her.

She straddled him. Placed her hands on his strong chest. "Ooh, I adore you." She gave him a big kiss on the lips.

Looking serious, he stroked her hair. "I adore you too, baby."

Her expression became reflective.

"What cha thinking 'bout, baby?" he asked, noticing her face.

She took a deep breath and laid down next to him. "Trey, I'm kinda scared."

"Of what?"

"I'm happy."

"And that scares you?" He looked thoroughly perplexed.

She took a deep breath. "This is the first time in my life, I've been truly happy. I have a wonderful guy. I've gone into business for myself. And the store is doing well. I'm going back to school to get my degree. I have a nice place to stay … For the longest time, all I thought about was getting surgery. Finding the right doctor. Round-the-clock, that was in my mind." She took a deep breath. "And then I had the surgery. Initially, I wasn't happy with the results."

"But you got it fixed. And we've been having some fun times with it."

She giggled.

"So baby girl, you don't have anything to worry about," he said.

"But you see, most of my life has been filled with complications and setbacks." She sighed. "And I don't know, call me a pessimist. But I wonder what's waiting behind the next door. I'm wondering if this supreme pleasure I'm enjoying is temporary or if it's here to stay."

"Well, when you've had a lot of setbacks and tough roads to travel," he said, "I guess you can become negative and jaded. But I think it's your turn to live the life you've always wanted. The life that you deserve … All that stuff you went through to get to this point was part of the journey. And girlfriend, you made it and together, we're going to live our lives. Love each other. And be happy.

Smiling warmly, Lenore thought, *Sounds good to me.*

About the Author

Pamela Hayes is a transsexual who would like to see more people like herself in mainstream fiction. She adores old movies, cooking gourmet food and traveling.

She can be reached at PamelaHayes70@Hotmail.com. Drop her a line.

978-0-595-43256-1
0-595-43256-5

Printed in the United Kingdom
by Lightning Source UK Ltd.
124592UK00003BC/73/A

9 780595 432561